A GOOD PLACE

A GOOD PLACE

J.R. Barnes

PALMETTO
PUBLISHING
Charleston, SC
www.PalmettoPublishing.com

Copyright © 2024 by J.R. Barnes

All rights reserved.

No portion of this book may be reproduced, stored in a retrieval system, or transmitted in any form by any means–electronic, mechanical, photocopy, recording, or other–except for brief quotations in printed reviews, without prior permission of the author.

Paperback ISBN: 9798822967328

For Gary, everyone misses you.

I would like to thank my childhood friend, Angela Zotto (the real "Dragon Lady") for patiently reading through the manuscript and giving her unbiased opinions and suggestions.

A special thanks also to Billy Phillips (Vietnam veteran and retired PPD) for answering all of my crazy questions at all hours of the day and night. You are a great man!

A proceed from the sale of this book will be donated to the National Veterans Suicide Prevention program.

"Who shall separate us from the love of Christ? Shall tribulation, or distress, or persecution, or famine, or nakedness, or danger, or sword?"

- Romans 8:35

"We are all broken, that's how the light gets in."

- Ernest Hemingway

Chapter One

Ben was standing over a cast iron skillet watching a large pancake bubble, he could never get over how soothing and inviting they were to cook and how great they smelled. He was a large man, almost three hundred pounds and stood six foot, six inches tall and his once thick dark long hair and beard was now gray. For the ripe age of sixty, he still had good muscle tone and a broad chest. A news segment came on the small TV in the kitchen that featured an upcoming Halloween costume party for local kids at Anson B. Nixon Park, the very place where he and his wife Lynne had met ten years earlier. Ben had been engaged in conversation with a buddy and was about to leave after starting his custom built Harley Davidson Road King, when he happened to look up and see a beautiful young woman running towards him and chasing after a softball. After smiles and a sincere greeting she invited him to join her friends who were attending a church picnic. Ben had never been a religious man (although he did believe in divine intervention and a higher power) but her eyes beckoned him. A month after they met, the pastor of Lighthouse christian church invited him to stand before his fellow parishioners and give his testimony. The front door bell rang and he removed the pan from the front burner, wiped his hands on a cotton dish towel and went to answer the door.

"Hexe stop!" He shouted down to the family's six year old German Shepherd, who had managed to make her way to the foyer from the second floor before Ben did.

"Good morning, Ben." His friend from church said with a solemn look upon his face, his township police hat was removed and in his left hand.

" Hey, Mark." Ben said, noticing the sad look in his eyes.

"Is Lynne home also?"

"She should just be getting out of the shower, is there a problem?"

"Yeah." Mark managed to say, looking down at the porch floor.

"It's Joshua, isn't it?"

"He's gone Ben, I just got a call from Philly PD."

"Accident?" He asked, rubbing the palm of his hand over his flattop.

"Ben." Mark said softly while keeping direct eye contact.

"Honey, who's out front?" Lynne inquired from the top of the stairs.

"It's Mark, Lynne, and he needs to talk to us."

"Be right down."

"Come in." He invited with a nod.

"Let's go into the kitchen." Ben suggested softly, taking her hand and waiving Mark inside. Lynne had a confused look upon her face, like a child that wasn't understanding a math problem and Ben's heart broke.

"Baby…" He began to say before choking on his words.

Lynne's eyes grew wide and an expression of frozen disbelief materialized, as her innate maternal sense of losing her child was realized. "Oh no!" She screamed in pain, and fell into his arms.

"My name is Benjamin Ladd, and I stand here this morning willingly and with an open heart to offer up my sins to the Lord."

"Hello Ben!" The congregants acknowledged enthusiastically.

"I was born to an unwed mother in Elizabeth, New Jersey in 1963, and a year afterwards was given up for adoption. At about a year and a half, almost two years of age, I was adopted by a family from Trenton. I don't really remember too much about my early years with them but I can tell you around the time the physical and mental abuse started. In those days, there really wasn't much follow up or any kind of visits from the state concerning a child's well being. I grew up in an alcoholic and dysfunctional household and then one summer afternoon ran away with a buddy of mine. We were fourteen and hitchhiked to Atlantic City, where we were soon picked up by the local police and thrown into 'Juvie' until our parents could come and get us. That's the slang name for juvenile detention, it's basically a jail for all you bad boys who are under the age of eighteen, so all you tough guys out there better smarten up!" He joked with a nod to his future stepson Joshua and his buddies who were not bad at all.

He looked at Mark but couldn't mentally process what he had just heard as Lynne's muffled screams gripped his attention.

"Gunplay Mark, what are you talking about?" Ben asked, with a dazed look on his face.

"The guy who shot Josh was fleeing from a shootout and wanted their van. Apparently, Joshua tried to fend him off but the weapon discharged. The round struck him above the right eye and killed him instantly."

Lynne's horrified screams escalated to an ear piercing level and Ben held onto her even tighter.

"I'm so sorry Lynne." Mark said with sadness in his voice.

"Next month is his twentieth birthday!" She shouted angrily, breaking free of Ben's protective embrace.

"Honey." Ben said softly.

"I want to know what happened Mark, tell me everything you know right now!" She demanded, wiping tears from her eyes. Her face was growing flush with anger and Ben looked over her head and nodded, giving Mark his approval.

"According to Roland, he and Joshua were on their way to a job on Frankford avenue near Kensington. Josh was driving and while they were slowing down to check on the address they heard gunfire erupt behind them. What happened next is a little hazy because Roland said it went by in a blur, but a dark colored small sedan crashed into a light pole just to their left and a young black male staggered out of the passengers side door. The driver was dead and hunched over the steering wheel, that much has been confirmed." There was a pleading look in Mark's eyes as if not wanting to describe the death of her son.

"Go on." Lynne said sternly.

"Then the guy approached Josh's side of the van and attempted to carjack them at gunpoint. He pointed the pistol nervously at them and then Josh reached out in an attempt to grab the weapon. The guy was able to grip Josh's arm with his free hand, overpowering him until it discharged, ultimately striking Josh just above the right eyebrow. Roland said he died instantly."

"I ended up back in Trenton and had the living tar beat out of me by both adoptive parents, but I already mentioned that they weren't very nice people so I'll move a little further ahead." He said, taking a deep breath and looking up at the morning sun rays that were gleaming down through the skylight casement in the cathedral style ceiling. "I was sixteen when he put his hands on me for the last time. He called me down to the basement and that familiar look came over his face, the look that he would get just before he would beat me." His voice cracked and for the first time since he was a child he began to weep.

"Amen, Ben. Go on honey!" Lynne cried out.

"Amen, Ben!" The parishioners encouraged.

"He looked around for something to hit me with, and in a second I grabbed a breaker bar that had been laying in an open tool drawer. The look he had on his face when he turned around and saw me, will haunt me for the rest of my life. He was shocked but his anger didn't go away."

"Put that down, boy!" He shouted, with a red face and murder in his eyes.

"I didn't say a word before I beat him half to death and left him lying on the basement floor." Ben said in a serious tone.

"Needless to say I was sentenced to five years and ended up in Mid State Correctional over in Fort Dix, New Jersey. When I turned eighteen, I was moved back to Trenton but this time to the toughest prison in the state, New Jersey State or what some past residents refer to as: 'The

University.' My first cellmate was none other than Micheal Stratter, he's dead now so I don't think he'll mind me telling you all this." Those in attendance chuckled and were totally captivated by his testimony as he continued.

"I'm sure that most, if not all of the adults here today have heard his name. A month ago, after walking into this church I could tell by some of your expressions that you had also heard of mine. Mike aka "The General" was the founding father and president of the one percent motorcycle club the Sworn. As fate would have it, I too would eventually become the president; the number one ranking man of the entire Sworn nation. Meeting him in prison began a life of reckless abandon, but also gave me something that I never had before. Love and loyalty"

"Who did it Mark?" She asked, swiping away her auburn hair that had matted to her wet face.

"Lynne." He whispered.

"Tell me!" She cried out.

"Lynne, they haven't apprehended anyone yet. This just happened within the last couple of hours."

"How long will it be until his body is released from the coroner's office?" Ben asked gently, in an attempt to steer her in a softer direction.

"About a day or two, but I can make sure that happens faster."

"Thank you, Mark." He said appreciatively.

"Ben, we should call Tom Deery." Lynne said, looking up from under his arm.

Tom Deery of Deery Funeral Home in Kennett was a well respected member of the community and an elder at Lighthouse.

"I've already taken the liberty of notifying him Lynne, I'm sorry if I acted too forthcoming." Mark stated with empathy.

"Mark." Was all she could manage to say before reaching out to him.

"Everything will be handled, now please take some time to rest and be with one another, all of our family have been notified and I can assure you that they're worried sick and sending out their prayers."

"I want to see my son." Lynne could barely say.

"Baby…" Ben quietly urged, trying to bring reason to bear.

"I want to see my boy, Ben!" She shouted passionately, as tears began filling her eyes again. He looked over at Mark who nodded back.

"Okay Lynne, give me just a minute to give them a call." Their friend said softly.

"Most bikers are genuine kind hearted people with hearty souls, just big kids really. They work hard, feed their families and pay their bills. They're the last folks on earth you'd hear complain and they'd be the first ones to stop and help you out in a pinch. Remember that flat tire you had last month Henry?" Ben asked one of the elderly members in attendance.

"I most certainly do, young man!" He replied.

"I really like you now Henry!" Ben joked back, stirring a round of laughter, as the rest understood the reference to being called young.

"We are what we attract. An outlaw motorcycle club is a business, no more and no less. It's based upon the fundamental principles of brotherhood, loyalty and honor but what keeps the lights on and the machine running is money. Every area, depending on its size, has chapter officers and above those are state level officers and then finally the whole nation." He looked around the church summoning his inner strength to continue onto the darkest part of his life's story. Lynne gave him a smile and a wink and Ben exhaled and began.

"I prospected (which is a probationary period) in jail and when I was released, I was taken to Baltimore to meet with Mike again. He took me under his wing and trusted me enough to start recruiting members in Virginia. Anyhow, I coordinated or actively participated in the manufacturing, trafficking and distribution of methamphetamine, cocaine and other hard street drugs throughout the East Coast. I actively participated or gave orders to have people hurt or their property destroyed or stolen. I served twelve years in a federal prison for shooting a rival gang member and transporting his body across state lines; this brought an attempted first degree murder charge which was pled down to aggravated murder. I pray to God with every ounce of my soul that He forgives me for half the sins I have committed and the ruin I have caused others." He couldn't hold it in any longer and in a split second all of the pain and torment he'd stuffed down under the guise of a hard man exploded outward in a burst of tears and despair.

"Please, Lord have mercy on me!" He cried out in agony.

Within seconds the entire congregation made their way to the elevated stage where he had given his ultimate testimony. They reached out putting their hands upon him, engulfing Ben with hugs and tears of love and acceptance. When silence fell upon the church he continued.

"I had a counselor in prison tell me once that life was like a cloud. Sometimes it's dark and ugly, sometimes it's white, fluffy and pretty. They can bring rain or snow and at other times they just float away. It's the dark scary ones that open up and pour down that usually leave a beautiful rainbow after they're gone. That's how I feel standing here in front of all of you today. My life up until now has been a dark scary storm cloud and now a rainbow has appeared out of nowhere." He said while wiping his eyes and smiling at Lynne.

Chapter Two

The two were being led down the long white tiled hallway by the coroner's assistant. Occasionally the bright overhead fluorescent lights reflected their cold sheen catching Ben's attention and bringing him back from the surreal.

"Just give me one moment please." The middle aged black man said with a sincere look in his eyes.

"Sure, go ahead." He replied, looking down at his wife.

"Oh honey, I just can't believe this…" Lynne said softly, breaking into tears.

He held her close until the large heavy door opened and they slowly walked in. At first, the innate reaction to intentionally avoid the obvious gripped them and they stayed in the periphery of the tragedy. Ben looked at her and she at him, both searching for the appropriate words to say while being held prisoner by this silent duress. Except for the black hard rubber collar which held his head slightly upward and a white sheet folded at his stomach, Joshua's body laid flat on the stainless steel table.

"I used to dream about you when I was a little girl and I just knew that you were going to be a boy when I found out I was pregnant. I was eighteen when I had you, and you were everything that I ever wanted. We watched each other grow up!" Lynne shouted in agony, feeling more pain than any woman should have to endure.

"Joshua!" Her high pitched shrill echoed to the far reaches of the building.

"Oh my God." Ben whispered, looking at his son's face.

Lynne reached down and removed the small white gauze that had been placed over the fatal wound by the coroner's assistant; a professional and considerate gesture. The bullet's entrance wound had been cleaned and a dark pinkish brown bruise surrounded a deep hole. She removed the white sheet and gazed at his entire body. Joshua was a stout young man who took after her side of the family. He had strong broad shoulders, thick forearms and a narrow waist. His mid-length, blondish red air fell in ringlets that laid upon the sterile stainless steel table. She gently placed her hands on both sides of his face before leaning in and kissing him on the lips, and finally his forehead.

"I love you, son." She whispered, as a teardrop fell upon his cheek.

"That young man and his friend did nothin' wrong, they did nothin' to deserve this!" An elderly black woman said, speaking loudly into the Channel 6 Action News camera.

"This is just crazy, when does the violence stop?" Her teenage niece added.

"They were right down the street and heading to my house to put in a new service panel. I just got off the phone with them!"

"At 11:00 o'clock this morning, shots rang out here on the 1200 block of Kensington avenue. This high crime corridor's latest victim is a nineteen year old electrical apprentice from Kennett Square, Pennsylvania. He and his work partner were on their way to a job at Ramona Jones's house when an apparent drug deal went bad. One of the two suspects tried to steal their work van and in the process shot nineteen year old Joshua Ladd, a second year apprentice with Central Electric."

"I was standing on the corner waiting for the bus and a young dude stepped up to the driver's side of that black Acura. Next thing ya know, he just starts blasting, pop, pop, pop."

"I saw that too!" A younger homeless looking white man added. "Then the car barely made it half a block and stopped against that pole."

"Yeah, then the passenger got out and tried to jack that van, and then there was another pop."

"The suspect is still at large and no further details are available at this time." A gray haired police sergeant said in a serious tone. "We're asking anyone who can provide us with any information about the shootings or if anyone knows who the suspected gunman is to please call Crime Stoppers."

"Reporting live from Kensington avenue, I'm Katie Katro with Channel 6 Action News."

"He's right here, hang on a minute." A young girl's voice replied.

"Yo, who's this?" A gruff sounding teen asked.

"I'm the motherfucker your tryin' to stomp on outta here that's who." The caller stated.

"Shey."

"That's right, ever since you GSM's come up here from DC, like you gonna take over…"

"Hey, fuck you Shey! Gold Sheik Mob got yo ass all day, motherfucker!" The young man threatened before letting out a moan of pain.

"East Coast Hood's all day punk, run a rocket right up yo nigga ass!" Shey challenged back.

"Bitch, please! And you got balls callin' me!"

"Listen up ya stupid motherfucker and you better listen good…"

"Shut the fuck up!" He shouted in agony.

"For real. You have any idea who's kid you killed?" Shey asked with a stern voice.

"What? I didn't kill nobody, nigga!" The teen answered, obviously lying.

"Yeah, well that young buck's daddy is like way high up in the Sworn, motherfucker! Ya feel me? You know, like the whole country high up!"

"Outlaw biker club."

"No shit?!" Shey asked sarcastically. "Your a fuckin' genius."

"And what about it?"

"Wow! Well the way I see it, your fucking dead and all you bitch's will end up in bags back in DC, where ya'll belong and I don't gotta do a goddamned thing thanks to your brain power!" Shey said laughing.

"Fuck outta here!"

"Aaaaaaaand I got your phone number from your babymom, bitch!" He taunted before hanging up.

Chapter Three

"Ben, have I ever lied to you?" The General asked, squinting his eyes to convey how serious the subject was about to become.

"No Mike, I don't think you have." Ben answered. He was one of the few members who was permitted to call him by name.

"I can assure you that I have not, brother."

"I believe you, Mike."

The two sat in the small cozy living room of the hunting cabin that Mike owned. It was in Warren Pennsylvania just North of the Allegheny National Forest, and was a dovetail and mud/clay mortured stout structure that sat on ten acres of rural hillside.

"I've been running this club for almost twenty five years. Do you have any idea what it takes to head a one percent motorcycle club?" Mike asked, while playfully rolling his eyes and flicking his tongue in and out of his mouth.

"Like that?!" Ben replied laughing.

"No man, a hundred times worse than that!" He joked back, joining him in the spirit.

"Look, when I first met you in Mid-State, I knew there was something different about you. You came across as a thinker, a young guy looking for direction and guidance but you also had that light and that's a rare thing Ben, seriously"

"And I felt the same way about you. I'll never forget the look on your face when you told me who you were and I said, 'Please to meet you.'" Mike let out a burst of laughter and began coughing so hard his face turned beet red.

"Holy shit! You just stood there waiting for a handshake!" Mike screamed with laughter.

"I had never heard of you in my life!" Ben shouted through his howling.

"Oh man! I mean what the fuck, I had to shake your hand right?!" The General could barely ask. "That was the moment you got your handle."

"Towers." Ben acknowledged.

Mike took another sip of the moonshine he had in a small tumbler and saluted his young friend. Ben lifted his longneck Bud and connected with the backwoods potion before he took a mouthful.

"I took over this club and assumed national president the year I turned twenty five. It was a piss-ant, ragtag bunch of bums but I built this club into the best and now you're about to become the youngest VP of the whole Sworn nation."

"What?!" He exclaimed, as if not hearing him correctly.

"You heard me, I'm making you vice president of the Sworn nation next week. You'll be the youngest senior officer this club has ever had, and you beat me out of that record by three years!" Mike said with a wink and a nod.

"What about Moogie?" He asked, referring to their current national vice president.

"Don't say a word to anyone, but they just gave him less than a year to live. Cancer."

"Jesus, Mike." Ben whispered.

"I'll handle all the details. Every chapter will send a representative when I announce the date and time."

"You really think I'm the man for it?" He asked, looking for reassurance.

"Ben, very rarely does a kid come along who has a brain, leadership skills and a heart like yours. Yeah, you can handle it. Not only do you 'get it' but you have a way of talking to others that helps them to get it too."

"Yeah Mike, but nation? I only held chapter level before."

"If I say so, it's done, and I say so." Mike said with a raised eyebrow.

"You got it."

"That's my brother. Now listen, we need to talk about something very important, something very serious, do you understand?" The General asked, narrowing his gaze while looking through the glass of moonshine he was holding up to the light.

"A hit?" Ben asked under his breath.

"Yeah, Ben, it's just business."

He awoke from a deep sleep and stared at the Hunter ceiling fan that was turning slowly and pushing light tepid air down upon them. Ben's eyes moved and he glanced over at Lynne who was still sleeping soundly, partly due to the amount of incredible stress she was under and also the Valium that Dr. Trainor prescribed. He smiled to himself remembering when he and Joshua had installed the fan, teasing the young man that a first year electrical apprentice couldn't possibly be up to the task. Ben ate that joke after returning to the bedroom with two ham sandwiches and Coke's.

"It's done." Josh beamed up at him.

"No way!" Was all he could say after placing their lunch's down on the end table .

"Yup, turn it on big daddy." He turned the variable speed controller switch and the fan slowly came to life.

"She's quiet too." Josh added.

"Wish I could say the same for your mother sometimes." He replied, as Lynne walked into the room behind him and playfully wacked his back.

"I heard that!" She scolded with a smile.

Hexe's head raised when she saw him slowly get out of the queen sized bed and put his slippers on. "C'mon, let's go to the garage girl." Ben whispered, gently petting the side of her head.

She followed him down the refinished oak steps, pausing occasionally to look behind her as if contemplating whether to go back and sit with Lynne. Ben had just finished the work on the barn planked upstairs hallway when Lynne had made the keen observation that it would really be nice if the steps were redone as well. After ninety trips to Home Depot (as he liked to tease) the agreed finished look and materials were purchased. His 'husband labor' did the rest and Lynne's happiness was more than sufficient payment, notwithstanding the bartered surprise given later that evening. They reached the kitchen and Ben gave the shepherd a chewy; she had been addicted to the treats since she was six months old and Lynne had to scold the pup on more than a few occasions for sitting next to the pantry closet door while whining. Hexe would protest by barking and letting out high pitched yelps which caused Ben to laugh hysterically, and ultimately sneak behind his wife's back and spoil the girl.

The clock on the coffee maker informed him that it was 2:35 a.m., as he put a filter in and added four scoops of his favorite brand, Cafe Bustelo. Ben walked into the dinning room and gazed out through the large bay window, the darkness was impenetrable and blinded all that could be realized. Hexe sat at his feet and looked up at him with her head cocked to one side and sadness in her eyes.

"I know baby, it's a tough time right now, huh?" He asked gently.

They made their way out to his workshop that had been converted from an old barn that once housed ancient farm equipment and seed. The floor hatch which led to an earthen sub basement used to store the large cut blocks of ice for the summer months had remained closed since Joshua turned fourteen. He claimed that it just wasn't cool building forts down in the abyss anymore. Ben removed the old white bed sheet and there standing before him was Josh's twentieth birthday present. The candy apple red, 1990 FXRS Low Rider was absolutely beautiful and Josh built the whole thing in his mind, never realizing that it was being made for him. Ben sent the factory 1340 cc jugs out to an old buddy of his in Dayton Ohio, who bored it out to a 1450 cc and installed Wiseco high performance pistons bringing the compression ratio to 10:1. Once back in Pennsylvania, the fun began and after the addition of an S&S Super E carburetor and a Feuling cam kit (which keeps the intake valves open longer, throwing more fuel into the cylinder heads) he started asking the young man what he thought about the particulars.

"What do you think, spokes or mags?" Ben asked, nonchalantly.

"I like spokes, the twisted ones like you have on your King." Josh replied.

"Chrome?"

"Yeah, definitely chrome." His son replied, transfixed on the machine.

When he gave Ben a confused look during one of these question and answer sessions, he would simply shrug his shoulders and tell Josh that the guy he was building the bike for didn't know his ass from a hole in the ground.

"That color would look bad, dad!" He exclaimed, using the old Delaware Valley slang which really meant cool.

Ben waited until Josh went to work one morning before he fired the bike to life and the sound of a bored out V-Twin with straight drag pipes exploded into the morning air.

The flat, cut and rolled California style rear fender exposed the wide tire and the Model A Ford style tail light illuminated and vibrated with the engine's pulse. He rolled it outside to his awaiting wife who stood in the morning sun with her arms folded and a smile on her face.

"It's gorgeous honey, he's going to lose it!" She shouted over the fury.

Lynne ran her hand gently over the high gloss candy apple red paint job and followed the contours of the fat split tank.

"These look a little low though." She remarked, touching the one inch riser drag handlebars.

"You're just like a kid Lynne, stop touching everything!" He barked.

After he put the bike back into its hiding spot (because Josh was told that it went off to its new owner) Lynne remarked how she thought

Joshua would be just as surprised as he was when he was given his tenth birthday present.

"What is it?" The boy asked while looking at the manilla envelope.

"Go ahead and open it honey." She replied, smiling over to Ben.

Joshua carefully tore open the sealed envelope and began to read aloud.

"By the power vested in me by the Commonwealth State of Pennsylvania, I, Judge Martin Andrew Davis, am happy to announce and grant the adoption of Joshua James (Hollis) to Benjamin Roger Ladd, on this day, June 1st. 2013." The boy burst into tears and ran into Ben's arms burying his face deep into his large chest.

"I love you son." He said softly, stroking Josh's hair.

Chapter Four

"And you are?" The rookie detective asked into the phone while typing a key pad with his index fingers and glancing up at a wall calendar.

"I don't want to tell you my name, but I know who shot that electric worker guy in Kensington." A young juvenile answered.

"What did you just say? I'm sorry, I was a little distracted."

"I said, I know who shot that dude in the work van." The teen stated again.

The detective cupped his hand over the mouthpiece and snapped his fingers loudly, getting the attention of those who were in close proximity.

"Yo, I gotta kid on the phone who claims he knows about the Ladd murder." He said quietly but with urgency.

"Go ahead, Clay." His senior urged softly, spinning his hand in the air motioning for him to continue.

"How did you get this number kid?" Detective Clayton asked.

"My name's Greg, and I aint no kid!" The boy exclaimed.

"I thought you didn't want to give me your name." He quipped, receiving a pat on his shoulder from his boss.

"Shit, I fucked up." The teen mumbled.

"No, you're talking to a detective Greg, and that's how we roll." Clayton said sarcastically.

"Ya can't tell anyone." Greg pleaded.

"Well, my name is Sergeant Clayton but you can call me Clay, alright man?"

"Okay." The teen replied under his breath.

"So, where did you get my number Greg?"

"Miss Ramona gave it to me, I told her that I'd ask around." The boy admitted freely.

"Ramona Jones, the lady on the news?" Clayton asked innocently.

"Yeah, you guys were passing out cards. Do you remember her house down the street from where it happened?"

"Yes, I remember her house because I grew up about four blocks from there." Clay said with a smile, realizing that he had just made a connection.

"In that 'hood?" The teen asked.

"Yup, in that same 'hood, brother."

"Damned." The boy said with a squeak in his voice.

Clayton looked up at his boss and both men began to chuckle.

"Who's that?" The boy asked seriously.

"Just another home boy who thinks he's a super pimp."

"Fuck outta here!" Detective Richards shot back with a laugh.

Greg began to laugh after he heard the whole room roaring in the background and the result was a magical release of his anxiety and fear.

"I'd like to meet up with you Greg, if that's alright with you?"

"Yeah, maybe but not down there." He replied, referring to the precinct.

"No, of course not. I could come to you though, and believe me man, nobody would know I was a cop, understand?"

"Yeah." Greg answered with skepticism in his voice.

"How old are you, for real?" Clay inquired, jotting down notes in a spiral pad.

"Thirteen." The boy answered as if he didn't want to be heard.

Clay put his hand over the phone again and looked up at Richards knowing exactly what he was thinking.

"You're going to have to bring someone from Child Services, even if they just sit and observe. He's a minor." Richards whispered off to the side.

"I know." Clayton said under his breath.

"Listen Greg, it's like this, your thirteen and I can't meet with you out there without having a parent or legal guardian present. Maybe even someone from Child Services, you know? They could even be sitting in my car or just watching."

"I thought you wanted my help." Greg stated with a hint of anguish in his voice.

"Greg, you have no idea how much we need your help brother, but there are rules man." Clay exclaimed.

"Well, if we meet how am I gonna know it's you and not a set-up?" The teen asked suspiciously. Richards tapped Clay's shoulder and chuckled.

"Huh? I'll be wearing that bright green Eagles jersey, that's how!" Clayton said proudly.

"Eagles?! Shit, I'll be in my Cowboys gear!" Greg taunted playfully.

"Oh, it's gonna be like that huh? Well, I don't think we can meet up then Greg!"

Chapter Five

The funeral attendees began arriving at 10:00 a.m., and were led by church elders to the large white revival tent that had been set up alongside the house the previous afternoon. There were more volunteers than needed, so the men began mowing and pruning the large expanse of the landscaped area while others still, chopped and split cordwood all the while directing their children on where and how high to stack. The women brought covered dishes filled with hams, casseroles, baked and mashed potatoes, pickled beets, greens and deviled eggs. At first both Ben and Lynne protested, insisting that they couldn't possibly accept this level of generosity and merely stand by and watch everyone doing all the work. Their church family, neighbors and old friends alike refused to back down as they continued to actively give from their hearts presenting unconditional love. Fall in the Pennsylvania countryside is clear, crisp and beautiful. The hardwoods are slowly changing from dark lush green to golden yellow and fire blaze red. Migratory waterfowl are in transit overhead and the Canadian geese who moved to the mid Atlantic region back in the 1980's, honk and flail about as if agitated to see the uninvited arrival of their distant cousins.

They sat down in the front row on the two chairs that were placed exclusively for them and their eyes gazed at the coffin sitting a mere six feet away, suddenly images of Joshua's life began to transpire on the large screen behind it. The still of a red faced, screaming newborn slowly faded to a baby sitting in a high chair covered with birthday cake and joy in his eyes. Photos of a child's life from the days when he sat on Santa's lap and cute Halloween costumes that Lynne made, to Little League and vacations at the Jersey shore. Ben placed his arm around her and lightly gripped her shoulder as she began to tremble and weep. The look upon her face was more than he could bear and he too began to cry.

"Good morning, friends, family and loved ones." Pastor Walt said with open arms. "We are all here today to give our love and support to Lynne and Ben as we send their cherished son home and into the arms of Christ."

"Amen." All in attendance said in unison.

"Let me first say to you both, how sorry I am and all of us are for the pain and sorrow your going through. Our hearts and prayers are filled with love and I know that there will be many days ahead when we will come together as a family to aid in the healing." Walt offered as he slowly walked from the lectern and over to Ben and Lynne. He then knelt down before them and the three embraced.

"Behind me are the moments of Joshua's life and make no mistake about it, he had a unique way of letting everyone know when he was bored. From the time when he was six years old, putting little holes in the bottoms of the styrofoam coffee cups after church and giggling while watching as a few of us complained about the leaks dribbling all over our clothes; to when he was around ten and he loosened the collars on all of the new urinals in the men's room!" A roar of laughter filled the air as Ben shouted out that he was Josh's first victim of the men's room caper.

"My new suit pants were soaked!" He shouted with a laugh.

"Josh!" a young woman pleaded, the pain in her voice could not be mistaken.

"It's alright love!" The pastor responded. "Can we see a show of hands from everyone else who is here today from his highschool graduating class?"

All in attendance turned and looked at the large section of about fifty young people who raised their hands identifying themselves, they all had tears in their eyes. After the blessing and a reading from the Bible, 'Good people pass away; the godly often die before their time. But no one seems to care or wonder why. No one seems to understand that God is protecting them from the evil to come.' Isaiah 57:1-2 (chosen by Lynne). Ben stood and walked to the podium.

"Thank you all for coming today and know that Lynne and I love you." He began while wiping tears from his eyes. "Joshua came into my life when he was seven years old and to this day I can't imagine what I ever did to deserve such a fine son. He was polite, gentle and kind; inquisitive enough to drive me crazy at times with a thousand questions but his heart was pure gold." Ben heard his wife let out a small giggle and he knew that she was remembering happier days.

Chapter Six

"Will you be ready in the morning?" Detective Clayton asked.

"Yeah, I'll be showing up." The teenager answered as if he was an undercover agent.

"I'll be on the number 89 tomorrow morning at 8:00 a.m., pick it up on the corner of East Russell street at 8:22, is that okay with you Greg?"

"Okay, and that lady who's gonna be on the bus don't know me right?" The boy asked as if rethinking the agreement.

"Chill Greg, alright young blood? Fuck no she don't you, she don't even know me!" He joked.

It had been previously arranged with the Department of Human Services to have a representative from Child Welfare along with a female detective to sit in close proximity, posing as passengers on the bus. Detective Clayton's boss had picked up the phone and explained with urgency how delicate the situation was. Considering the probability that the incident was the direct result of gang activity, within an hour a court order had been granted. All of the requested personnel were notified, the stipulation being that the Child Welfare supervisor and the policewoman would be present only as observers and Detective Clayton's capacity was strictly to gain information (while wearing a wire) concerning the Ladd homicide.

The extruding interior air blew back her jacket lapels as Juliet stepped up into the bus, and immediately the driver noticed her state employee's badge; he then motioned for her to pass the fare box and take a seat. She thanked him before proceeding to the rear and after passing a few riders who were standing along the isle holding onto hand grips, she noticed the young auburn haired woman wearing a Jack O'lantern sweater and bluejeans.

"May, I?" Juliet asked, pointing down to the empty seat.

"Of course." She replied with a smile.

"My name's Julie." she said, after sitting and placing a bookbag at her feet.

"I'm Kim, and it's nice meeting you." The woman responded before nodding in the direction of Detective Clayton.

"Got it Kim, thanks."

Three stops later a young juvenile wearing a Dallas Cowboys hoodie and hat got on the bus, paid his fare and walked slowly to the rear. His sunglasses were straddled low on the bridge of his nose as he gazed over the frames carefully scanning for the man in an Eagles jersey and a cigarette tucked into his right ear. Without warning, a large and severe looking man stood up in the aisle and waited momentarily until he was sure that the kid saw the detective who was sitting by the window. Suddenly, their eyes met and Clay gave Greg a wink before he nodded to the empty seat.

"What's up Greg?" Clayton asked softly while keeping his eyes forward.

"She, here?" The teen responded nervously.

"She, who?" Clayton inquired, leaning toward the kid to make room for a passenger walking past them.

"The lady from Child Services?" The teen asked with a hint of sarcasm.

"I told you man, I don't know who she is. It's way easier this way bro."

"Okay, you gotta badge?" The teen asked, looking over his sunglasses.

Detective Clayton shot him a sarcastic grin. "Some days I wish I didn't." He said, lowering his right hand and opening the badge wallet.

"Cool." The boy whispered.

"Now, you have something for me Greg?" Clayton asked with a raised eyebrow.

"My name's not Greg." The teen stated, as if getting one over on the detective.

Clayton's mouth dropped and he let out a chuckle. "Are you fucking with me kid?"

"Nope, my name's Jerome Wilts, but you can call me Jelly."

"You got some balls, I'll give ya that!" Clayton exclaimed, trying to keep his laughter under control. "You can call me Clay from now on, if you like."

"What, you think I'm an idiot?" Jelly asked rhetorically.

"No man, not at all Jelly." Detective Clayton responded with a fast wink.

"Look, you grew up out here, you know what this shit's like." The teen explained.

"Yeah, I lost a few friends myself back in the day." Clay agreed.

"The motherfucker who killed that Ladd dude aint no joke either, he's straight up GSM." Jelly stated.

"Out of DC?" Clayton asked, glancing over at an elderly woman who was standing up to exit the bus.

"Yup, and he aint no foot troop either, ya feel me?"

"How high up, Jelly?" Clay asked, trying to invoke a street feel.

"Like, about upper management here in Philly."

"Killer?" Clayton asked, checking to see if the kid was being sincere.

"That's a stupid question, Clay." Jelly responded, cocking his head over quickly as if saying, 'What do you think?'

"Sorry man, had to ask. How do you even know this guy?" Clayton wanted to know, using a softer tone in the hope that there was still a little bit of a kid inside Jelly that he could talk too.

"I'm friends with his lady's brother, I see him all the time." Jelly answered, looking up at an advertisement for young mothers to get counseling.

"What's his girl's name?"

"Trina." Jelly whispered.

"And what's the shooter's name?" Clayton asked, thinking that the kid would choke out.

"Blaze. His real name is Andre Pelts." Jelly said coldly, looking directly into Clayton's eyes.

He slowly began to show the teen that he cared, and was listening intently through the use of his body language. Clayton slouched lower into his seat so as to appear smaller and leaned his head in closer to Jelly's, guaranteeing the boy that he was paying close attention.

"DC." Jelly repeated under his breath.

"No shit, an original GSM gangbanger up in here?" .

"Yup, and a nigga named Shey aint to cool with that." Jelly continued.

"Shey?" Clay asked with a confused look.

"Yeah, he's with the 'Hoods,' they're a brand spanking new crew." The boy giggled. "Punks, really."

"You know him too?" The detective asked with a surprised tone.

"Naw, but I seen him around. Usually cruising up the block tryin' to represent." (This is a common tactic that shows a rival gang member that they're not intimidated and will stand and fight).

"So, you know what he looks like?" Clayton prodded further.

"Yeah." Jelly certified with a nod.

"And you know for sure that Blaze shot and killed Joshua Ladd?" Clay asked, giving him a serious stare.

"Yup, no doubt. Right after him and Cleats got shot up." Jelly certified his answer with a quick nod.

"Okay, here's a hundred bucks, go buy lunch and we'll talk later." Clay said with a smile.

"I aint doin' this for money, my mom got killed in a driveby the same way." Jelly answered, looking away.

"I get it." The young detective acknowledged after shoving the bill into his hoodie pocket.

The silver, 2018 BMW 3 Series slowly cruised up West Glenwood avenue in the city's North section and slowed down at the corner of West Cambria. The passenger's side window buzzed down and the driver called over to the young female who had been standing at the bus stop. She was completely unaware of the driver in a 2016 black Mercedes GL sitting behind a line of parked cars watching her.

"Yo Trina, get in." Shey ordered. She opened the door and sank down into the warm and inviting saddle leather seat.

"What do you need to see me for?" She asked, with a hint of attitude.

"You know goddamned right well what I need to see you about!" He shouted. "Did Blaze kill that Ladd kid or what?"

"All this because I got caught with two ounces of dope?"

"You agreed to the terms girl, now I need to know the truth."

"Fuckin' Feds!" She exclaimed.

"That's fuckin' Special Agent Moss to you!" He quipped, hoping that she would laugh at his sarcasm.

"How the fuck do I know?" She asked sharply.

"Oh girl please, I got people sayin' he was the motherfucker in the car that got shot up just before Ladd got murdered."

"Well then go talk to those people, 'cause this aint got nothin' to do with dope, asshole!" Trina shouted back.

"If I find out your playin' girl!" He threatened.

"Pull this damned car over!" She demanded with the look of a wildcat.

"Fine, get the fuck out and I'll see you next week."

"What you wanna do Blaze?" The driver of the Benz asked into his Iphone.

"Stay with that nigga, and stay hid, you get a chance, bust one in his ass."

"Okay, boss."

Trina slammed the door and flicked Moss the bird before turning quickly and storming off towards the bus stop.

"Fuck you bitch." He hissed as he pulled away from the curb and banged a U-turn.

The driver of the Mercedes did likewise after making sure that the BMW was far enough ahead so as not to notice the tail. Moss then proceeded West on Glenwood and jumped on Rt. 611 Southbound (Broad street) until getting off at the Thomas Jefferson University Hospital exit on Chestnut. He pulled the BMW into the hospital staff parking lot, exited the vehicle and got into a newish maroon Jeep Grand Cherokee XL. All the while the black Mercedes was sitting across the street parked on South 10th, and its driver was videoing Moss's every move. The Jeep eventually made a hard left at 600 Arch street and pulled into the underground parking garage of the William J. Green Jr. Federal Building.

"I fucking knew it, he's a Fed!" The GL driver said to himself as he pushed the red stop icon on his phone's camera.

Chapter Seven

"Believe it or not, this Harley is up here because it was meant to be Josh's twentieth surprise birthday present, which is next month. He never knew that I was building it for him and all the questions I asked about what he thought might look good on it actually began to drive him crazy!" Ben exclaimed. A hint of jovial mischief appeared upon his face.

"Yeah, that's right kiddo, take that!" He joked as the entire tent joined in laughter.

"I'll never forget the first night you brought me to this great house baby. Of course, I didn't realize at the time that you already had a 'Honey-Do List' hidden away in your head but…" Lynne looked up at him and smiled her genuine loving smile and Ben almost broke down.

He looked out to the open and barren vast field that had recently been harvested of feed corn. The noon day sun had long burned off the early morning dew and there was a touch of humidity in the Pennsylvania air.

"This is the most fertile earth in the Eastern United States, if not the whole country." Lynne mentioned, just before they began turning one of the four large fields.

Ben glanced over at the guests and smiled to himself while taking in the sight of the old two story, stone home that he and Lynne had completely renovated themselves.

"Let's take a moment to close our eyes, bow our heads and send up a silent prayer to Joshua."

"Wow, how old is this place?" He asked as the headlights from his Dodge pickup illuminated the entire front of the 18th Century farmhouse, after bumping along the fifty yard roadway that led up to it.

"It's older than me, and I was born here." Lynne joked.

After shutting the truck off, he leaned over and kissed her and she accepted by wrapping her arms around his neck and squeezing him tight.

"You think maybe this could lead to something? I mean, would you really be interested in an old, has-been biker like me?" Ben asked seriously.

"A fine reformed honest man who is finding his way to the Lord? No, absolutely not Benjamine. I want a fake, greedy, womanizing liar who will mistreat me and make me write bad checks!" They both howled laughter while looking at each other and her smile and flushed cheeks made his heart melt.

"I swear Lynne, you are a smartass!"

Just then a flashlight beam burned into the truck cab and a young boy's voice shouted out with authority. "Alright, hold it right there Mr. Buddy Boy, I got ya surrounded!" The boy squealed laughter.

"The question is, would you really be interested in a single mom who has a lunatic seven year old kid!"

"Hi Ben!" Joshua shouted with excitement. "This is where we live and it's a good place!"

"I can see that Josh!" He responded, opening up the truck's door and getting out.

They walked up the three granite slabbed low front steps that ascended to the porch, and upon stepping on the floor Ben could feel the sagging, aged deteriorated wood underfoot. Once inside the main door, he noticed a clean and warm home that was in need of some TLC. Wallpaper that looked like it had been hung sometime in the 1980's peeled away from the corners of the livingroom and where the seams met, revealing the original plaster and lath walls behind it. The barn planked hardwood floors had scuffs, gouges and stains; in high traffic areas the varnish had worn away completely leaving it naked and raw looking.

"It's been in my family for six generations, and my brother Craig and I were going to farm again someday but he was killed in Iraq."

"I'm sorry, Lynne." Ben said softly.

"It's okay, that's his picture on the mantle."

The three had sat down to dinner at the dining room table and Lynne began to cut into the homemade lasagna. Joshua was excited to see Ben and began asking him a hundred questions ranging from motorcycles to how come he didn't shave his beard sometimes.

"You're a good boy, Joshua!" Ben stated after noticing him passing around the sliced bread.

"He was about two…" Lynne said. "And one morning after I had wiped down the kitchen counters and mopped the floor, I decided to go out back and water some plants that I had hanging on the clothesline." The boy let out a high pitched laugh and stared lovingly at his mother waiting for her to tell this famous family tale.

"I heard the teapot whistling, so I sat the garden hose down and went back inside to turn the burner off. What do you think I saw as I was about to open the screen door and go back outside? This little bugger in Huggie Pull-Ups, mud up to his belly button, standing there with the orneriest Jesse James grin you ever saw while gripping the hose gun and pointing it at me!" Ben began laughing so hard he had to hold onto his stomach which in turn started a ruckus.

"Don't you squirt mommy, Josh! Put that down right this instant!" I shouted to him and yup, the next thing you know he let out a yell and blasted me with it! I mean, I was soaked from head to toe, hopping up and down in one spot screaming my head off and the entire kitchen looked like it had been in a flood. There was water running off the counters, the refrigerator was streaming and the floor, oh my God, Ben you should have seen it! The whole time, this kid was squealing his little pants off!"

"What did you do?" Ben asked after he was able to catch his breath.

"I spanked the crap out of him, then sprayed him off with the garden hose, dried his butt off and in the playpen he went, until he cried himself to sleep."

"Now you listen to me Josh and you listen good. I know you're excited and I can tell by the look on your face that you think you've really got the hang of this bike. I get it son, believe me, I get that one hundred percent. You're ten years old and you've got your clutch, shifting and braking down but always remember one thing, you can never let it get ahead of you, not ever. It will kill you for sure and the very second you lose respect for these things will be the moment your wrapped around a tree. I bought this for you because I love you and believe me, your mother was dead set against it from day one, so don't let me down boy." Ben said in a serious tone while staring at Joshua without blinking.

"I won't dad, I promise." He replied seriously.

"And don't ever take it out on the main road, cagers will run you over sure as hell!"

"Joshua, grab me the broom out of the closet would ya?" His mom asked from the porch. Ben had appeared at the end of the hallway silently walking up behind the young teen in his stocking feet while holding his cell phone and videoing the whole scene.

"It's a puppy!" Joshua's voice squeaked in true puberty fashion. "And it pooped on the broom!" He added, laughing as he picked up the shaking and squirming six week old female German Shepherd.

"The little witch!" Ben exclaimed, while Josh held the puppy up close to the phone's camera lens.

"Say hi to Ben, baby." Joshua said, lifting the puppy up to him.

"Witch, is a really good name actually." Lynne added.

"Well, she is German so look up the translation?" Joshua asked, while the dog licked the side of his head.

"It says here that in German it's 'Hexe' or 'Hexen' depending on how it's used and in what context." Lynne explained, reading the definition from her Babbel app.

"You like that name girl?" The excited boy asked as the pup squirmed around in his arms and licked his chin. "'Hexe' it is then!"

"It's not fair dad, she said she loved me!" The sixteen year old exclaimed, his voice was filled with confusion and angst.

"Joshua, listen to me son. There are going to be many young women in your life before God sends you the one who will be your true mate."

"But, I love her!" He said, bursting into tears.

"I know you do, and right now your heart is breaking up and it feels like you've been gutted…"

"Why did she break up with me, is there another guy or what? She won't tell me!" He asked in pain.

"There could be many reasons Josh, maybe she just wanted to be free and not be with anybody or maybe she thought this was the easiest way, if she didn't want to see you anymore." Ben said in a consoling tone while avoiding the possibility that Joshua's ex girlfriend, Rachel had met another guy.

"You don't think she's with someone else then?" He asked with wet pain filled eyes.

"No, my guess is she's just trying to be decent about her reason and she doesnt want to hurt you any more than necessary. She's going to work down at the beach soon Josh, I really think that she just wants this time to be free."

"My son, you were a better man than I." Ben announced, looking down at the casket. "You were a loving, caring and decent young man. You applied yourself in school, studied, passed exams and played sports. You worked long hard hours here on the farm and that never got in the way of you taking night classes and working on your apprenticeship. Your mother and I love you more than you'll ever know."

"I would like to finish by saying to all of the young folks here today, that Josh would want you to go out into the world and get on with your lives. Go to college, get good jobs, marry, settle down and have children. Do all the things in this life that he'll never be able to do. Someday, when you're older and wiser, I hope that you'll look back on this day if you can and remember Joshua as a friend. He was a good person who was taken away from us too soon, but will never be forgotten by those who love him."

After he finished, Ben looked out over the guests and noticed four men getting out of an older Cadillac. All were wearing black suits and one had a charcoal Stetson Seneca with silver conchs. They donned sunglasses, gray and white beards and stern expressions. He smiled to himself after seeing them intercepted by Mrs. Bryce, the eighty eight year old church widow who had a soul as pure as God's Word. She no doubt was welcoming the four to the funeral service and reporting all they had missed. The man leading them into the banquet tent removed his hat and the others stood solemnly with their hands folded in front of their stomachs. Suddenly, as if on some sort of karma que Ben's eyes met Lucy's for the time in fifteen years.

"I'm sorry to hear about your boy, brother. Beth also sends her love." He said, gripping Ben's hand in a coded hold.

"Thank you man, and it's good seeing you too Lucy." The two embraced and were soon joined by the other three.

"Towers." The oldest looking man announced.

"Hey Bones, thanks for coming out, it means alot to me." Ben answered, accepting his hand shake.

"We heard about it on the news, then read the obituary in the paper." Lucy explained.

"Is it all right that we came, Towers?" The largest man, who had a Teddy Bear cuteness about him, asked.

"Absolutely Mickey, are you kidding me?!" Ben assured them all. "Hey brother, how the hell have you been?" Asked the last friend who was waiting.

"You look good Towers!" He exclaimed, giving Ben a big hug.

"Oh Jocko, seeing you all brings back so many memories!" His voice cracked as the five of them stood together arm in arm not taking their eyes off of one another.

"Let it all out brother." Jocko encouraged, giving Ben a pat on the back.

"Yes sir, Towers, get rid of that poison man." Lucy urged.

"The two guys you assholes blew up in Fredericksburg were good brothers and they meant the world to me!" The General was referring to the attack on one of his clubmate's houses shortly after their weekly chapter meeting had ended. The Sworn had just moved into the region about a month earlier, when the established but much smaller motorcycle club from Northern Virginia and Western Maryland, Odin's Order, got the bright idea of throwing two sticks of dynamite through their living room window. The sticks were taped together along with a brick and after landing in the middle of the room exploded, killing the two men who lived there. The General shouted down to the two naked and beaten men who were hog tied and laying in their own shit and piss on the wet, cold concrete floor of a leaky and abandoned old gas station. The only telltale sign that remained of the Phillips 66 service station, was a faded and broken light sign standing dark and alone on the corner of South Maryln avenue and SouthEast boulevard. Ancient exterior oil paint peeled and rolled away from the cracked moldy cinder block walls and weeds grew from the separated blacktop. It was two o'clock in the morning, and not much happened at this hour in Essex, Maryland.

"I knew them boys for a long time and Towers here even recruited one of them. I know that the motherfucker that ratted you out was there when it happened too! You know how we found that out?! Brother Lucy, down in Virginia got a call from one of our chapters and they said that a nice old neighbor lady described the truck leaving the house just before it went up, and the patches on your jackets. So, we grabbed the easy piece of shit first and he sang us a nice little song about you two. I had a road flare to his feet, so I knew he was telling the truth!" The General screamed at the top of his lungs to the point that his voice cracked.

Ben stood next to Mike with his arms folded and his presence alone was nothing short of awesome and terrifying. His long black hair that was pulled back in a ponytail left his sharp chiseled face plain to see.

Large dark eyes were set in an angry squint. His full dark beard faded to his thick muscular neck and his broad chest, shoulders and biceps spoke for themselves. The six foot, six inch Ben 'Towers' Ladd was as smooth as ivory and built like a turbo diesel powered Frieghtliner.

"Which one do you want Mike?" He asked, looking down at his president and best friend.

"I want em both!" He shouted with rage in his voice before raising the .357 Smith & Wesson K-Frame and shooting them both in the head.

"Dead." Ben whispered gruffly, kicking one of them in the ribcage.

"Jockey rider, circle back, dinner's ready." The General ordered into the Motorola walkie-talkie.

"10-4, in five." Jocko's voice cracked through, answering his boss.

Ben awoke in the middle of the night, a cold sweat covered his body and the sheets were damp. He heard the echo of a crow squawking off in the distant recesses of his consciousness, and tears began streaming from his eyes.

Chapter Eight

"Yo Trina, Marcus out front, says there's a big surprise party gonna happen for yo girl, Amara!"

"When Blaze, now?" The excited teenager asked.

"Yeah c'mon girl, grab ya shit and let's go!" He insisted.

"Oh, I know dats right!" Trina exclaimed joyfully.

Blaze suggested that they sit in the back seat before ordering Marcus to drive them to the spot. Shortly after he pulled the black Mercedes Benz away from the curb, he asked Blaze if he had seen the latest prank video on Youtube.

"No man, what's that some funny shit?" Blaze answered, smiling at Trina.

"Yo man, y'all gonna rip!" Marcus exclaimed, looking back at the two through the rearview mirror revealing his two front gold teeth.

"Let me see?" Trina asked, after Blaze had taken ahold of the cell phone.

The video captured every moment of Trina and Special Agent Moss's time together. It started with her getting into the silver BMW, continued with her exiting the vehicle and finally it showed Moss switching cars at Jefferson and driving to the federal building on Arch street.

"No Blaze, you got it all wrong, I thought he gonna buy dope!" She pleaded, shaking her head.

"Lyin' bitch! How long have you been talkin' with the Feds?!" Blazed demanded, reaching for the Glock in his waistband.

"No baby, please!" Was the last thing she managed to say before he pistol whipped her, rendering her unconscious.

"Yo, I kinda feel bad Blaze." Marcus said in a low voice.

"What about this snitch here?" He responded, while grabbing the back of the girl's hair and lifting her head up to show his friend.

"Naw, not that dumb bitch." Marcus answered, glancing back over his shoulder. "Are you sure that it was Cleats and not me who shot you at the hit?"

"Yeah bro, Im positive, he panicked and got me as I was tryin' to get out of the way. Now c'mon man, let's go do this thing!" Blaze ordered, motioning for Marcus to stomp down on the gas.

A hazy morning sun cloaked itself underneath a veil of grayish white sky as it came into view over the Betsy Ross Bridge. Through the light fog that permeated the skyline, the blurred car lights and exhaust smoke corrupted this scene with endless rows of commuter traffic. The air was dense and damp as Detective Clayton got into his white 2020 Toyota Tacoma. He reached for the roll of paper towels (that he always had on board because his two year boy, Corey was a perpetual mess) tore off a sheet, and blew his nose.

"Feels like sandpaper." He mumbled to himself just before his phone rang.

"Clay?" Richards asked sharply.

"Yeah, boss?"

"Sending you photos."

"Okay, go ahead."

Clayton was horrified at the images that he was seeing on his phone. The first one was a close up of an amateur tattoo that simply read, 'Trina' in black ink. Another photo (taken approximately ten feet from her remains) revealed that the girl had been hacked into three or four pieces. Last was the shot that actually disgusted Clayton the most for it screamed silent brutality and was sheer evil. Blood was splattered on every surface of the kitchen and it sprayed in an arch-like fashion streaking most of the ceiling.

"I need you to get down here to 3161 Custer street, off Allegheny." Richards ordered. "And bring me a Wawa coffee, please."

"You got it."

"I've called forensic and the coroner, they said they'll be another hour or so. Right now all I got is two Motor Unit's out front." Richards informed him in a far away voice.

"Okay, on my way." Clayton assured him.

A cold steady breeze out of the North blew dust and trash across the desolate and dirty streets of Kensington, and the particle board covered windows of the vacant graffiti laden abandoned row homes slid past him as he made his way to Custer. Occasionally, a homeless person would waddle out into the gutter and glance up at Clay with a look of hopelessness and despair. Lines of drug addicts sat huddled together, side by side and he even saw a young female with her sweat pants pulled down around her ankles squatting back and urinating from a curb.

In the mid 1800's Kensington had a booming textile industry that produced mostly carpets; along with iron and steel manufacturing, machine works and tool making. The entire residential community consisted of hard working, middle class Americans until deindustrialization in the 1950's brought population loss and high unemployment. The area never regained economic balance and as a result, social degeneration continued to erode these streets, and Kensington was left to sink into the abyss.

"Heads up sir, it's a mess in there!" Corporal Delano called over to Clayton who was getting out of his truck.

"Yeah. so I've heard. When the other units get here, shut down this side of the street. The whole row." He ordered, thumbing from one end of the four unit row of attached homes to the other.

"Yes sir, no problem."

"George?" Clayton called out as he entered the abandoned, boarded up house.

"Back here, Chris!" Detective Richards replied.

Without realizing it both men had dropped all formalities while addressing each other. This happened in most instances when the occurrence or circumstance was visibly brutal and heinous. It was as if the fragile human condition preceded anything else for those that felt empathy and had a soul.

"Dear, God." Clayton whispered.

"They hacked her up, the sick fucks." Richards added, not looking over at him.

"More than one attacker?"

"Note the two different, smudged sized footprints on the floor and the direction of the blood splatters on the walls. Right handed attacker sprayed blood to the left and the left handed man carried it to the right; after the initial strikes of course." Richards surmised while looking up at the rookie detective.

"What do you think they used, boss?" Clayton asked, stooping over to examine the cuts that separated the girl's limbs.

"Probably machete's."

"Hey fellas, four units just rolled up and we're taping off now!" Delano called in through the front door.

"Okay, thanks!" Richards replied.

"Chris, grab my pack there, and give me those print kits." He ordered.

"What are you serious? Forensics will be here any minute." Clayton warned.

"Fuck em. Besides, they're backlogged until the second coming. If this is who we think it is, I want to move on it now, so let's go."

They donned latex surgical gloves and didn't make eye contact or utter a word during the grizzly process of lifting up the teen's separated limbs and pressing her fingers, palms, and footprints to the kit's print board that they had neatly laid out on the decrepit linoleum. Detective Clayton's flashlight beam reflected off of something near the bottom of Trina's torso and he froze dumbfounded and horrified as if not believing what his eyes were seeing.

"George." he whispered. "There's a cellphone jammed up in her vagina."

"What?" Richards replied while crouching down near the floor aiming his light at it.

"I was looking around her remains and it gleamed in my light."

"I got it, we'll check it out when we get back. This one's between you and me Chris, understand?" Richard asked as if making a pact.

"You bet sir." Clayton winked.

Steve walked over to his partner and pulled a pack of Marlboro's out of his leather jacket making sure that he was facing him directly and intentionally blocking his view before giving him a wink.

"Got a light Craig?" He asked, putting the cigarette in his mouth.

"Yeah." His partner replied, reaching for his zippo. "What, you need fluid?"

"No man listen, and don't look when I tell you." Steve whispered.

"Go ahead." Craig nodded, acknowledging the dynamic at play.

"There's a black GL about thirty yards behind me, he's been sitting there since we first rolled in. I thought that maybe he was picking someone up or on his phone, but he's watching us." He explained, staring at his partner with narrowed eyes.

"What do you want to do?" Craig asked softly.

"I want to check him out." He said under his breath, exhaling smoke through his nostrils.

Craig moved his eyes in the direction of the other four officers that were talking out front of the rowhouse, and Steve slowly shook his head 'no.'

"I don't want to scare him off, if he doesn't bang a u-turn, act like you're heading toward your bike and step in front of him. I'll hold him at his door." Steve suggested. "And we got him, man."

"Okay, but we need to be quick about it." Craig agreed.

The Mercedes pulled away from the curb and headed in their direction, luckily a large PECO (Pennsylvania Electric Company) cherry picker pulled out from a side street and rolled directly in back of the GL.

Steve Delano saw his partner nod before he walked out to his bike then into the middle of Allegheny avenue. Craig put his left hand up and the other was on the butt of his Glock G22; he stood with his hip cocked to one side and the polished riding boots and spurs gave the impression of a high noon standoff.

"Stop the car!" He shouted, the order echoed off the buildings in the cold dense air.

Immediately the driver put the vehicle into reverse but the utility truck had managed to get within six feet of the Mercedes, blocking any attempt from backing away. The late morning sun reflected off the GL's windshield, and the glare was blinding for both cop and criminal. In the blink of an eye, while Steve was approaching the driver's side door, Officer Craig Dane Jr., saw what every street cop on the planet feared in a suspected vehicle.

"Gun, gun, he's got a gun!" Craig yelled excitedly.

"Let me see your hands motherfucker!" Steve ordered at the top of his lungs while pointing his gun directly at the side of the man's head through the window.

The other four officers ran to the scene and two took cover behind Steve, Another managed to get between the utility truck and the GL before finding an optimum firing position across Allegheny avenue; the fourth one stepped out in front of the car and stood next to Craig. Marcus's gold teeth flashed while giving a 'go to hell' smile just before he raised his Bond Arms Bullpup 9mm and pointed it at the windshield. Steve got off three quick shots in succession, disintegrating the driver's window and killing the driver instantly. Marcus's head rocked violently as the rounds impacted into his cranium, and a pinkish red mist mixed with glass shards and gunsmoke sprayed the car's interior.

Chapter Nine

They sat on the leather couch in front of the stone hearth holding hands under the warm goose down comforter. Ben occasionally got up and stoked the fire with the hardwood that he and Joshua had split and stacked the previous season.

"Do you want anything from the kitchen Lynne?" He asked.

"No, just you." She replied gently, smiling with sad eyes.

Hexe managed to shmooze her way to the couch, and she placed her head between them before gazing up at Lynne. She could sense the loss and fragile state of her owners, she herself would whine and enter into Josh's bedroom periodically through the night checking to see if he had returned home.

"She can feel your pain." Ben whispered, gently petting the dog's head.

"I know she does and I hate not seeing her happy or playing. She never leaves my side, do ya baby?" She asked, a thump on the hardwood floor answered as Hexe's response was through her tail.

"I saw those four men today Ben." Lynne whispered.

"Old friends who heard about what happened. They just wanted to stop in and pay their respects."

"Club?"

"Yeah honey, they're old and retired club like me." He explained, hoping that his inclusion would cease any concern.

"No, not like you Ben, not like you at all." Lynne rolled her head up from under his arm and gave him a serious look.

"How's that?" He inquired with a frown.

"You found the Lord."

"Yeah, that's true, but it's also an ongoing process."

"Little by little, you are gaining, and your soul is healing Ben, I can tell."

"I can feel it too." He assured her.

"Was there any talk about them wanting you back?" She asked, a hint of suspicion was just under the surface.

"Lynne, first of all, the rules say that I can't go back. I'm retired and I left in good standing. And don't forget, I'm an old fart now!" He boomed, causing her to laugh.

"I needed to hear that." Ben whispered softly in her ear.

"What?" She asked.

"I needed to hear you laugh, because the sadness on your face is killing me." He answered before giving her a kiss on the top of her head.

"They're no different than anyone else, Lynne." He explained with a serious gaze.

"I know Ben, because if there was never a sinner born, heaven would be empty."

"Amen. If I can do it, anyone can." He said with a grin.

"Yes, and I'm sure you remember our conversation the first time you came here, after Joshua went to bed."

Lynne had made a carafe of decaf coffee and invited him to come into the kitchen and join her in a bowl of Breyers vanilla ice cream. She warmed up some Hershey's chocolate syrup and Smucker's butterscotch topping sauce in a small water filled pot before placing the sugaree banquet on the round table.

"Your testimony last Sunday really moved me, Ben and I respect your honesty." She said, scooping out the icecream from the cardboard container.

"Thank you Lynne, and I also want to thank you for inviting me back to your home after our shopping date. I'm horrible in the grocery store!" Ben exclaimed in mock disgust.

"Now, it's my turn to confess my past." Lynne offered with raised hands.

"You don't have to tell me anything." He interjected.

"No Ben, please let me finish, I want to. There was once a day when I sold my body, a day when I was a drug addict trapped in a very physically abusive relationship, I can't tell you how many times that I went to the ER and got x-rays. I got pregnant by a man I didn't even know, that guy turned out to be Joshua's father and I only met him once. I slept in seedy motels infested with bed bugs, the back seats of abandoned cars and homeless shelters. I shoplifted and sold stolen items, panhandled for dope money and ate in soup kitchens and out of dumpsters. My mother (God rest her soul and embrace her) told me that when I was ready to surrender and offer myself up to the Lord, I could come home. I returned here spiritually, mentally and physically bankrupt. I had Hepatitis C and Gonorrhea, not to mention the best part, I was also three and a half months pregnant. After going through hell being dope sick and attending meetings at Lighthouse, I was invited to speak one Sunday and give my testimony. After that day Ben, I never looked back."

He slowly reached across the knotty pine table and took her hands in his. Lynne didn't try to pull away or change her demeanor, she openly accepted his small gesture of kindness and affection. Later that night, he laid awake in the basement efficiency apartment that he had been renting from a nice young Mexican family. Maybe, it was all the sugar he had consumed or maybe it was their first date. The pullout mattress with the world famous dip from hell didn't help with his insomnia either, but deep down in his heart he knew the real reason that he was unable to sleep.

Ben closed his eyes and a teardrop streaked down the side of his cheek as he recalled a situation similar to what Lynne had spoken of earlier.

"You've been ripping us off Barb!" Towers shouted down to the girl hudling on the edge of a metal fold out chair.

"Towers please, I needed the cash bad!" She exclaimed in fear.

"Yeah, so do we ya dumb bitch! You know, like we hire you to mule dope for profit?"

"I know, I fucked up and it won't happen again! I promise Towers!" The scared, dirty and emaciated young woman pleaded.

"Oh Babs please, everyone on the planet is going to know not to trust you!" Ben barked, while removing a pair of pruning shears from his back pocket.

"Give me her right hand Jocko." He ordered sternly.

"Nooo!!!" She screamed in horror as his mate slapped her hard and grabbed her right wrist.

Her shrills filled the double wide trailer and the windows vibrated. With one quick snap, the sheers removed her right index finger and Ben tossed the digit down into the garbage disposal. He grabbed her throat firmly and made her flip the switch, and the grinding, crunching sound of what was once Barbara's finger disappeared into the septic tank.

"What are you thinking about Lynne?"

"I'm not sure, my head is spinning and I still can't grasp all of this." She replied, putting a tissue up to her mouth holding back her emotions.

"Do you want one of the pills that Dr. Sharp gave you?" He asked, rubbing her shoulder.

"No, I think I'm going to try and get some natural sleep, I don't want those to be my go- to."

"I've replayed the whole scenario a thousand times and the ending always comes out the same. All I keep asking myself is, why did this happen to him, what was the point? It just doesn't make any sense at all." Ben stated, shaking his head slowly.

The fire had burned itself down to tiny flames that danced above the dark red ambers and occasionally a whiff of smoke lifted and floated away up into the chimney. He walked her up to their bedroom and then with Hexe's help, checked the entire house before he himself climbed the steps. Ben paused briefly to look into Joshua's room and slowly closed the door but the thought of the dog not being able to enter and mourn him in her own way made him leave it ajar. He remembered what was in his wallet and removed the small handwritten note that was folded inside.

'Loyalty forever brother, if you want this handled, we'll be there.'
-Lucy

Chapter Ten

"Good afternoon this is Detective Richards with the Special Investigations Unit, and I need to speak with someone in your Field Director's office please."

"If you could just give me your ID number please?" A young man's voice asked.

"Sure, it's 4510. Hope that's today's number." Richard's joked.

"It is and you win a cookie, hang on just a moment please." After a short pause and the usual bizarre, electronic gadgetry noises that occasionally came through the secure line, a serious sounding woman answered."

"Agent Timmons here."

"Good afternoon, this is Detective Richards over at Philly, SIU." He announced.

"Okay detective, shoot." She responded.

Richards could hear her tapping on her keypad and talking with another person off to the side, he imagined that her office environment was similar to his. Snack time in the romper room.

"We received a call very early this morning about a young woman's body being found in an abandoned row home on Custer Street in Kensington. She had been murdered and her corpse mutilated and left on the kitchen floor, we're not sure if the cause of death is one in the same with the condition of the body. Upon further investigation, a cell phone was discovered lodged in her vagina."

"Nice." Agent Timmons quipped flatly.

"Yeah, well it gets better so hang on. The phone only has one thing on it and that's a homemade video of the victim meeting with a black male in his mid-thirties driving a silver BMW 3 Series. It then goes on to show the victim getting out of the car and seemingly upset with the male. Then he proceeds to drive to Jefferson Hospital, where he gets into another vehicle, that being a newer maroon Jeep Grand Cherokee. Indiana plate 892WCS."

"I see and…" Timmons began.

"Yeah, and then he drives to your office. He's a Fed, and we believe that she was his snitch." Richards stated as if saying, 'The ball's in your court lady.'

"He drives to my office?" She asked sharply.

"Well, that maroon Jeep just rolled right on into the William J. Green underground, and right on past your guard booth. I mean, that's what the video shows anyway."

"Okay, let me get your cell and give me some time to find out who's on my end." Timmons suggested with urgency.

"Ma'am?" Richards asked, with a confused tone.

"Look detective, I don't have a list in front of me of who's driving what on any given day and I have a couple hundred people down here."

"I get it Timmons, believe me." He replied, with professional courtesy.

"I'll be honest with you, this isn't even my slot but I figured since I had so much 'connect the dots' to catch up on, and was going to be by the phone anyway…"

"You figured what the heck, right?" Richards asked, finishing her expletive.

"Exactly, so please bear with me and I'll get back with you asap. Oh, and good work, I'll be sure to give this info to our field director personally. One more thing, detective, we're going to need that phone and a copy of your report."

"Understood and thank you Agent Timmons, I appreciate it."

"Call me Deb, and we'll have someone stop over in the morning." She stated softly.

"Nice chatting with you Deb, I'm George, and if you like I can send you what I have to your email?"

"That would be great George."

After giving him her email address she hung up and got on her office line, and then punched in three numbers.

"This is Pool, Taylor speaking." A young man answered with a tired voice.

"Goodmorning, this is Timmons from Field and I need to know who had the maroon Jeep Cherokee, Indiana 892WCS. Another vehicle was picked up at Jefferson two days ago."

"One sec ma'am…" He replied while humming under his voice and typing the information on his keypad. "Okay, that would be Agent Moss, he was driving a silver '16 BMW 3 Series and yes, the secondary would've been the brand spanking new Jeep."

"Thanks son and that was fast!" She complimented.

"Oh shit!" Agent Moss shouted at his laptop, he had just nuked a family size Stouffer's meat lover's lasagna and cracked a can of Coors light when the alert popped up on the screen. Staring back at him were the horrible images that were taken by Detective Richards. The last photo featured was the tattoo of the victim's name, it was in black-work ink and read: "Trina" in a one inch, cursive style font.

"Looks like someone got your girl Moss, I need you in now." Was all the email read.

He immediately selected the interior security camera icon which was located in a secured app on his personal Iphone. The undercover address was on the corner of Erie and K streets and had been Moss's (Trey's) house for the past three years, while he was investigating the gang activity of the Gold Sheik Mob. The live feed showed him nothing out of the ordinary and everything seemed to be just as he had left it two days prior. Moss then scanned back through the timeline and all appeared as it should be, except for the gray rat walking along the living room baseboard and disappearing behind the old red couch.

"Awesome." He said sarcastically.

"In the news tonight, the gruesome discovery of a young woman believed to be in her late teens or early twenties. During the early morning hours a call came into the Special Investigations Unit after officers responded to an anonymous call regarding a dismembered corpse found in an abandoned row home on the three thousand block of Custer street, here in Kensington. Also at the same location, while detectives were inside the home, gun fire erupted out front and a man brandishing a weapon was killed by police. No further information is available at this time, but Channel 6 Action News will keep you posted. Reporting live from Kensington, I'm Katie Katro." The lovely raven haired reporter signed off with her characteristic cute pout.

"Good morning, I'm Agent Lee and my boss, Special Agent Timmons, volunteered me to come over and pick up something that you have for us?" The young attractive Korean American said while holding up her credentials in one hand, and offering a handshake with the other. Both Detectives Richards and Clayton gave her a double take and were instantly smitten with her natural beauty and charm.

"Well good morning to you Ms. Lee and please call me George." Richards said, accepting her hand.

"Yes, good morning ma'am, I'm Chris." Clayton added, playing the good boy role while smiling from ear to ear.

"I'm, Jane." She said with a slight giggle.

"Would you care for a cup of coffee or tea?" George asked.

"No thank you, I have to get back soon and I'm double parked out on Whitaker."

(The PPD, East Police Division Headquarters; 24th/25th Districts, East Detective Division is located at 3901 Whitaker avenue).

"Well, I've already had your car towed, so you'll have to stay and have breakfast with us!" Richards cracked. Jane let out a girlish squeal and blushed while waving off his flirtatious joke.

"This is everything that Timmons asked for," Clayton said, handing her the paper office mail bag that contained the cell phone and crime scene report. "Please excuse me just one moment, Jane." He exclaimed, holding up his index finger and answering his cell phone.

"Yes, Jelly relax and stay put, I'll scoop you up in ten minutes." He said into his phone.

Agent Lee got behind the wheel of the navy blue, 2022 Chevrolet Malibu that she had double parked out in front of the division. The only telltale sign that the vehicle was official in nature was the black four inch stick style antenna on the roof, just forward of where the top of the rear window met the body of the car. A light rain began, and faint droplets of water covered the windshield in small specks clouding the outside world and converting the city scene into a haze of blurred traffic and street lights. When she first turned on the wipers it looked as if an invisible artist's fan brush had stroked across a clear canvas smearing and blending soft muted oil colors.

"They have the kid." Lee said into her phone while putting the car into drive.

"I wonder how they got to him?" Timmons inquired.

"I'm not sure, but I'm heading in now."

"Okay Jane, let's bleed this to Moss slowly."

"Yeah no problem, but he's starting to act a little suspicious." Agent Lee warned, reaching into her purse and pulling a cigarette out of the pack.

"Right, or maybe it's disillusionment?" Timmons asked hypothetically, feeling Jane out and checking on her confidence.

"It doesn't really matter, he'll keep playing as long as I do." She assured.

"That's my girl! Okay, we'll see you back here soon."

Detective Clayton parked his Tacoma at a public pay lot two blocks up from Rittenhouse Square on Chestnut street, then walked around the corner and into the Dunkin' Donuts on South 20th. The rain had tapered off leaving the sidewalks and anything else stationary with a high gloss sheen and as he shook his jacket and wiped his black suede Nautica shoes on the large doormat. He looked up and saw Jelly sitting on a stool at the far end of the counter.

"You know he's gonna fucking kill me right?" The scared looking teen asked, glancing over at the door.

"How would he know about you and me?" Clayton asked softly, referring to Blaze.

"You can't think like that man, you know how these gangsta's are! C'mon Clay!" He exclaimed, shaking his head in disbelief.

"Jelly, would you just stop?!" Clayton raised his voice, getting the attention of the young Indian woman working behind the register. "Listen, I'm a black cop who's seen, heard and been in every shit hole situation and place that the devil himself could put a man in, understand? I'm telling you, your fine bro, stop worrying. No one knows shit, and you're safe, so be cool. Do you think I'd let anything happen to you? Do you think I'd ever put you in danger? I'd shoot that motherfucker in a second if I thought he was coming for you."

"They chopped her up." The boy whispered before breaking down into tears. "They just carved Trina up, Clay."

"Evil." Clayton agreed, reaching over and gently gripping Jelly's wrist.

"Clay, I'm scared." The boy said, looking at him through his intertwined fingers that screened his eyes.

"Listen man, I served three tours in Afghanistan as an Army Ranger, and I grew up in the same 'hood as you, no different. You want to know, how I knew that I was getting out of that shit hole someday, Jelly?"

"How?" He asked with pleading wet eyes.

"I knew that someday, I'd be able to leave all that behind because I have a brain. You also have a brain Jelly, and you also have the best of both worlds. You're street smart, which means you have common sense and you have intelligence. That means you're smart and that also means that you can be dangerous, if you don't use it right."

"Yeah, I'm so smart that I'm caught up in that nigga's drama!" Jelly exclaimed, wiping a tear from his cheek.

"Well, I got news for you man, with your help that's all gonna change." Clayton whispered, giving him a wink while shaking his wrist. "I ain't gonna lie to you bro, not now and not ever, but you're the only eyes and ears I got on this guy out there." He said thumbing over to the glass door.

"Blaze is a straight up psycho killer Clay, and you know it." Jelly whispered nervously.

"Blood, this is so secret that the cops don't even know. They knew about our little bus ride sure, but they don't know that we're here right now. All I need in order to grab this fucker is for you to text me when you see him. Put three stars at the beginning of your message then tell me what you see. Where's he at, who's he with and what kind of car is he in, info like that." Clayton urged with a squint in his gaze. "Then leave the rest to me Jelly, because when I bust his ass, he ain't getting away and if he runs or goes 'hood… Ya feel me?"

"Yeah, I feel ya." Jelly nodded back.

"They got nothing on him yet but believe me, in a very short time, every cop and Fed this side of his mama's ass crack is gonna be looking for him." Clayton exclaimed, flashing his boyish grin.

"That's probably a big area on the other side of this one then!" Jelly cracked, letting out a squeal.

"You know those kind of women!" Clay joked back. "Listen Jelly, what I want to ask you is really important shit, okay?"

"What?" The young teen asked under his breath.

"Why did Mickey leave Minnie?"

"Huh? I don't know!" Jelly said, shrugging his shoulders.

"Because she was fucking Goofy!"

Detective Clayton got behind the wheel of his Toyota and started it before calling Richards.

"Yeah, Clay?" He answered.

"I waited an hour, boss but the kid didn't show." He explained, while adjusting his rearview mirror.

"Damned, he's probably scared out of his mind." Richards replied under his breath.

"Yeah, that's what I'm thinking too. Alright, I'm headed back in."

"Hey, Clay…"

"… I know, stop off at Wawa and grab you a coffee!" Clayton joked back.

"Thanks." Detective Richards said with a chuckle.

"I'm going to put your ass in the dirt, if it's the last thing I do on this earth." Clayton promised aloud, looking at the District of Columbia DMV drivers license photo of Andre Pelts.

Chapter Eleven

"Good morning dear friends, before we start today's service Ben has an important message that he would like to share." Pastor Walt announced to the parishioners.

"Good morning family and thank you for allowing me this time." He began.

"Good morning Ben!" They all called back.

"As most, if not all of you are aware, Joshua's twentieth birthday (or what would have been) is this coming Thursday, November 9th., and the Annual Philadelphia 'Toys for Tots' run is on Saturday the 11th. Lynne and I would like to extend an open invitation to all, whether you would like to ride up or not and participate by meeting up after the rally, at the location where he lost his life. Pastor Walt has volunteered to trailer Joshua's motorcycle along with toys, blankets and canned goods. If anyone would like to make a donation please feel free to contact me beforehand and bring anyone else who would like to attend this awesome event. We're planning on a prayer vigil and we'll be handing out the toys and the other items while we're there also. Let's spread the word of the Spirit and bring joy!" He exclaimed with his arms opened wide.

"Lynne honey, I'll meet you after church and we'll talk about a bucket load of food!" Mrs. Hostetter, who was on the North side of eighty called out.

"Me too, Lynne!" Her mother's old girlfriend Judy added.

Lynne became overwhelmed with emotion and before she could turn around in her chair to thank everyone, she broke into tears.

"And I have a huge cooker and enough venison that'll grind into about two hundred good sized patties!" A friendly voice boomed.

Ben, who had been distracted while looking around at all the folks who were offering to bring food to the event, glanced up and saw Mickey. He was now standing in the center aisle in the middle of the church wearing a black two button suit with an open collared dark violet shirt. His fresh flat-top and trimmed beard gave him the appearance of a retired NFL linebacker. Ben had him by a few inches in height but the two always had about the same weight and broad chest. Mickey always had the look of a little kid who was at summer camp, and his broad genuine smile, rosie cheeks and dimples attracted more than a few young ladies back in his hay day. As innocent and gentle as his nature seemed to be, there was a time when Mickey was a heavy hitter in the club. He was the past state president of Virginia, and he used to give and follow orders to the letter. After serving six years in FCI Cumberland for drug trafficking, he retired honorably from the Sworn and started an online used motorcycle parts store.

"Mickey!" Ben exclaimed with joy. "How in the world did you …"

"I got Pastor Walt's number, he gave me the address and told me when church starts!" He explained with a wide grin.

"Looks like ya might have another reformed man here, Mark!" Ben yelled over to his friend who was wearing his township uniform, due to the fact that he had to report to work directly after the service.

"Welcome, and there's always room in here brother!" He called over with a wave.

"Ben, I'm going to ask you to please step down now or I'm going to be out of a job!" Pastor Walt joked while approaching the stage. His remark caused such a roar that it took another five minutes for the entire congregation to settle down.

After the service ended and most of the congregants gathered for coffee hour (which was held in the church's large expansive basement) Ben introduced Mickey to all. His warm and boisterous voice called out, "I'd like everyone to meet Mickey, he's an old buddy of mine and I can't tell you all how surprised and happy I am to see him here this morning!"

"Hello, Mickey!" They all shouted back with smiles on their faces.

"Thank you, and hello to you all as well!" Mickey exclaimed, his cheeks blushed and his eyes danced with delight.

"He's a big Teddy Bear!" Ben teased.

"It's true, I'm just a big old goofball really!" He agreed, receiving a brotherly hug from his old friend.

"Lynne, everyone, c'mon over here and let's talk to Mickey!" Ben invited.

Their church family approached him with smiles and handshakes, and Lynne got a big hug. Mickey felt his trousers being tugged on and he gazed down to see three year Rebecca Cole smiling up at him.

"What's a goofball?" She asked with a squeal, and love in her sky blue eyes.

"Your gonna steal my heart, aren't ya missy?" He teased just before she tore off, skipping after one of her girlfriends.

"I've been thinking, Mick…" Ben stated.

"Yeah, well ya know where that got us before!" He cracked back, igniting a round of laughter.

"No seriously, I think it would be really cool if we could ride through the area where we lost him and show support for ending the violence."

"Now that sounds like a wonderful idea!" Pastor Walt said, walking over to those surrounding Ben and Mickey.

"Yeah, honey!" Lynne agreed. "Joshua will be there handing out the toys too!"

Lynne insisted that Mickey follow her and Ben back to their place for a Sunday afternoon brunch, and after he was reminded by his old mate (in a joking manner) that he was still an underling, he accepted.

The golden and red leaves that had fallen onto the long gravel entrance road that led up to the house were turning brown, and clusters of crows landed in the cleared corn fields hoping to grab every last kernel that could have possibly been left behind by previous visitors. Just inside the front door Hexe was barking excitedly and waiting in anticipation for her parents to enter the house. Her high pitched bark, mixed with whines suddenly converted into a threatening and deeper sounding alarm. She knew that a stranger was out front with them.

"Give me a second while I put the dog up Mickey." Ben said.

They were waiting for Lynne, who was grabbing choir robes out of the trunk. She had volunteered to do alterations and light mending on the garments a few years ago, and the choir seemed to turn into a 'Lynne can fix that' kind of thing.

"No, don't honey." she replied to Ben. "I want Hexe to meet him, a little distraction might be good for her."

"Oh I see, let's invite Mickey back to the house and feed him to our werewolf!" Mickey shouted, laughing.

"No, Mickey!" Lynne responded with a squeal.

"Right, I bet!" Mickey playfully mocked.

"Alright listen, Lynne stand next to him and I'll let her out. You know she's gonna go to you Mickey, but she won't bite." Ben assured him, before opening the front door.

"There's my girly!" Ben said to the shepherd. She stopped momentarily to lick his hand, then bolted around him.

"Hexe, sit now!" Lynne ordered sternly. She sat in front Lynne and received a loving stroke between her ears, before placing all of her innate and protective attention on Mickey.

"Here Mick, give her this." Ben whispered, giving him a chewy treat from a cupped hand.

"You like these, Hexe?" Mickey asked in a little kid's voice, opening up his hand.

Hexe's tail began to immediately thump on the porch floor and her head cocked over to one side as if contemplating the possibility that this guy might not be that bad after all. Sam the mailman had chewies too after all!

"Go ahead and get the treat girl." Lynne said with a motherly tone. The dog slowly inched its head into Mickey's open palm and gently took the chewy.

"Pet her, it's okay." Ben said, standing next to his friend for moral support.

"You sure man?" He asked shyly.

"Yeah Mickey, I'm positive."

Hexe looked up as Mickey's hand came closer and she didn't flinch a muscle or bat an eye. She was well trained by a loving and caring family that understood the animals general nature and characteristics. Ben wanted a good all around dog, child friendly but also able to protect and attack (if necessary) anyone with bad intentions. This unique quality was not limited to the boogie man either. Rustling leaves, UPS delivery drivers knocking on the door and far off imaginary night sounds were also fair game. From the time she was a few weeks old, Hexe would be put in a cage down in the basement if guests were coming to dinner or friends stopped over to visit. This was an old and proven German Army training technique that was established before WW I, that taught the animal to be one with its owner, forsaking all others unless approved by him. It built an unbreakable, loving and loyal bond between them.

"Hey Mickey, maybe someday you could show up over here wearing one of those padded attack suits." Ben joked.

"Yeah, and maybe some day you'll get some psychological help." He replied, trying not to burst out laughing. Lynne however, couldn't contain herself and Hexe jumped up on her and began licking her face.

"Stop!" She half yelled and half giggled. "It's not play time, she always does that if I start laughing!" Lynne explained, speaking more to the dog.

"It's good seeing you laugh honey." Ben said.

"Yeah, it feels good being the mom too."

"I love this house you guys!" Mickey exclaimed after following them into the living room. "I mean, check out the stained and polished barn planked floors!" He looked around and noticed that the entire first floor had a beautiful, refinished high gloss sheen. True to its colonial period design the first floor was divided in half. The gray marble tiled foyer, just inside the front door acted as a functional entrance way by allowing foot traffic to keep mud and dirt from their shoes to a minimum. The idea being that after guests had wiped their feet and walked across it, most of the grime would be removed before proceeding further into the house. Just to the left of the foyer was the living room which had a large stone hearth; a cut and polished granite slab acted as its mantle. Through French doors one could see the parlor, which had been redesignated as the family room. The right hand side of the house (from front to rear) was the large dining room complete with an antique, twelve foot Victorian dining table and 12 reupholstered maroon velvet chairs. Gazing through the large arched open passageway one could see the kitchen and just beyond it was the narrow back deck and to its far left was an enclosed mudroom.

"Yup, and it's all original or reclaimed lumber throughout." Lynne replied, taking her black quilted North Face coat off.

"It's amazing what one can accomplish when they're clean and sober." Ben said smiling. "And when the labor is free!" He finished, giving Lynne a poke in her side.

"Oh please!" She giggled back at him.

They wandered into the kitchen and immediately Mickey was awestruck at how rustic, yet clean looking and functional the room was planned out. In the center of it all stood a large antique sidebar that had been modified and converted into a cutting block for food prep. A small stainless steel sink and trash shoot were on one end, allowing the remaining surface to be free of any clutter. The mahogany sidebar (which was used as the piece's base) still retained all of its silverware drawers and flatware cabinets, which permitted extra storage space. Above it all was a Victorian era wrought iron fence that had been fabricated into a pot holder, complete with adjustable sliding hooks.

"Amazing, Ben." Mickey whispered.

"Check out the small woodstove in the corner." He encouraged with a wave of his hand.

"We still have no idea how old it is." Lynne added.

"Oh yeah, that's an old boy right there!" Mickey walked over to the cast iron pot belly stove and crouched down to take a better look. "My guess is, it was once in somebody's workshop or cabin."

"That's what I thought too." She agreed.

"How do you like my ceiling Mick?" Ben asked with pride in his voice.

"Hardwood?" Mickey inquired.

"Yup, it was Lynne's idea actually. We had a bunch of pallets left over from the building material that we had delivered."

"I thought hey, there's plenty of good hardwood here, and if Ben could run those through a planer they would make a great ceiling!" She explained.

"Totally salvaged lumber and stained with a satin finish. The indirect lighting around the four sides was Josh's idea. The kid was an electrical genius." Ben said, his voice trailing off.

"Well, I think this place should be in Architectural Digest if you ask me!" Mickey claimed with a bright smile. "Now, how can I help with brunch? I'm starved!" He exclaimed, bringing his friends back to the present moment.

"Of course you are, I'm sorry." Lynne offered.

"C'mon, let's do cakes, eggs, french toast and oatmeal! The whole shabang!" Ben suggested excitedly.

"Let's do it people!" Mickey said in a deep baritone voice causing Lynne to laugh and Hexe to growl.

The three of them sat at the end of the long table, with Ben in the middle and Lynne and Mickey facing each other. Hexe laid on the floor between her parents at the ready for Ben to sneak her a piece of bacon or sausage. They looked down at the breakfast bounty before them, and Ben said grace. "God, bless this food to give us strength for your purpose for us. We thank you for our friend Mickey being here today and we pray that we may be comforted Father, during this time of sadness and loss."

"Amen." Lynne and Mickey responded softly as he reached for Lynne's hand.

"Thank you." She replied with a smile. "Oh, I almost forgot, Mickey, hold on a second."

"C'mon Lynne the food is getting cold." Ben urged, before taking a piece of bacon off a serving plate and holding it low under the table.

"Ben stop feeding her, she's going to get fat!" Lynne called back from the living room. She returned with a bible and offered it to Mickey.

"Do you have a bible?" She asked.

"To be honest, I haven't seen one since I buried my father, Lynne."

"Well, it's never too late to start now, is it?" Lynne asked in a playful voice.

"No ma'am, I suppose not."

"Let's eat!" Ben announced as if summoning them to feast.

"My dad told me just before he died, that one of the happiest days of his life was when I got away from the outlaw lifestyle that I had been caught up in. One of the last things that he told me about two days before he died in a hospital bed from stomach cancer, was that he had hoped for the day that I would see the light." Mickey stated, looking at the NIV (New International Version) bible with a smile.

"What did your father used to do for a living?" Lynne asked, crunching a piece of toast. Ben looked over and grinned at him, already knowing the answer.

"Oh, he was a Baptist Minister." He replied nonchalantly.

Lynne coughed on a swallow of orange juice that had managed to make it half way down her throat, before bursting into laughter.

"What?!" She exclaimed, covering her mouth with a napkin. "I bet that made for some interesting family reunions!"

"Ya got that right girl, let me tell ya!" He answered, joining her in the laughter.

After brunch, Ben invited Mickey to go out and see his shop and catch up a little on each other's lives. The late afternoon gray sky was dark and to the West a storm front could be seen slowly moving in their direction. Rain was guaranteed instead of the original forecast that called for snow; the air was a tad too warm and moisture clunge in the air.

"Reminds me of Jocko's old Shovel Head." Mickey remarked looking down at the customized Low Rider.

"Yeah, a little bit I guess." Ben replied.

"What year was that, do you remember Ben?" Mickey asked, trying to keep his friend in the moment.

"Sure I do, I built that bike for him. It was a '75 FLH and Bootsie over in Jersey bored and stroked it to a 1450, it was a nice old motor too."

"Yup, and almost the same candy apple as this one." Mickey said with approval.

He looked over at Ben after the conversation stalled and noticed that his back was turned and he was weeping.

"Hey brother." Mickey whispered, walking over and giving him a hug. "You don't ever have to cry alone."

"I just can't believe it Mick, I just can't believe what happened to our kid." Ben said through his tears as he grabbed ahold of his old friend.

"I can't imagine that pain brother, and I'm here." Mickey managed to say before he choked up.

"Lucy gave me a courtesy note." Ben added, referring to the coded invitation to have payback handled.

"I know he did, I saw him write it down in the car just before the funeral."

"I just can't go there again Mick, I don't want to think that way anymore." Ben said with a serious look on his face.

"Me either, it's no accident that I showed up in church this morning. I've been thinking a lot lately, and I know I've been searching…"

"That's a good place to start, Mickey!" Lynne announced, walking into the old remodeled barn carrying a tray of hot chocolate.

"It is at that, old friend." Ben said softly, wiping away the tears before releasing his embrace.

"Maybe it was coming out here that day or meeting you Lynne and well, Pastor Walt too? I don't know, but I felt like I wanted to be part of it, part of you two and feel like I belonged. Something has been missing inside of me for most of my life." Mickey confessed.

"Oh, I get it, Mickey, believe me." She said, sitting the wooden serving tray down on Ben's work bench.

"I have more good news too." Mickey offered. "I'm moving to Oxford, it's about…"

"We know where Oxford is MIck!" Ben shouted with joy as he cut him off.

"Oh, that'll be wonderful for you two!" Lynne exclaimed, giving Mickey a hug.

"My Aunt's not well, so I volunteered to stay with her. She really doesnt have anyone to take care of her."

"Very cool, and you'll be in range of us, and Lighthouse!" Ben said with approval.

"After today, I'm doing it, my mind's made up!" Mickey stated to Hexe who was sitting inside the doorway. "And I'll remember to bring treats too!"

Chapter Twelve

Jane was on her back before him, her arms held high above her head and her perky dark nipples stood at a half inch high. She opened her legs to reveal her thin labia and smooth shaven pussy. "Fuck me, Moss." She ordered with a cheeky smile.

"Chinese bitches." He grunted before sliding the length of his cock into her.

"You love it, nigger boy." She moaned as he held her right leg back and thrust harder. He tossed her over onto her stomach and she immediately lifted herself up and assumed the doggie position. One quick hard slap to Lee's ass was all it took for her to go into hyper-fuck mode, and within a few fast minutes (and with the help of his fingers rubbing her clitorus vigorously) she came in a gush.

A soft yellowish light from somewhere down the hallway could be seen through the open bedroom door; Moss was on his back and she was stretched out alongside him. Jane's long, sleek firm muscle toned arms and shoulders revealed that this kitten had the potential of being a killer. They shared a Newport 100 while gently caressing each other. Occasionally, Jane's white Pomeranian, 'Gigi' would have to be shooed away in order to prevent her from jumping up and getting in between them. They were on her queen-sized bed in a unit on the tenth floor of the Rivers Edge Condominiums, which sat on the East bank of the

Schuylkill River. She had lived there for the past four years while working out of the Philadelphia office, and she thought it was a clever idea to lease it under her deceased aunt's name.

"Any thoughts as to how Clayton got ahold of Jelly?" Moss asked, playing with her hair.

"No idea, my guess would be that the kid reached out to him."

"Yeah, probably." He consented.

"The kid would definitely know you as 'Shey'?" She asked looking up under his chin.

"Sure as hell, seen me driving past Blaze and Trina's a million times." Moss assured her.

"Do you really think that Blaze hacked her up?"

"Yeah, him and Marcus too I bet." He said under his breath.

"I kinda thought it was strange that they left Marcus out of their report." Jane mentioned.

"What, about him getting shot up outside the place they found Trina?" Moss asked after blowing a smoke ring.

"Yeah." She whispered, kissing his neck.

"I didn't think it was strange because they've known somethings been going on since the Ladd murder and that's probably around the time Jelly came into their world." He stated reaching over and putting the cigarette out before he got under the sheets to face her.

"What does Timmons want to do?" He asked her while staring into her dark and mysterious Asian eyes.

"Wash it, just sweep it under the carpet." Jane answered with a frown.

"That's the feeling I get too." Moss replied.

"Trina never said for sure that Blaze killed Joshua Ladd?"

"No, she got pissed off and jumped out of my car and that's the last time I saw her alive." Moss answered with a heavy exhale.

"Timmons is going to pull you Moss, you know that."

"I want to meet Detective Clayton." He stated flatly, ignoring her claim.

"I don't really think that's a good idea, I mean you'd just be exposing yourself again."

"Again? What the hell is that supposed to mean?" Moss asked, lifting himself and sitting upright against the headboard.

"I remember the night you told me about calling Blaze, and accusing him of killing the Ladd kid. You also mentioned that you knew that Trina was in close proximity during the phone conversation right?" Jane asked with a raised eyebrow.

"Yeah, that's all true. He fucking denied it too and that pissed me off badly." He answered, looking away from her inquisitive gaze.

"Clayton was Army Airborne in Afghanistan, served three tours, then came home and went directly into the academy."

"What's that got to do with…" Moss began to say.

"It's got to do with the fact that he has Jelly like a big brother and if you come out, he's going to put one and one together. In his mind, and it's the truth; the reason Blaze had her tailed was because he suspected that she got scared. Clayton's going to single you out as the one that got Trina killed and Jelly's life in jeopardy." Jane explained in a rational way.

"Especially if he finds out that the only way I got to operate in Blaze's peripheral, was to bust her on a bullshit trafficking charge." He added.

"Yeah, I'm sure that would go over real well with him and his boss also." She said sarcastically.

"Who's that?"

"Detective, Sergeant Richards. He served in the first Gulf War, also Army, and he's about a year away from hanging up his badge." Jane informed him, as he rubbed his temples.

"These fucking cops, I always end up having to deal with these old school niggers!"

"Maybe you should try to be a little more covert then." She suggested.

"Fuck you, this shit happens. You'd last about ten minutes out there girl, you've admitted it before, it's the nature of the business!" Moss said angrily before throwing off the sheets and getting out of bed.

"Honey!" Jane pleaded with a guilty girlish look on her face.

"I'm getting in the shower, I'm sorry baby but I'm balls deep in stress right now." Moss walked down the short hallway and through the open air linen closet before entering into the master bathroom. He loved the layout and the contemporary look of this room; the walls were 12" x 24" dark gray marble Bardiglio tiles, and the twenty four inch polished black marble sink sat upon a sharp lined, teak wood table. All of the fixtures were chrome and his favorite piece of it all was the large square rainwater shower pan that hung directly over the center of the immense oblong walk-in.

"Moss, an alarm's going off on your phone!" Jane called out.

"Shit!" He growled, turning the water off and marching back to the bedroom. "I can't even get a fucking shower!"

He opened the app for his cover residence security camera, and there in front of his very eyes was the image of a lean male, hooded up and dressed in black. The intruder pointed behind him to the spray painted wall that was clearly visible, and the message read: 'Your fucking dead Fed!'

"Goddamned it!" Moss yelled aloud.

"What is it? Let me see." Jane inquired nervously. "Wow, we better nail this one down!" She suggested.

Just as she was about to hand back Moss's phone, the hooded man on the screen raised what appeared to be a Glock G19, Gen3 and fired a round at the camera.

"How in the fuck did they find out where…" His voice trailed off.

"Jelly." She answered, looking down at his phone.

"I don't think they know my real name." Moss said flatly.

"You don't think?" She replied, staring entranced at the black phone screen.

"Sit your ass down, shut the fuck up and don't even breathe!" The tall and pumped aggressive looking man shouted. He was wearing a wife beater t-shirt, hip hugger Levi's and powder blue Timberlands. "And listen very carefully to my questions, before you open your mouth!" He warned after removing the dark Oakley's that had been hiding his angry eyes.

All Blaze could do under these extreme circumstances was nod back, because he knew what the outcome would be if he didn't listen to his president. Blaze had witnessed the man's wrath more than a few times and the end for GSM members was way more severe than for those who played for the other teams.

"What in the fuck were you thinking? Why did Cleats get shot up? Why did you and Marcus cut Trina up? How the fuck did Marcus end up dead, outside the very spot that you and he carved her up like a primerib? And lastly, how did you let a Fed into your world?!" He yelled while staring Blaze down.

Breach was thirty four and had been raised in the street gang culture by his stepfather who had also been the president at one time. He grew up in a middle class section of DC and his mother insisted that the family attend church every sunday. He killed his first man when he was seventeen after his stepdad handed him the weapon to commit the act; and what most people didn't know was that he had a bachelors degree in economics from the University of Maryland. Breach was the perfect example of a gangland leader, he was hard, fast, smart, had class and the wearer of many hats.

"You got exactly five minutes, motherfucker, so I hope you highlighted your script!" Breach finished while pointing at Blaze's forehead as if his hand was a gun. "And, go!"

They were in a newly constructed apartment complex just outside of Arlington. The painters had just finished up with the large three bedroom ground unit that the meeting was being held in; the air was dry and smelled like fresh latex. Dried clumps of joint compound that the sheetrock contractors had dropped and small specks of paint that had been flung free from the three foot paint rollers littered the otherwise clean concrete floor. Blaze was sitting on a lawn chair that had been placed in the empty living room prior to his arrival and standing behind Breach was another notorious man who went by the name of Buttons.

His face was completely expressionless. A sixteen cubic foot, 48" Knaack job box on wheels (used primarily to hold tools and other gear on large job sites) sat out in the open against the wall. This was for Blaze's body to be removed from the location if things didn't jive well with his boss.

"Cleats got killed while we was meeting up with a motherfucker who was supposedly a big boy, Cleat himself set it up and vouched for the nigga. Dude's name was Darren, from North Philly; anyhow, we rolled up to the connection and he tried to stick us. Cleat went for his nine and it was over, dude shot his ass up and got me once in the back of the left thigh. After that, I ran and tried to take the van to get away." Blaze said, as he stood up and pulled down his black Adidas track pants to reveal the scar from the bullet wound.

"I see it." Breach acknowledged.

"The undercover Fed, goes by the name of Shey, called me from a phone (probably a Five-O rig) and said he got my number off of Trina. Right after we hung up, she started acting strange, like she got spooked or something, ya know? Then she asked me if I killed that Ladd kid. Anyway, I put Marcus on it and he followed her, he videoed Trina hooking up with Shey." Blaze looked up at the ceiling and took a deep breath. "It got out of control, it's my fault Breach, it was my idea to take her to a spot and strap her down."

"Why not just cap her, why did you decide to go medieval on her ass?" Breach inquired, moving in closer and staring Blaze in the eye.

"We was smoking dippers." He answered as if confessing to a sin.

"Smoking that fucking embalming fluid again?!" He shouted down to the teen.

"I knew…"

"You knew what, the fucked up shit it got you into down here?!" His boss screamed angrily, referring back to the time when Blaze and a couple other youngins showed up to a party in Georgetown and shot up a girl's apartment, killing two of the guests.

"Yeah…" Blaze began to say.

"Fucking idiot!" Breach shouted with dancing eyes.

"Man, let me tell you somethin' blood, back in the day that woulda been it, right then and there." Buttons guaranteed, by this time he had made his way to the conversation and stood next to his president.

"Marcus got shot up outside were Trina was, because he was down the street waiting to see if Shey was gonna show up."

"Oh I see, and you were just going to handle him right there in the middle of the street, in front of like what ten cops? You're fucking brilliant!" Breach shook his head in mock amazement.

"You saw the video of Trina getting out of Shey's car, before he went and swapped that one out for another whip. He eventually pulled…" Blaze tried to explain.

"I know what the fuck he eventually did! Buttons, are we alone in this bitch, because this motherfucker might as well be a stick on the floor?! What in the hell ails you Blaze?!" Breach demanded waving his hand in front of Blaze's face, "Hello?! Is there anything in that coconut skull of yours boy?!" Both he and Buttons looked at each other and laughed.

"Coconut skull, I love it Breach!" Buttons added.

"How come you didn't know that Trina got jammed up on a bullshit trafficking charge? Maybe that's how this dude, Shey entered onto the stage?" Breach suggested with sarcasm in his angry voice.

"She lied…" Blaze whispered.

"Oh please, cut me a fucking break! Of course she lied, she's a woman!"

"She didn't say anything to them and they aint got nothin' on me Breach." Blaze said with an assuring nod.

"Your positive about that boy?" Buttons asked, moving in closer to stare him down.

"You better be sure as hell they don't, Blaze!" Breach added, pointing directly into the scared young man's face.

 "I got one last thing to say to you before I let you live. Your my nephew and I love you with all my heart, I always have, but if I ever find out your going rogue on me, I'll kill you in a second and if the Sworn decides to hit you, I'm walking away from that, you feel me?"

"Yeah, I feel you Breach." Blaze replied in a somber tone, focusing on a lump of caked, dried up spackle on the floor.

Chapter Thirteen

"Ben, honey I love it!" Lynne yelled out excitedly. She had just returned to the bedroom after the two had one of his famous pancake lunches.

"What's that Lynne?" He called back from the foot of the stairs.

"You know what!" She scolded in a teasing tone.

"And these?" Ben asked her while holding something behind his back.

"What is that, another surprise?!" She asked while attempting to sneak around him and get a peak.

"Ah, back with you then wench!" He playfully growled in his English pirate's voice, "And don't try gettin' outta' the dish's either, or it's the Cat 'O Nine!"

"The jacket is beautiful honey!" Lynne replied with a giggle.

She was referring to the Branded Leather women's high collar riding jacket. It was hand made out of premium quality cowhide to race specs, thickness and weight. It featured a one inch collar with a neck strap and brass snap enclosure; the strap could also fold back (within the collar) and fasten to a hidden snap. Heavy brass zippers on the outside of each forearm closed the garment snug to the wrists which aided in preventing air from riding up into the sleeves. Two other zippers on the lower flanks of the jacket brought in the back and stomach sections to form a perfect fitting, classically styled riding jacket. It was the women's version of the very jacket that Ben had and used for the past thirty years.

"Now close your eyes." He insisted with a smile. "I'm going to need to see you naked in these, sometime!"

"Benjamin Ladd!" She squealed after Ben revealed the pair of women's riding chaps that he had been hiding.

"Or, I can borrow Mark's uniform and we can step out as The Village People some night!" They both howled laughter, then Lynne blushed and Ben's heart melted.

"I love you, Lynne." He said softly.

"Oh my goodness, they're gorgeous. I must try everything on now, so shoo!" She giggled, motioning him away with whisking hands.

"Okay baby, let me know when the fashion show starts!" He encouraged.

"Here I come, biker boy!' She called out from the first floor landing. Ben was sitting in the living room reading the morning edition of the Philadelphia Enquirer.

"Wow, your one sexy tough chick, I'll tell ya!" He exclaimed with approval. Lynne stood there with one leg slightly bent and her hands on her hips. She had braided her dark auburn hair, and for effect made sure that one was draped out in front. She pivoted from side to side and eventually turned around giving Ben his favorite view; that being her firm tight ass which was perfectly formed in the tight Levi's visible through the rear of her chaps. Lynne was a petite woman who stood at around five feet tall, and weighed a hundred and thirty pounds. Her upper body strength provided by strong shoulders and biceps (that she kept in tune by attending Planet Fitness twice a week) and her occasional temper earned her the pet name, 'Little stick of dynamite.'

"Lynne from the first moment I saw you, I thought you were the sexiest girl in the universe." He said lovingly.

"Well, I thought you were a dirty old biker who needed saving!" She joked back, causing them to laugh into each other's eyes, "And, you didn't even look down at my feet!"

"Oh wow, the Texas roach killers that Santa brought you last year!" Ben said, pointing down to the black pointed Alvies, Rio Grande cowgirl boots. They matched her new riding chaps perfectly.

"Yes Ben, and thank you! I love you too!" She said in a motherly tone.

"No you don't!" He teased back with an intentional pout. "You only wanted my candy!"

The day started early and the forecast called for sunshine, a crisp mid 50's temperature and light winds coming out of the Northwest; a perfect clear day for a motorcycle event. Ben was up at 6:00 a.m. (as he had been all his life) making final preparations for the ride. Hexe followed him around, first to the kitchen to make coffee and then the shop to check the tire pressure on his Road King. (During the colder winter months the air is much denser and the result is low tire pressure, many younger inexperienced riders discover this natural phenomenon the hard way while leaning into a turn or down shifting). He then unscrewed the large fittings for the oil dipstick and transmission. Lastly, Ben plugged in his twelve volt, ten amp battery tender before walking back to the house.

"We'll pick up fuel in Kennett, just to top her off." He said to Hexe, before stooping over to pet her.

He went to the kitchen and pulled a large stainless steel mixing bowl out from under the island and turned on the front gas burner of the JennAir Rise, thirty six inch range. Hexe sat patiently awaiting a nibble as Ben cracked a dozen eggs into the bowl, added whole milk and small cubes of Alpine Lace Swiss cheese that he had sectioned on the cutting block. Whisking the contents vigorously (which added air to the dish) and with perfect Chef Ben rhythm, poured it carefully into a sizzling olive oil and garlic laced All-Clad D3 frying pan. The sound of the mixture when it first hit home was like none other and Ben had to grin.

"That's right. That's how you do it girl!" He exclaimed to the whining dog in a little kid's voice. "You want a treat, treat?"

"Honey, when are you going to let me cook?" Lynne asked, as she entered the kitchen wearing her white terry cloth robe.

Her hair was wet and rolled up under a towel and her feet were bare, this is when she was in her most beautiful state he thought. No makeup, clean and fresh while allowing all of her many natural blemishes to be seen and adored by his eyes only.

"When you learn to cook!" He answered, with his ornery smile.

"Ben, stop!" She squealed.

He playfully grabbed her robe's sash and yanked it open before pulling her body close to his. Lynne physically answered by pressing against him and grabbing the back of his head, forcing him into a deep passionate kiss. Ben's hands immediately went to fondle her small tits, before Lynne intentionally exhaled a large plume of breath into his mouth causing him to gag.

"I hate it when you do that!" He scolded back, shaking his index finger at her.

"That's what you get." She replied in a bratty tone. "You'll just have to wait until later."

After she left to put some clothes on, Ben folded the omelet and set three place settings at the round breakfast table. He then fed Hexe before putting another layer of cheese, cracked pepper and fresh minced cilantro on the omelet; lastly, He placed a glass cover over the masterpiece and cut off the gas.

"Need any help?" She asked.

"No honey, I'm good."

Hexe barked three times (the last one included a long drawn out warning growl, this had been her standard response to an impending invasion since she was a puppy) and ran for the front door. Eventually the sound of a big bore V-Twin came into earshot and shortly afterwards, rumbled down to an idle before falling silent.

"C'mon girl, give old Mickey a break!" Mickey pleaded through the door.

"Hexe, come now!" Lynne ordered from the kitchen.

"I'll go and let him in." Ben said, volunteering to let his old friend in without being mauled.

He opened the front door to see Mickey's broad smile and behind him, resting on its kickstand was his vivid black and chrome, 2018 Road Glide. It was a bagger built for grunt and she sat low and wide; the Vance & Hines PCX Big Shot pipes and the large Screamin' Eagle air breather, along with the low profile sharknose fairing gave it the look of a two wheeled stealth fighter jet.

"Yeah, I finally went and had the 131 cubic inch, Milwaukee 8 Stage 4 kit installed, so she's probably pushing around 125 horsepower." Mickey boasted.

"More like 119 to 120 Mick, but that 517 Cam sounds bad as hell." Ben said with a wink, "Who did the work?"

"Dude named Freddy Stewart out of Arlington. He's got a nice shop and works an honest program." Mickey answered, looking down at his bike.

"He has a Dyno too?"

"No, that he had to send out, but he knocked a few beans off the tab so the whole job cost me just under ten grand."

"That's not bad at all!" Ben exclaimed with raised eyebrows. "I would have only charged you around twelve!"

"Gee, thanks brother, it's always good seeing you again!" Mickey cracked back, causing them both to laugh.

"Ben, breakfast?!" Lynne asked sharply from the doorway.

"Okay boss. C'mon Mick, let's eat." He invited.

"Good morning Lynne!" Mickey shouted happily over the Shepherd's barking.

"Good morning to you Mickey, and Hexe stop now!" She commanded. The commotion ceased immediately and the dog sat with her ears at attention awaiting for the visitor to present himself.

"Good morning, Hexe." Mickey said calmly. She cocked her head over to one side as if not understanding what this large man had just said.

"Can I give her a chewy, Lynne?"

"Of course, Mickey." She replied, smiling.

"Look what I got girl." He said, extending his reach and opening his hand. "Your favorite!"

"Go ahead Hexe, get the treat!" Lynne exclaimed in a motherly tone.

Ben stood in the doorway with his arms folded and a broad smile upon his face.

"I really like the message that you posted on the church's Facebook page, brother." Mickey said, wiping his lips after eating a strip of Canadian bacon.

"Well at first I thought it might sound a little weird, but after she read it Lynne agreed." He answered, reaching for her hand.

'I want to personally thank everyone for their love and support during these days of sadness and loss. Lynne and I are amazed and truly humbled by all of your cards, phone calls and visits. We would also like to express our heartfelt gratitude for all of the toys, blankets and canned goods that have been donated for Joshua's prayer vigil. I'm sure that all of you are aware that not only is our mission to donate these items to the less fortunate, but also to bring a message of love and ask everyone, everywhere to stop the violence. Please do not donate any toy guns of any kind! Once again, we look forward to rendezvousing with all who will be participating, in the parking lot of Lighthouse church this coming Saturday morning at 9:00 a.m.'

Lynne saw Mickey pull up his hoodie sleeve to scratch his arm, and immediately noticed the black diamond one percent tattoo just above the one in Bold Old English that read: 'Sworn Motorcycle Club.'

"Just like yours." She said to Ben, nodding over to Mickey's forearm.

"No, my arm's don't have all that baby fat." He joked back with a wink. Mickey coughed into his napkin and looked over at him while shaking his head.

"Your ass." He replied, with a smirk and a chuckle.

"Mickey, be honest with me." Lynne stated, narrowing her eyes.

"Yes ma'am, shoot."

"Is there any girl out there with Ben's property tattoo on her ass?" She asked, trying to be serious. Both men burst out laughing and her timing couldn't have been better, as Ben had just taken a giant gulp of milk.

"What?!" He asked his wife while sopping up milk slobber off his beard and shirt.

"You heard me bubby boy!" She teased back, wagging her finger.

"No Lynne, I can tell you that there is no other." Mickey answered her through his laughter. "Both he and I were not the settle down, keeper kind of guys."

"Well, until I met this nut!" Ben teased, thumbing over at his wife.

"Yeah, I suppose my chance will come too." Mickey said with a pout.

"Mickey honey, there are a lot of single women at Lighthouse and I just know you'll meet the right one!" Lynne promised.

"Now Lynne, don't go playing…" Ben began to say.

"Oh, I'm playing matchmaker Benjamin Ladd, so don't you worry about that!" She shot back with a grin.

They rolled into the parking lot of Lighthouse church at approximately 9:15, fifteen minutes before the scheduled kickstands' up time. Both Ben and Mickey were amazed at how many bikes there were and by the number of participants who had showed up with trunk loads of items for donation. They cut their engines after backing the machines up to the curb, fitting them snuggly in between others who had done the same. A casual observer would note that the line of parked motorcycles looked neat and organized, as if a squadron of planes were parked and waiting at the ready.

"Hi goofball!" A girl shrilled from behind them.

Mickey turned to see Rebecca standing on the sidewalk with her mother. The little doll was wearing a white puffy coat, a white knit cap and fuzzy pink mittens were on her little hands.

"Hey girlfriend, what are you doin'?" He asked, getting off his bike.

"Nothing, but this is my mom!" She exclaimed, pointing to the attractive blonde crouched next to her. She was bending down and zipping up the three year old's coat that Rebecca didn't seem to want it zipped.

"Stop mom, I'm hot!" The girl ordered with a frown.

"I think I remember you from last week ma'am, my name's Mickey." He said, walking over to the pair.

"I'm Amanda, and I remember seeing you too but I was probably in and out of the choir room a lot." Rebecca's mother said with a smile.

"Hi, Manda!" Lynne called over, after taking off her helmet.

"Lynne, you look great in that outfit!" She replied.

"My early Christmas, 'will you ride with me now?' presents!" Lynne exclaimed, "Ben knows I'm not crazy about it, but I'm getting more comfortable." She then walked over and stood next to Mickey and gave him a wink of approval.

"Can I sit on your motorcycle Mickey?" Rebecca asked with a pleading look.

"Rebecca..." Her mother started to say, with a 'shame on you' tone in her voice.

"No, It's alright Amanda." He assured. "C'mon girl, let me give you a hand on up there!" With one sweeping grab, Mickey scooped the child up off the sidewalk and plopped her down on the queen seat.

"No, up front Mickey!" She insisted with a squeal.

"Of course." He replied, lifting her up, squirming legs and all, placing her on the front section of the large seat.

"Smile!" Lynne encouraged Rebecca who was distracted by all the sights and sounds of the dashboard cluster and playing with the radio volume buttons.

"Well, I'm sure we'll see you up at the prayer vigil, and thank you for letting her sit on your bike." Amanda said with a smile as she reached out and lifted her daughter off the seat.

"Can I see the picture, mom?" Rebecca asked, reaching her hands skyward, "I love it!" She shouted while staring into Lynne's phone.

"Your welcome doll." Mickey said, leaning over and patting her head, after she ran to him and hugged his leg.

"I noticed your truck and bike trailer over there, I see you brought the cooker and cooler too. You weren't kidding about the venison burgers!" Ben exclaimed.

"And you weren't kidding about the pretty ladies here either, Lynne." Mickey said softly, looking at Amanda."

"Thank you Mickey, we'll see you up at the vigil." She replied, offering her hand to her daughter.

"I look forward to that." He assured her.

The twenty or so bikes headed North up Route 1 with Ben and Lynne at the head of the staggered single lane formation. Mickey rode twelve feet behind him and off to his right because Ben had told him earlier that Lynne was still trying to get comfortable on the back of his motorcycle, so he stayed a little further behind to give the couple more breathing room. They had been married ten years and she had only let him convince her a half dozen times to go for a summer night putt. Lynne said that she enjoyed it, and it reminded her of flying but there was something about being out there alone and vulnerable with nothing around but the world. "That's the whole point honey." He said, after they stopped to get ice cream.

The pack got off Route 1 at Concordville and headed East on Rt. 322 for another eight miles until they jumped on the entrance ramp to I-95 North. Ben waited for everyone behind him to get into the merge lane and immediately noticed the droves of Harley's already out thundering down the highway. He patted Lynne's leg before he put the boots to the 117 cubic inch, customized Road King and blasted out beyond 75 mph in the blink of an eye. Ben kept his left directional button pressed signaling his intentions to all behind him, and also to give advance notice to cagers that the other bikes with him would also be following. They were all together and riding as a pack.

What seemed like thousands of motorcycles converged on Philadelphia, many had toys bungeed or strapped to their windfarings and more than a few single riders had large teddy bears sitting as passengers. The Lighthouse church riders awaited their turn and after being given a wave by PPD patrolmen to proceed, maneuvered their way into the multitude of bikes and continued with them along the ten mile parade route. Motorcycle clubs (both weekend and one percent) from as far away as New York and Pittsburgh, cruised slowly next to one another down Broad street. They were joined by veterans, retired law enforcement and first responders. The 'Widows Sons' (a Freemason MC) and Christian Fellowship clubs were also in attendance. They all melded into one.

The destination (besides pulling over on occasion to get their photographs taken) was the U.S. Marine Corps Toys For Tots depot which was located at Rivers Casino on North Delaware avenue. A sea of bikers donned in black leather and winter riding gear filled the area. Old friends hugged and laughed while others made new ones, all the while holding onto the toys they had brought to be donated. Lines formed and people began taking the gifts to the receiving area and occasionally a cheer would come from the crowd calling out the name of the organization and where they hailed from.

"Towers!" Members of the Sworn camp yelled out.

"Hey, fellas!" He exclaimed boisterously with a broad grin.

"Mickey!" Another shouted.

"That's our ex National President right there, and an ex State President with him." A senior club member mentioned to a prospect.

"National?!" The young man asked with awe.

"Yup, the whole Sworn nation, son." The heavily patched elder stated proudly. "He was directly under The General, our founder. You'll learn more history in a few weeks."

After stretching their legs and having a smoke (while Lynne showed off her new riding gear with some of the other women) the Lighthouse ensemble regrouped and made a graceful exit, before heading over to Kennsington.

Chapter Fourteen

Jelly sat on the torn ragged couch in the dark living room of the small three bedroom row home on East Elkhart street, where his mother had also once lived. Trina's kid brother Dante (also thirteen years old) and he had lived there together for the past two years. On occasion, (especially if she and Blaze were arguing or she needed to go upstairs to weigh out heroin) Trina would stay over and cook for the two. By the time Jelly was twelve, he had witnessed more devastation and horror than most adult men would ever be subjected too in their lifetime. It was on the steps of this very house where as a sixth grade middle school student, he witnessed the death of his mother. Shouts of anger began flooding the city side street, resonating through the hot balmy night air, and car horns blasted aloud just prior to gun shots coming from half a block away. "Jerome, come!" His mother screamed with fear in her high pitched voice. He turned around just in time to see a stray round punch a hole in her left temple before she fell back onto the small concrete stoop.

When he was seven years old, Jelly entered the tiny upstairs bathroom to find a man (who his mother later confessed was his father) dead on the toilet. He was hunched over and leaning against the grimey yellow tiled wall with a syringe in his arm. Through it all, he had managed to not only stay in school but also achieve and maintain excellent grades. Jelly was a smart kid and learned by watching interviews of famous people who came up under the same circumstances, that the only way out was to get good grades and work hard.

He was holding a plastic bottle of mint Arizona ice tea, and in his other hand was the Mercedes AMG supercar that he had constructed from the Lego Speed Champions kit. It was a Christmas present that had been given to him by Joshua Ladd's mom, Jelly remembered her waving from across the street and inviting him to come and pick out a toy. The little kid in him won over of course, and he accepted Lynne's offer. The teen looked up from the model car when he heard the sound of motorcycles coming through the small television. In an instant, the smiling faces of children and adults alike filled the screen as hundreds of bikes rumbled past the reporter.

"Thursday would have been Joshua's twentieth birthday and we thought this would be a good day to memorialize him." Lynne said with a smile, as a light breeze blew back wisps of her auburn hair from her rosy cheeks.

"He would have loved this, and I know he's looking down on all these kids with a smile on his face." Ben added, putting an arm around his wife.

The news segment then featured the earlier broadcast from mid October, it showed the overall crime scene from street level. A black Acura sat against a large aluminum traffic light pole and the work van rested haphazardly near the curb, while Joshua Ladd's photo sat inset on the upper right hand side of the television screen.

"As many of you may remember, this was the horrible scene and the tragic end of a young electrical apprentice's life. Joshua Ladd, nineteen years old from Kennett Square, Pennsylvania, was gunned down last month, the victim of an attempted car jacking. His family and friends thought it would be a good idea to gather here today after the annual toy drive, and pay tribute to their fallen loved one." The reporter narrated over the footage.

"Josh was a great kid." Pastor Walt exclaimed while flipping burgers from a smokey open grill. "I remember him as that kind, and loving boy who had a heart like a lion."

The news camera then focused on the 1990, candy apple red Low Rider leaning elegantly and sparkling in the midday sun. A cross was strapped in place with wide black ribbons at the front of the low deck trailer and gift wrapped boxes and bags were stacked around the machine.

A large sized portrait photo of Joshua was sitting on an easel in the bed of Pastor Walt's Chevy pickup, and underneath a white poster board was crammed with the signatures of loved ones. Jelly's eyes began to water and a tear trickled down the side of his face. His nose started to run and as he wiped away the tears with a shirtsleeve, the news camera suddenly zoomed in on Lynne's face. "Momma!" He cried out and burst into tears, before reaching down into the side pillow of the couch and pulling out the Ruger P series, 9mm pistol that had been there since his memory served. "You never know son, and I'll be damned if some nigger's gonna lay a hand on us!" His mother would occasionally joke while spinning the trigger guard around her index finger like a gun slinger. "You only go near this if your life is being threatened and that's it, ya hear me boy?" She would ask him sternly. "Yes, ma'am," he would always answer back, assuring her that it would have to be a serious situation before he picked up the weapon.

"What's up Jelly man?" Clayton asked, picking up the phone.

"I'm gonna kill that motherfucker, I swear to God!" He shouted back. His pain and anger could not be mistaken for it had come from his honest and broken heart.

"I feel ya, but if you go and do that you'll end up being the same thing he is, a piece of shit. You hear what I'm sayin'?" Clay asked with concern.

"I know Clay, but I was on Kensington avenue today and Joshua Ladd's family, and church friends had a big gathering for him. It's got me tore up bad!" The teen exclaimed while crying.

"Have you seen him?" Clayton asked, trying to steer the topic in another direction and ease the kid's pain.

"Who Blaze? Naw, I ain't seen him since before y'all found Trina." Jelly replied, wiping his nose again on his shirtsleeve.

"What were you doing over there today, did you hear that there was a prayer vigil going on or something?"

"I was meeting up with Jayvon." Jelly replied in a low voice.

"Who's that?" Clayton asked back (knowing of course who he was) with the intention of helping the boy by keeping his focus on other scenarios.

"Trina's brother, he's living with his aunt now since she got killed."

"Yeah, this shit affects a lot of people bro, ya know what I'm saying? It always hits hard, hell it's hit us like that too. Everybody's human, ya feel me?" Clayton stated softly.

"I feel bad for the Ladd mom and Trina, it's messed up." Jelly replied in anguish.

"Feeling bad stems from emotions and apologies don't make anything better. They don't fix what happened, and in these types of situations that's where justice comes in. Ya hear?"

"Yeah, I feel ya Clay, and revenge can fix this shit too." The teen declared, looking down at the Ruger.

"Well yeah it can, but in alot of ways it's like suicide. It's a permanent solution to a temporary problem. Justice by law brings the light in and exposes all the cockroaches." Clayton's statement caused Jelly to laugh, and that in itself was enough for a breath of fresh air to be brought into the conversation.

"What are you doing right now?" Clayton asked.

"Nothing, just sitting here in my living room watching the news and eating Cool Ranch, Doritos."

"I'll meet you at the spot close to you and bring you back to my place, I'm off tonight and me and the family are going to watch a movie."

"Watch a movie with you, at your house?" Jelly asked in a sarcastic little kid's voice.

"Well fuck you then, if you don't want pizza, hot wings and icecream cake for desert that's on you!" Clay shouted back playfully. "Alright young buck, suit yourself then…"

"Yo! Wait, hold up! I didn't say I didn't want to, did I?" Jelly cut him off.

Clayton smiled on the other end of the phone as his wife nodded over to him and winked.

"You're a mess, you know that kid?"

"I aint no kid!" He taunted back.

Clayton parallel parked six inches from the curb in front of the four bedroom brick house on 49th., street in Cedar Park. The plum and rose painted ornate porch pillars matched the second floor tri-window dormers, which added a touch of quirkiness to the nostalgic Victorian slate roofed brownstone.

"This is your house?" Jelly asked in an amazed tone, staring out of the passenger's window.

"Yeah, sure is. Well, me and the wife's." Clayton responded, looking at the home and smiling. "It seems like a lifetime ago that I lived in that old 'hood."

"Man, it's nice." Jelly complimented.

"Thanks, but it's expensive too."

"Shit, better than being back on the block, don't bullshit me Clay!" The young teen exclaimed with awe.

"C'mon man, let's go in and eat. Oh, and by the way, watch your language, my wife's a born again christian. Ya feel me?" Clayton asked with a serious look.

"I get it." Jelly answered assuringly.

Clayton opened the large front door after peering downward through the wavey windowpane. He always did this to make sure that his toddler son wasn't standing in front of the doorway or hiding there intentionally waiting to scare dad. His boy had been creamed a couple of times while attempting to pull off this trick, but it seemed that his two year old brain didn't quite get it yet.

"Hey Alicia, this is Jerome but you can call him Jelly." Clayton announced, walking into the living room.

"Hello, Jelly. It's nice to meet you." The slender light skinned woman said.

Jelly was completely caught off guard by Alicia's natural beauty and her warm sensuous eyes.

"It's nice meeting you ma'am." Jelly said, while blushing and shaking her hand.

Clayton burst out laughing and Alicia could see that it made Jelly momentarily uncomfortable. "Chris stop now, leave that boy be!" She scolded, giving her husband a light slap to his shoulder.

"Never mind him Jelly, your going to sit next to me when we put the movie on!" She ordered, in a playful manner.

"Yes, ma'am!" He exclaimed with a broad smile.

"Who are you?" Clayton's son, Corey asked while peering around the corner of the couch.

"Jelly, what's yours?" The tot's head disappeared before he let out a high pitched squeal.

"Corey, c'mon out man! This is Jelly, now are you going to introduce yourself?" Clayton asked in a fatherly tone.

"No!" The kid responded, as he continued to giggle.

"Oh don't worry Jelly, in about ten minutes your going to wish that little bugger would go back behind the couch!" Alicia exclaimed, making her way to her hiding son.

"Kitchen or living room?" Clayton asked his wife, who was in the process of getting her son in a Superman onesie.

"Kitchen, Chris." She responded, while Corey had a hold of her shoulder, all the while gazing at Jelly.

"Would you just put your leg in here please?" She asked her son.

"Now comes the important question." Clayton announced. "Minions, Angry Birds or The Lego Movie?" Because Lord knows, it has to be one of the three doesnt it son?"

"Yeah!" The toddler shouted back with a shrill.

"I like the Minions too!" Jelly exclaimed, crouching down to Corey's eye level. "I mean it, they're cool!"

"The Minions it is then!"

"So Chris tells me that you're a straight 'A' student, is that correct?" She asked, placing paper plates and napkins on the table.

"Yes ma'am." Jelly answered proudly.

"Please, call me Alicia."

"Call me Jerome, I kind of miss that." He said softly, smiling up at her.

Clayton looked up while finishing off a hot wing and gave him a nod of approval.

"Well Jerome, it so happens that I'm an English teacher at Mount Calvary, Christian."

"No kidding?" Jelly asked with raised eyebrows.

"That's right, I also have something for you to study, and it also comes with practice tests." Her voice sounded enticing.

"What is it?" The teen asked earnestly.

"All the material you'll need in order for you to take your SAT's." Alicia beamed, excusing herself from the table and returning with a large white mailing envelope.

"Wow, thank you but I'm only thirteen!" Jelly said with excitement.

"Yeah, and he ain't no kid!" Clayton poked back.

After they ate, Alicia began cleaning up Corey while Clayton and Jelly cleared the kitchen table. Clayton then asked the teen to follow him to the rear of the house where his small office was located. It had the typical look of any home work space; a PC desk was against the back wall and on one side of it was a file cabinet and on the other, a tall narrow bookshelf. Framed photographs on the walls captured the smiling faces of the young men he proudly served with in Afghanistan. One in particular that really stood out was a close up shot of Clayton with a serious look upon his face as he gazed out of the rear of a C-130, which was high over the barren rock faced landscape below.

"Airborne?" Jelly asked while looking around at the photos and at the awards that were displayed on the bookshelf.

"Yeah, 4th Brigade, 82nd Airborne." He answered with a nod.

"Wild man, jumping out of airplanes?"

"Oh yeah, and a lot of action too!" Clayton exclaimed with a wink.

"Like what, bad?" Jelly inquired.

"Yeah, It was hot and heavy most of 2011 through 2013. I served three tours and on my second mission after they dumped us out, my team ended up out in the middle of nowhere." Clayton let out a slight chuckle and looked up at the drop ceiling. "Man, I ain't shittin' you, it had to have been a hundred and ten degrees out there, and no wind at all; we were wide open. Did I mention that we were lost on top of it all?"

Jelly laughed, seeing the look on his face. "Damned." He said with a grunt.

"So anyway, we're standing in the middle of this dust patch and there's about four or five clusters of trees and overgrowth out there." Clayton explained as he held his hand open and downward, momentarily plopping an invisible landscape from his imagination. "Then my boss, Sergeant Master Santos, asked for the binoculars and held up a fist.

"You notice anything funny, Chris?" He asked me after we had all crouched down getting as low as possible.

"No sir, what's up?" I answered, in a whisper.

"Turn that fucking shit off back there." He ordered our radioman.

"You see what's in those trees over there, and over there?" Santos wanted to know as he pointed to a couple of the small patches of overgrowth.

"All I see is birds, Juan." I replied, calling him by his first name.

"Exactly, and are there any birds in that spot right there?" He inquired, squinting his eyes.

"No, there is not." I answered, handing over the scope I'd been looking through.

"He ordered me and three others to circle around to the left of it and wait for his call, then he sent two others halfway up the right side. He wanted to see if we could draw fire from them."

"What happened next, Clay?" Jelly asked with excitement.

"Me and my guys got about fifty or so yards parallel to the patch, and Rice and Torillo, the other two guys, got about seventy and below our line of fire." Clayton looked at the boy with a slight grin then continued. "All of a sudden, I see this one stand up and he's holding an RPG."

"Wow!" Jelly cried out.

"That's right, and don't you know that my boss had us covered so well that he saw it before we did!"

"Go, go, go!" Sergeant Santos shouted through the earpieces.

"I dropped the one shouldering the RPG and then we saw their muzzle flashes." He explained while pointing out and shaking his index finger. "Then we opened up on them, and it was over in about thirty seconds."

"Thirty seconds?!" Jelly asked with awe.

"Yup, tore the shit out of them. Then we marked it off and called it in."

"Did you like the Army?"

"Yeah, I did. I mean it had its moments but shit, I was young, dumb and full of cum!" He shouted out causing Jelly to laugh hysterically.

"Why Airborne though?" The teen asked, shaking his head in amazement.

"Honestly, because me and some friends were talking after boot and a big fat dumb hillbilly I knew, said I wouldn't be able to hack it." Clayton smiled proudly. "So, fuck him!"

"I thrive on challenges too." Jelly stated with a nod.

"You ever heard the saying, 'Free your mind and your ass will follow?'" Clayton asked as he pointed down to the boy. "Well, in the Army it's, 'Move, get your ass in gear and your head will follow.' It's all about repetition, Jelly, it's all about staying in motion, it's all about building strong character."

"Look, this is what I wanted to show you right here, man." He said after a brief pause, handing Jelly a 5 x 7 photo. "You see those five kids? Out of all of them, only two of us, including myself, are still alive."

"How?" Jelly asked, looking up over the photo.

"The two on the far left, Caleb and Lekan were shot, basically dumb street shit and the one in the Ravens jersey, Tritchy, died from a heroin overdose about six years ago. He was a junkie most of his life." Clayton replied in a serious tone as he shook his head.

"Wow, I'm sorry man." Jelly said, staring down at the photograph.

"And you want to hear some shit? The cat next to me there with the black hat on backwards, my best friend Tamar, he's serving life up in Camp Hill for first degree murder. Shot his girlfriend's ex in the middle of the street in broad daylight!"

"My mom was killed during a fight that was going on down the street. She was shot out in front of the house." Jelly whispered.

"I know she was son, and there's a reason that I'm showing you all of this." Clayton explained, pointing at the memories on the office wall. "You listen to me Jelly, you stay in your own lane, ya hear? If it ain't yours then don't pick it up. Your not a gangsta or a 'hood rat, I knew that from the first time we talked, and your not a nigger. You're a guy who has a lot of potential, and your way smarter than I was at your age. With your brain, you can get into a really great school!"

"You really think I'm smarter than you were back in the day?" Jelly asked with a grin.

"Shit man, my interests were football, basketball and cafeteria!" Clayton joked. "Well, and girls too of course!"

"Thank God you added that, I was getting a little worried Clay!" Jelly joked sarcastically.

"Okay boys, we're going to put the movie on now!" Alicia called out from the front of the house.

"Coming mom!" Clayton yelled back with cute sarcasm in his voice.

Chapter Fifteen

"In three years time, while working undercover you have produced absolutely nothing. You never made physical contact with the primary subject, Andre' Pelts and you have failed to bring any tangible evidence or anything else relevant that is needed for an indictment. Would you agree, Agent Moss?" Field Director, Art Schilling asked after removing his glasses and looking up from his laptop. His dark gray suit jacket rested over the back of the large executive chair and his freshly pressed and starched Brooks Brothers white dress shirt; whose sleeves were folded to mid forearm fit him perfectly. Strapped for business over a set of Maroon, Jacob Alexander suspenders was his brown Massimo shoulder holster that held a 1911 .45 Springfield Armory. He was seated at the head of the long conference table and to his left was Special Agent Timmons (who was quietly reading the case profile from her notepad) and off to Schilling's right was Moss and his boss, Special Agent Nolan. At 7:00 a.m. the sun hadn't quite met the Eastern horizon and the view through the large office windows was a muted blend of dark gray sky and interior lights from the neighboring high rises that were slowly announcing their awakening. City hall's five hundred and forty eight feet spire loomed to the West, and a dim silhouette of William Penn stood sentinel high above the Second Empire style building.

"Sir, I'm sure that we can recraft and find a way to maneuver ourselves…" Nolan began to say with a hint of yearning in his voice.

"I need to hear from Moss." Schilling responded gruffly. The fifty eight year old FBI veteran of many assignments and very bad situations, was not one to mince words or be fucked with. He had a reputation of being a maverick but when it came to business or his command being questioned the Missouri boy in him kicked into high gear. On this particular morning his diverticulitis was flaring up, due to the jalapenos he had eaten the previous evening (after his wife told him not to) and he wasn't in the mood for semantics.

"Sir, with all due respect our chief objective was (and I believe still is) to infiltrate and shut down the Gold Sheik Mob; not just here in Philadelphia but also across the country. My closest asset was killed…"

"Brutally tortured and murdered." Timmons stated solemnly, looking up at him from her laptop.

"And what kind of progress have you made in meeting that objective, Moss?" Schilling asked.

"She got caught out…" Moss tried to explain.

"You fucking exposed your informant and yourself Moss!" The field director barked back. "You underestimated your opponent's intelligence and the measures to which he'll take to guarantee his survival."

"Sir, during the course of our investigation we have gained valuable information regarding how their organization is funded through the sales and trafficking of narcotics and firearms; the structure and hierarchy of their management and also the means by which they recruit new members." Special Agent Nolan stated, as if reasoning with an angry parent.

"Timmons, call Agent Lee in." Schilling ordered, looking back down at his laptop.

"What?!" Moss exclaimed in disbelief. "Your fucking kidding me right?"

"I'm advising you to settle down and shut up." Schilling said, glaring at him with severity.

"Jane, Schilling wants you to come in now." Timmins announced into her phone.

Moments later Special Agent Lee entered into the conference room and after closing one of the double doors behind her, pulled a chair out from the far end of the long polished table. Her seductive and alluring nature that held Moss a sexual prisoner, along with her usual enticing form fitting attire had been replaced. She now wore a black, faux styled double breasted Smythe business suit and underneath, a purple colored Milano silk blouse was opened to her breastplate which revealed a white pearl necklace. Black satin, Saks Fifth Avenue pump stilettos were on her small feet and every step that Jane took was one of confidence. The woman who had just entered the room was once a U.S. Olympic gymnastics team member, a 3.8 GPA Syracuse alumni and the recruit who graduated top of her class at Quantico. By the time Jane had turned fifteen she had visited over ten countries and fluently spoke eight languages. Jane Lee was a bright girl.

"Please Jane, come sit here." Field Director Schilling invited with a motioning gesture.

Jane slowly walked around the end of the table and sat to the left of Timmins. She made no attempt whatsoever to make eye contact with Agent Moss, who was in the chair directly across from her. He had a bewildered look upon his face as if he was stuck in the middle of a bad dream and couldn't wake up. In reality however, Moss was seeing another side of someone for the very first time, and he immediately understood what it must be like for suspects, after his undercover veil had been lifted.

"Can you please give us a brief narrative of when you were first assigned to Agent Moss?" Schilling inquired, as Jane removed her laptop from her black leather Gucci briefcase.

"Good morning everyone." Agent Lee announced professionally and for the first time made eye contact with Moss. "I've been with the office of internal affairs for eight years and approximately a year and a half ago I was assigned to monitor and investigate Agent Moss under Agent Timmons direction. This all stemming from allegations of professional misconduct, misappropriation of expense accounts and failure to report on his direct involvement while engaging in criminal activity."

"And where did those allegations come from?" Schilling wanted to know.

"Trina Brooks. Agent Moss's informant contacted our office after she witnessed him engaging in illicit activity." Jane answered while momentarily shooting Moss a stern glare.

"Were you aware that DEA also had an operative working inside in an attempt to infiltrate Andre' Pelts?" Schilling asked in a low tone.

"No sir, not at first." Lee answered flatly.

"What the hell is going on here, a DEA operative next to Blaze?" Moss asked, turning his attention to the Field Director.

"Cleats, the guy that was killed just before Pelts attempted to carjack Joshua Ladd. Deceased also." Timmons answered with narrowed eyes.

"Jesus." Agent Nolan whispered to himself.

"Why wasn't I briefed on this?" Moss asked, with a look of disillusionment.

"You? We didn't know about it until after he was killed." Timmons responded.

"Jane, can you tell us what Agent Moss told you, regarding his interactions with Andre' Pelts and GSM?" Schilling asked as he leaned back in his chair.

"Moss informed me that on several occasions he drove past Andre's house, knowing that he and other GSM members would be out front. Moss also mentioned that he honked his horn repeatedly at times, and would shout out threats challenging 'Blaze to fight. He also admitted to brandishing his weapon and would wave it out of his car window, a couple of times pointing it at Andre." Agent Lee stated, as if she were a witness in a courtroom.

"Agent Moss, would you agree or disagree with any of this?" Art Schilling asked. He had his hands folded in the back of his head and stared directly into his eyes.

Before answering he took a deep breath, nodded and then looked across the table at Jane. "Yes sir, I told her all of those things."

"Fill us in on the items that were purchased with the expense account and documented money requests please?" Timmons asked, as she opened a file that Jane had handed her.

"Agent Moss took me out to dinner several times at Prime, in the Philly Live casino last year, and we spent two or three weekends at the Borgata Hotel casino in Atlantic City, in the spring of 2022. He always rented a Mercedes or a Cadillac whenever he took me out and we also flew to Tampa on September 25th 2023, to see the Eagles play the Buccaneers." Jane answered, looking up at the ceiling while counting the memories on her fingers.

"Yes, I see that all of your entries correspond to the dates and times that you have documented in your report." Timmons noted, nodding over to Agent Lee. "Then there's also a little issue here of a five thousand dollar discrepancy, regarding cash that you requested in order to make a narcotics buy off of Cleats, this being of course behind Adre' Pelts back."

"Which brings us back to the DEA operative of course." Schilling exclaimed as he leveled himself in the large executive chair while folding his hands on the table. "Dwayne Trainer, whose cover name was 'Cleats' reports here in this suspect file (that was given to me by his boss) that a DeShawn Shey made contact with him to discuss the purchase of five thousand dollars worth of fentanyl. The first entry that contact was made between you and Trainer regarding this matter was July of 2023, and the last was a week prior to his death in mid October. Now, we obviously can't talk to Trainer about the dinner dates or the Eagles - Buccaneers game, but I'm pretty sure that if his boss provided us with an itinerary, there would be nothing to substantiate your written reports justifying these expenses."

"I remember you requesting that money, Moss." Agent Nolan added with the look of a man who had been betrayed. "I thought we were friends."

"I thought at the time that I could work an angle on…" Agent Moss began to say.

"Oh horse shit, Moss!" Schilling burst out startling everyone seated. "Why in the hell would a specialist in the field, such as yourself, inquire about making an arrangement to purchase drugs? You mean to tell me that after three years, you were oblivious to GSM's line of operation?!"

"Or, were you just cuddling up to Cleats, so you could get the information that you couldn't get off of Trina?" Timmons inquired with a hint of sarcasm. "We've all seen the video from the phone that was found inserted in her vagina, and we'll be discussing the other video that Agent Lee brought to our attention in just a moment."

"Where's the phone?" Schilling demanded with a raised eyebrow.

"Phone?" Moss replied, as his gaze left the field director's and landed on Jane.

"You know Goddamned right well what phone Moss, and don't fuck with me!" The Missouri boy in him warned. "Timmons, play the thread that Agent Lee recorded on her dictaphone. The highlighted version, in regards to the night he called Blaze?"

"Yes, sir." Agent Timmons scrolled down through the saved items on her laptop before tapping on several options and raising the volume. "Here it comes now."

"I called Blaze and before I hung up on him, I told him that I got his number off of his girlfriend. I had no idea that he would react the way he did or that he would have me tailed." Moss's voice sounded as if he were coming through on someone's speaker phone.

"Why the fuck did you tell him that?" Jane asked in disbelief.

"Because I was pissed off. I accused him of killing Joshua Ladd and he wouldn't addmitt to it, so I thought fuck it, I'm gonna bust his balls."

"Christ, Moss you shouldn't have taunted him like that, I mean it was a little much don't you think? You knew he was a psycho."

"Yeah, and I feel like shit because Trina was the one who answered the phone. I could hear her in the background so I knew she was standing next to Blaze the whole time." Moss's voice began to trail off as if he were visualizing the scenario.

"Stop the thread," Schilling ordered. "Where's the phone you used to call Blaze on this particular night?"

"I was using a burner." Moss answered flatly.

"That's not what I asked you! Where is the phone…" Schilling pressed harder as he leaned in closer to show Moss how volatile he was about to become. "You are a fine hair away from being locked up." He hissed.

"I threw it in the river!" Moss exclaimed, his voice cracking with fear. "I don't know what I was thinking!"

"Well, you know what I'm thinking?! I'm thinking that you're a disgrace to this agency and all it represents, that's exactly what I'm thinking Moss!" Schilling had enough and his needle on the snap meter broke into the redline. He forced the large chair backwards and suddenly stood up before turning and gazing out the window. "Let's see Moss's latest TV show: 'This old dump gets remodeled by a ghetto rat!'" Schilling then spun back around, his head cocked over to one side and his eyebrows raised, warning Moss to tread very carefully.

"I think it's suffice to say that you have bastardized this whole operation, not only by your actions of gross misconduct and the embezzlement of allocated resources, both of which being unprofessional and completely irresponsible, but also allowing yourself to be exposed. All of this led up to the death of Trina Brooks and more than likely, got a DEA operative killed." Schilling stated while looking at the frozen image of a hooded individual pointing a handgun at the surveillance camera in Moss's undercover residence.

"Sir?" Nolan asked, with a confused look.

"DEA, has reason to believe that the botched drug buy that got Cleats killed, along with Joshua Ladd, was actually a hit. They think that Blaze was tipped off and the primary shooter was a GSM gangbanger named Marcus. He was shot and killed by a PPD Motor Unit officer after pulling a gun, outside the abandoned residence where Trina's body was discovered. The reason PPD didn't divulge any information about Marcus was because DEA wanted ballistics. The test results revealed that Marcus's gun was the same one used to kill Cleats."

"Oh my God." Moss whispered, dropping his head into his hands.

"Sergeant Clayton!" A man's voice called out from across Whitaker Avenue. "Can I have a word with you for a moment?"

Clayton had just gotten off work before walking to his truck which was parked across from Division Headquarters. As usual, he momentarily sat his oversized briefcase in the bed while wrestling with an Igloo lunch cooler, coffee thermos and his winter coat that Alicia had given him for Christmas. He hated wearing it because of its bulk, and only put it on before leaving the house.

"Just a moment buddy, I'm almost late for dinner!" Clayton responded, not turning around.

"My name is Agent Moss, and I'm with the FBI."

"Are you sure your name's not Shey?" Clayton responded with a smartass grin.

"Yeah, very funny." Moss said, nodding his head.

"What's up?" Clayton asked.

"I'd really appreciate it if you could turn me on to Jelly, I could use…"

"Whoa man, what did you just say?" Clayton asked, throwing his gear into the opened truck.

"Chris, I need to know if…" Moss beckoned with open arms.

Before Agent Moss could blink, Clayton grabbed a hold of his left wrist with his left hand before punching Moss's elbow joint with his right fist, forcing it to bend. With one sweeping maneuver he twisted his unbalanced weight and folded his arm around his back. Moss let out a shout of pain before Clayton slammed his forehead into the hood of the Tacoma.

"This is the only thing you need to know." He growled into Moss's ear while pressing down on the side of his head. "If you ever go near my kid, I'm gonna put a bullet in your fucking head, stick you in a freezer and wait until spring. Then I'm gonna thaw you out, cut you up and feed you to the crabs. This ain't no bush league bullshit, and if you haven't noticed, this case is getting people killed, Moss!"

Chapter Sixteen

Mark Hess met Ben and Lynne at the Giant grocery store on Scarlet Road in Kennett at 5:30 p.m., Monday evening. Ben had approached him the previous day after church and asked if he had heard anything further about Joshua's killer. After the two quietly left the after service coffee hour and stepped outside for a breath of fresh air, Mark assured him that he would contact his friend up in Philadelphia. He noticed their vehicle alongside a shopping cart stall in the middle of the parking lot; this would allow Ben to get out of his vehicle quickly if he was pressed into action. Mark had to smile to himself, remembering that he was a past president of a one percent motorcycle club. "You're still a careful man, Benjamin Ladd." He said to himself, stepping out of his wife's VW Touareg.

"I like you in jeans!" Ben exclaimed, after seeing Mark in the driver's side rear view mirror.

"Hey guys." Mark announced, opening the rear door and sitting behind Ben. He was wearing what he called his normal clothes. A pair of faded old work Levi's (that his wife Rhianne had tried to throw out on several occasions), a well worn Eagles hoodie, oil stained Timberlands and a reproduction of a A-2 Army Air Corps flight jacket that fit him perfectly.

A GOOD PLACE

"Thank you for meeting us, Mark." Lynne said with a smile, turning around in her seat.

"Don't mention it, you two." He replied, cleaning his glasses with a handkerchief and placing them back on his face.

"Lynne, I've known you since we were kids, long before highschool and Ben, I think you know that you're my brother in Christ." Mark stated, offering him a handshake..

"Mark, I can assure you that whatever is discussed here tonight in this car, will stay in this car." Ben promised, with a serious gaze. "Believe you me brother, Lynne and I both appreciate this from our hearts."

"I have a good buddy at a precinct up in Philly, and as it turns out, as it often does in this line of work, he has a good friend in the investigative division. Now look, none of what I'm about to tell you has been proven, and the investigation is still ongoing."

"We understand Mark, don't we honey?" Lynne asked softly.

"Okay, so this is what I was able to find out. On the morning that Joshua was killed an alleged drug deal went bad down the street from where the work van was parked. The driver of that car was found shot to death and hunched over the steering wheel, and a passenger in the car fled before attempting to steal the work van at gunpoint. He had what witnesses described as a gunshot wound to his buttock or left thigh." Mark brushed his hair back with his fingers and looked up to see Ben's unblinking eyes in the mirror.

"Go on." Lynne whispered, squeezing Ben's hand.

"This is where it gets a little weird. A nineteen year old female was found hacked up in an abandoned row home in Kensington, and apparently the killer or killers inserted a cellphone into her vaginal cavity…"

"Oh, my God!" Lynne exclaimed in horror.

"Fucking savages." Ben hissed, shaking his head with disgust.

He became momentarily distracted when he saw a young father who appeared to be in his mid, to late twenties pushing a shopping cart. His toddler son was sitting in the seat in front of the handrail and his head bobbled about as the cart's hard rubber wheels spun around at random and thumped over the uneven surface of the parking lot. The boy was dressed for a Siberian expedition wearing a one piece navy blue, baby spacesuit with an attached hood that was pulled over-top a red knitted cap. The only thing that revealed that there was a human child in there was his little wet, red runny nose. Ben's heart filled with sadness as he immediately realized that Joshua would never know what it would be like to push that shopping cart.

"This is the strange part, and it's still a little loose at this point in the investigator's thinking." Mark continued to say after muting his phone's ringer. "It's Rhianne, calling me to not forget something, no doubt. Anyway, a source my buddy has over at division, told him that they had heard that the driver who was shot and killed during the botched drug deal was a DEA agent and they suspect that it was actually a hit. A few days later, while detective's were gathering crime scene evidence from the location where the girl's remains were found; a shoot out ensued out in front of the house. They ran ballistics tests on the perpetrator's weapon, and it came back positive for being the same weapon that was used to kill the alleged DEA agent."

"Street gang, punk shit." Ben mumbled. He had a look on his face that Lynne had never seen before. "Our boy was killed because of some nigger bullshit!"

"Benjamin Ladd!" Lynne scolded with pain in her eyes. "They killed Joshua, Mark, and I am so sorry that Ben said that…"

"Don't apologize to me, I won't hear of it from either of you. I told you both from day one that I will be with you two until this is solved, and I mean to stand by that!" Mark exclaimed assuringly.

Mark patted Ben on the shoulder. "Hey, I understand and feel your frustration, it's completely natural. At this time, let's try and remember that as Christians we are meant to forgive our transgressors. Mathew 6: 15 "But if you do not forgive others their sins, your Father will not forgive your sins."

"Amen, Mark." Lynne said softly, reaching over and grabbing ahold of Ben's hand.

"God's Will." Ben whispered, clenching his fist.

Occasionally a patch of star cluttered night sky would momentarily peer through the voided openings of the dense tree canopy that seemed to loom overhead year round on this stretch of windy country road. The bare yet crowded branches that reached high above came from an unseen source that was hidden by the darkness of the earth. They sat in silence holding hands while staring through the windshield to the farthest reaches of the headlights.

"I'm sorry for my outburst honey, I'm just so pissed off right now that I can't see straight." Ben whispered over to her.

Tears began to fill Lynne's eyes and he could tell by her breathing that she was about to start crying.

"In the ten years that we've been married, I've never seen that look on your face. It was as if the devil himself swept in and took hold of you, Ben." She said softly, wiping her nose.

"I never wanted you to see that side of my personality, Lynne. The day I met you was the happiest day of my life and when I made the decision to become born again, I felt as if a giant weight had been lifted from my soul." Ben exclaimed, shaking her hand gently. "I love you with all my heart, and I am not proud of rancor. I'm sorry."

"You had red in your eyes honey, it was pretty scary." Lynne remarked in a low tone as if she were speaking to a naughty child.

"The old me resurfacing, after all this time." He replied, with shame in his voice.

"You would have murdered whoever's responsible for killing Joshua, back in your day wouldn't you?" She inquired. "It's okay Ben, I can handle the truth."

"In a second." He said with a nod.

"To be honest with you Ben, and God forgive me for saying this, but I fantasized about you doing just that." Lynne admitted while staring out of the passenger's window. "Making him pay for what he did."

"What?" He asked, with a confused look on his face. "Are you serious? Your the spiritual love glue that keeps me bound in happiness!"

"Oh, stop it!" Lynne squealed back before blowing her nose again.

"Hold on Lynne!" He shouted, after a large buck leapt out in front of them from where the forest met the road. Everything happened so suddenly that Ben didn't have time to hit the brakes and the last thing he saw before the violent impact was the shiny black eye of the deer. An explosive loud boom mixed with the sound of metal and glass being torn away echoed through the woods, as the energy from the impact was dissipated and released. Ben's seatbelt instantly locked before he saw a flash of light and heard the 12 gauge charges that deployed the airbags. Tiny flecks of plastic sealant from the steering wheel's housing and the slight odor of spent cordite filled the car. The large buck had been thrown up and over the hood of the SUV and a rack of its antlers penetrated through the windshield puncturing Lynne's airbag. Ben was still in a daze, as he looked over at his wife and asked her if she was asleep.

"Lynne, it's time to wake up now." He could barely say. "Lynne! Oh my God Lynne!" He shouted out with fear, remembering what had just taken place.

Lynne's head was slumped forward and her chin was resting on her upper chest. Blood soaked the depleted airbag and smeared her hair that covered her face. Lynne's body was limp and lifeless and leaned over towards the passenger door. Directly in front of her were the antlers that shattered through the windshield and ended up in an inverted position. Its severely severed head revealed dead red eyes that peered back through the window.

"911, what's your emergency?"

"Please send an ambulance, my wife and I have been in a bad accident and she's in and out of consciousness!" Ben explained with urgency.

"What's your location and what are you driving, sir?" The dispatch operator asked in a monotone voice.

"We're Northbound on Rt 162, just to the left of the Natural Lands ChesLen Preserve. I have a road flare burning at the rear of the car. It's a 2023, electric blue Subaru Outback. A large buck jumped right out in front of us!"

"Help is on the way…" The woman started to say before being interrupted.

"Baby, stay still, there's an ambulance on the way now." Ben assured her, while holding her head in his lap.

"Look, lady, get that unit out here now because my wife's going to be in a lot of pain soon, you understand me?!" He ordered.

"I understand sir, please stay on the line with me until the paramedics arrive." The dispatcher replied with a professional and mild voice. "Hit a big buck huh?" she asked, attempting to relieve his angst.

"Yeah, he's pretty big, he broke his neck and half his head went through the windshield; his antlers ripped through my wife's airbag!"

"Oh my Lord, how big is he, do you think?" She asked Ben with girlish curiosity.

"He's a big ole boy, probably close to two hundred and fifty pounds or so." Ben answered, looking up from Lynne and craning his neck to try and surmise the animal's size.

"My husband would be furious, I can tell you that!" The dispatcher joked softly.

"She's fully awake now!" Ben exclaimed joyfully. "Just hold on a bit, you okay honey?" He asked her.

"Sir, paramedics should be there in less than five minutes. Is your wife in any pain?"

"No, right now she's looking up at me and smiling!" Ben responded, choking up.

"Well, your test results are in." The young attending intern at Jennersville Hospital announced with a grin. He looked to be about sixteen years old and had the swag of rich brat beach bum, hanging out at his parents summer vacation home with his buddies. Ben had been standing next to Lynne and stroking her hair as she rested on an examining room table that was off to the side of the ER, when the doctor slid open the privacy curtain with one swift pull. He slid a series of x rays on a white screen and pushed a button illuminating the images and walked over to the bedside.

"Mrs. Ladd, your CT scan came back negative for any brain or spinal injury but you do have a broken nose, it's a clean break and it doesn't look like it needs to be set." He then pointed at the x-ray. "Right there, smack dab in the middle of the bridge."

"You lucked out honey." Ben whispered, patting her hand.

"I'll say, considering the beast's horns could have ripped her face off." The doctor agreed. "You also have a slight concussion that should be gone by morning, so I'll need your husband to check on you throughout the night. If your pupils are still dilated, which they shouldn't be, we'll have to see you first thing tomorrow, okay?" The doctor asked, flashing a small light beam across her eyes."

"You know it doc." He assured the young physician with a nod.

"I'll give you four sedatives to help with your discomfort and anxiety." He mentioned, as Lynne waved off his offer.

"I'm in recovery, so I won't need anything but Ibuprofen." Her muffled voice came from underneath the white towel that held a bag of ice.

"Last, but surely not least, you're pregnant!" The intern shouted with joy, raising his arms in the air.

"What?!" Ben asked, as if he was just informed that he had won the lottery.

"I was going to tell you that I skipped my period." Lynne said groggily after removing the towel.

"Let me guess, you were just waiting to see if the faucet would come back on next month, huh?" The young doctor joked.

"I'm sixty years old, doc!" Ben shouted with excitement.

"Well, she's thirty seven and by the rules of nature your wife is about six weeks into the process." The physician cracked. "The buns a cookin' in the oven old man!"

"Your going to be a what?!" Mickey yelled out with a laugh after he had gotten the phone call from Ben informing him of the accident and Lynne's test results.

"I'm going to be a father, Mickey! Can you believe it?!" Ben exclaimed. He sounded as excited as a little kid on Christmas morning.

"Let's see, both of you were almost killed when Godzilla deer crashed through your windshield, and the next thing you know Lynne's pregnant! How does this happen brother?!"

"I don't know the answer to that one, the only thing I can say is that everything happens for a reason. All in God's time." Ben said, after his laughter settled down to a chuckle.

"How's she feeling?" Mickey asked with concern.

"She's a little tired and achy, but the real fun house party starts in the morning. That's why I'm going to try and get her in a hot bath soon."

"Put the phone up to her ear, would ya Ben?" Mickey asked.

"She can hear you Mick, go ahead."

"Hey girl, sorry to hear about the accident, but you better get in that bath because the morning's going to be rough, let me tell ya!" Mickey suggested with a fatherly tone.

"Thank you, Mickey." Lynne replied, sounding muffled.

"Tell Ben to take that sock out of your mouth, I can't hear you Lynne!" He teased her.

Lynne was so caught off guard by his joke that she immediately burst into laughter.

"Hang on Mickey, I'm pulling it out now!" Ben chimed in, tickling her.

"Stop!!" Lynne squealed. "That hurts!"

"I'll swing over tomorrow morning sometime, do you two need anything?"

"No, I think we're in good shape here. Hexe's trying to crawl up inside of her and I'm off to start the bath water." Ben said, throwing another log into the wood stove. "Oh yeah, maybe we can take a ride into town to AJ's Garage & Towing, so I can empty out what's left of the Subaru."

"Totalled, huh?" Mickey inquired in a low tone.

"Yup, she's gone. Our agent said everything will be handled by next week." Ben said, looking down at Lynne and giving her a wink.

Chapter Seventeen

"Blaze just pulled off with another dude, they're in a white mid 90's Honda Accord whip. I couldn't really see the license plate but it's definitely a Pennsylvania tag." Jelly said into his phone.

He was looking out a heavily decorated window of a twenty four hour store off of East Lehigh avenue. The large cigarette posters and lottery ads provided perfect cover for surveilling Blaze, especially when the whole occurrence was by happenstance. The fact that the store's security cameras were out of order (useful information gained through a friend) and that the Pakistani man behind the bullet proof glass at the register didn't understand a lick of English, made the entire scenario priceless.

"Where are you now?" Clayton asked, looking around at the relatively empty early morning office.

"Old 'hood, off Lehigh. " Jelly replied, cupping his hand over the phone's mouthpiece.

"You good?"

"Yeah Clay, I'm good. There's no way he saw me in here with all this shit covering the windows."

"What was it, one of those love at first sight thangs?" Detective Clayton teased, knowing that Jelly would understand his reference to the entire episode happening completely by chance.

"Oh yeah, definitely Clay!" The teen said sarcastically before laughing. "You know how G-Money pimp he is!" Jelly's smartass comment made Clayton spit out a mouthful of coffee before letting out a raspy howl.

"Jelly, your a fucking nut!" He exclaimed, wiping his tie with a napkin. "I'll get with you later on young blood, and I'll try to get that Honda. If you see him again, get some looks on that plate."

"Alright, later on." Jelly replied before hanging up.

"Chris, can I have a word with you for a moment?" His boss asked. Richards had been standing around the corner of a series of highback cubicle desks that were set in long rows and placed back to back in the center of the large open expanse. He had called him by his first name, and that was indicative to Clayton that he wanted to have a man to man chat, rather than a strictly professional one.

"George, I didn't know you were here." Clayton said apologetically, making sure he didn't spill any of his coffee while walking over to him.

Senior Detective George Richards, was one of the old boys who grew up on the streets and played hard ball when he had too. He hated politics, racism, and rank and file. George felt more at home leading from the front or sitting at his station in the office amongst his staff (or as he fondly called them, his kids).

"Let's go in here." Richards said under his breath, while flipping on the light switch to one of the interview rooms.

They sat across from each other at the small stainless steel table, and Clayton glanced up (mostly out of habit and partly out of curiosity) at the one-way window glass that was strategically cut into the wall, up close and next to the table.

"I think you know me well enough by now Chris." Richards mentioned, nodding to the open door. The office was beginning to come to life as small chat and far off laughter could be heard from somewhere on the floor.

"I'm sorry George, it's just that I'm so used to working in this box and always having to be careful handling the bad guys." Clayton responded, calling him by his first name.

Richards took a sip of his Wawa coffee, then sat the twenty ounce red cup on the table before removing his reading glasses. His gray, slowly turning white hair was receding and his broad forehead and round face that seemed to never age was now tired looking and a bit ashen. George Richards was steadily approaching sixty one years of age and the young man who was once built like a linebacker, now toted a pot belly and had a limp when the weather was damp and cold.

"I don't think that I ever told you this before Chris. You know that I was an E5 (Sergeant) Tanker in the first Gulf War of course, but I don't remember telling you that I was with the 3rd Brigade, and what happened on the night of February 27th., 1991." Richards said, momentarily looking up at the acoustic ceiling tiles.

"'Friendly Fire, 3rd Brigade?'" Clayton asked softly.

"Yes. I was just about to turn twenty eight and in the middle of my third hitch, God I loved it man!" He said, causing Clayton to let out a chuckle.

"Anyway, that morning was dark as a bitch I'm telling ya, and fucking cold." Richards exclaimed, rubbing his shoulders as if reliving the frigid temperature. "We were working alongside the 2nd Battalion, nicknamed 'Hell On Wheels.' We were about two miles apart when we started taking RPG hits from the Iraqi Republican Guard. Through their infrared imaging, the 2nd Battalion thought that the grenades hitting our armor were muzzle flashes from our guns shooting at them. We were mistaken for Iraqis." Richards stated, shaking his head.

"Damned." Clayton whispered.

"My unit lost seven men, three of which were good buddies of mine, along with two Abrams, (tanks) and three Bradleys, (fighting vehicles). It was a shit show." Richards looked into Clayton's eyes. "It was the first time in my life that I saw, and experienced death on such a nasty level. It was very personal."

"I understand, George." Clayton whispered.

"I've been in this business since those days Chris, and I can tell when an assignment is getting too personal. Our demeanor changes and sometimes passion blind sides us. Maybe we're afraid our ego's, that cloak our insecurities, will fade or in my case when I was younger, a lot of repressed anger will resurface and I'll do something dumb." His boss said in a fatherly tone. "I think you're getting in too deep with this kid."

"He's just like we were George, growing up tough, with a brain. He lost both his mother and father and he's all alone out there. I just want to help him out a little bit, maybe mentor him." Clayton replied, raising his palms.

"Getting him killed ain't gonna help him out man, c'mon."

"He's safe at his mom's house and Blaze doesn't suspect anything. He's the only eyes and ears we got George…" Clayton tried to reason.

"And we don't have shit Chris, let's be honest. DEA had a man inside who was with Blaze almost twenty four seven, they were trying to establish GSM's narcotics distribution network and trafficking routes. Blaze never held on to so much as a gram of dope, and the operative drove every mile to and from the meeting locations. The operative, aka Cleats, ended up dead because Blaze found out he was a narc. Apparently, Blaze got injured during the hit before attempting to carjack the Ladd kid. The gun that was used to kill Cleats was found in the vehicle that our motor unit shot up in front of the house where Trina's body was discovered." Richards looked at his wrist watch before continuing. "The fucking FBI had a harebrained scheme to start a bogus gangbang outfit with the objective of gathering enough intel to shut GSM down. Then their agent popped Blaze's old lady on some bullshit charge before getting himself exposed and ultimately hacked up. All because he thought he was dealing with a bunch of freshmen."

"Jelly told me that Blaze killed Joshua Ladd, for sure." Clayton said, tapping his index finger on the stainless table top.

"Chris, how the fuck would he know that? Did he overhear Blaze telling someone about the shooting? What could that kid possibly know that we don't know? How do you know that he isn't just looking to impress you?" Richards inquired, looking over his glasses.

"I don't, but I trust him, George. He's gone out of his way for us, starting with the SEPTA bus ride meeting and calling me when I asked, and even coming to my home for supper." Clayton nodded with assurance.

"You had him over for supper?" Richards asked, rubbing his forehead.

"Well yeah, pizza and wings." Clayton responded nonchalantly, taking a sip from his Eagles coffee mug.

"Which brings me back to my point that maybe you're getting in too deep, and possibly putting him in harm's way?"

"Blaze isn't watching him George, because he's too busy making sure that everyone is noticing him taking Trina's kid brother, Jayvon out and about; the zoo, movies, the Franklin Institute and nice restaurants. The sick fuck kills his sister, then parades the boy around as if he feels bad for his loss!" Clayton said, raising his voice with anger and disgust.

"I'm not going to get into the legalities here Chris, he's thirteen years old as you know, but also by law, Jelly shouldn't be living alone as a minor in his deceased mother's house, and they know that too! He shouldn't be in the possession of a firearm, that information was disclosed to us by a neighbor, because they knew his mom had one. I'll be Goddamned if I wouldn't want my kid having one either in that spot. He also shouldn't be running around the streets playing I-Spy." Richards wagged a warning finger accompanied with a grin. "I'm going to just come out and say it, FBI wants you to work undercover as a surveillance operative."

"What?!" Clayton asked, as if his boss had just asked him to take his clothes off and run around the office.

Richards burst into laughter after he saw the look on Clay's face.

"Your fucking kidding me, right?!"

"Shhh… Quiet down now Chris, we don't want to expose you before you accept their offer." Richards joked.

"There's that motherfucker, get around him and bang back at Franklin!" Blaze ordered the driver of the stolen white Accord. They were traveling West on Luzerne street when Blaze spotted his target.

"C'mon, Cruz, get past his ass man!" He shouted over to the skinny, GSM gangbanger.

"I got oncoming cars man, chill Blaze!" He answered in a nervous voice.

Blaze punched him hard in the side of his head, causing Cruz to momentarily lose control of the car. "Tell me too chill nigga?! Who the fuck you think your talkin' too?!" Blaze yelled with rage. "Now I said, pass his ass and bang around at Franklin!"

Cruz stomped down hard on the accelerator and flew past a line of slower cars, narrowly missing an oncoming minivan as he cut back into the proper lane. He cut the wheel hard to the left and spun the Honda around in the middle of the intersection at North Franklin street, and tucked in behind a SEPTA bus. Blaze then put on a full black hood with a facemask and reached for a .38 snub from under the passenger's seat. He gripped the pistol's handle with his left hand before shoving it into a heavy white plastic bag. Lastly, he took ahold of a long stemmed window washing squeegee and jumped out of the car.

"Go back two blocks the way we came and scoop me up over there." He ordered over to the excited looking teen, while pointing out his intentions.

Agent Moss stopped for the red light at North 7th street and saw a lean looking man wearing a black Adidas tracksuit approaching his vehicle and carrying window cleaning gear.

"No thanks man, I don't have time!" He exclaimed through his half opened window.

Moss didn't realize who it was until it was too late. Blaze then pulled down his face mask before winking at him.

"Fuck you, asshole," he hissed loud enough for Moss too hear, before shooting him twice in the head at point blank range.

Blaze kept low as he hunched over and pulled the magnetized mini GPS tracker from the rear left wheel well of Moss's gold Toyota Corolla..

Chapter Eighteen

'My name is Jerome Wilts but you can call me Jelly. I'm the kid that was across the street from the prayer vigil, and you invited me to come and pick out a Christmas present. I thought that I'd 'Friend Request' you and sent a message of thanks!' Jelly thought about sending his message through Josh's Facebook Profile but changed his mind when he realized that his family might think that it was too personal. He scrolled down through Joshua's contacts and came across a photo of Lynne standing next to her son and husband. The three stood in a row (Joshua in the middle) on the porch, and sitting in front of them with its head cocked over to one side was a large female German Shepherd. Jelly could see that it was a girl dog because of the pink collar around her neck and the small, well loved white teddy bear dangling from her mouth. He was surprised when Lynne accepted the request so soon (considering the fact that his profile picture was a SpaceX rocket taking off from a launch pad, and his username was 'Skydancer') and noticed that she had also messaged him back saying that he was welcome and that she would keep Jelly in her prayers.

'What was the gift you picked out?' Lynne wanted to know as she smiled into her phone's screen.

'I got home and opened it right away, lol. It was a LEGO's Speed Champions, Mercedes AMG. Of course I put it together that night!' He answered, looking down at the car on the coffee table.

'Wow, that sounds great and I'm happy that you like it Jelly!' She giggled to herself, imagining the look on the kid's face when he saw the kit. 'How old are you, may I ask?'

'Thirteen.' Jelly replied, hoping that she wouldn't think that he was just a kid.

'That's nice, and where do you go to school?'

'I'm in my senior year at Conwell Middle school.' He stated proudly.

'Wow, and do you get good grades?' Lynne let out a laugh knowing that the boy was on the verge of adolescence and wanted to be treated like a young adult.

'Yes, straight A's. My friend's wife is a high school English teacher and she gave me a SAT prep exam. I passed with a 1220 score on my practice test and she was really excited!'

'A 1220?!' Lynne asked with amazement. She remembered when Joshua studied and took his SATs his junior year in highschool, and with a score of 1210 one would be in the top twenty five percent of all test takers. 'Jelly, that is an excellent test score!'

'Thank you!' He answered, smiling down at her text.

'Please stay in touch Jelly, and I'm very proud of you! I have to run to the grocery store now.'

'Yes ma'am, and thank you again!' Jelly signed off.

As usual, he hid the phone and placed one earbud in his ear so that he would know if the phone rang. Before he slid the neatly cut and tight fitting baseboard back into place (which was positioned behind the couch in the living room) he removed a large Ziploc freezer bag and stared down at the gun that was used to kill Joshua Ladd.

Although it had only been a week since the car accident, Lynne's muscle aches in her neck and upper back had subsided to occasional spasms and the horrible looking swollen black and blue contusions that aggrandized her upper mandible had faded to a blend of yellowish grays.

The bridge of her nose was as wide as a banana and breathing through her nostrils was still next to impossible. Dr. Ben (as she liked to tease) insisted that she apply Neospouran liberally to her face and forehead and she had to admit that the lotion treatments every night after a hot bath seemed to be working. Lynne slowly walked up the stairs while holding on to the handrail while Hexe stayed on her free side taking every ascending step in time with her. The dog's unconditional love and loyalty could never be matched or bested by any human or another beast. She had the best of intentions of getting out of her 'hang around the house' get up, (which usually consisted of tight yoga pants, one of Ben's old hoodie's or Harley Davidson T-shirts and Crocs or barefeet) pulling her hair back into a ponytail, putting on a pair of jeans and going to the grocery store. Instead, something called her into Joshua's room, and after passing through the doorway Hexe nuzzled Lynne's hand as if telling her that she missed him too and that it was okay to enter.

She found herself sitting Indian style in the middle of his bedroom surrounded by the knick-knacks, old photographs and the childhood artwork that he had saved. The love of Josh's life smiled back at Lynne from a class picture and in another, the two young teens appeared to be laughing while sharing an icecream cone. She saw the large manila envelope laying in the bottom of a banker's box and inside was her son's school report cards that dated back to when he was in first grade. There was also another sheet of paper that was addressed to Mrs. Ladd, and she immediately burst into hysterical laughter.

"You did what?!" Lynne asked from one end of the supper table with the look of a Marine Corps drill instructor, while Ben laughed so hard that he couldn't breath or look at Josh.

"I don't like her mom, she's always trying to boss me around, especially in biology class!" The fourteen year old pleaded back.

Holly Shultz and Joshua had been classmates since preschool and they had a love- hate relationship since day one. If they weren't telling on one another, or teasing each other to the point of driving everyone around them crazy, then out came the dirty tricks that never failed to amaze.

"Maybe that's why Mr. Harlow paired you two together as lab partners?!" She asked angrily, with a hint of sarcasm.

"I dont care mom, she always starts!" The boy shouted, crossing his arms and stomping his foot on the floor.

Lynne had enough of his backtalk and reached across the table. With one swift and sudden motion she backhanded him on the cheek.

"Ow, mom!" He cried out, rubbing the sting away from his face.

"Lynne!" Ben interjected with a warning. "C'mon honey stop, it was just a kid's joke." He said softly, trying to calm her down.

"I don't think that stealing a lamb's eye and putting it in a girl's purse was the right thing to do Joshua, whether you like each other or not!" She scolded with dancing eyes and a wagging motherly index finger.

"I'll apologize." Josh assured her with a whine.

"Oh, you'll do better than that young man! You're going to walk her to and from the bus stop every morning, and after school you're to carry her books!" She ordered. "Did you read this Ben?" She asked, but he had to turn away before he started laughing again. "It's not funny!" Lynne exclaimed, as if he would be next.

'Dear Mrs. Ladd, It has been brought to my attention that your son and Holly Shultz were recently paired together in Mr. Harlow's Biology class. The assignment (on the day that the offense took place) was the dissection of lamb's eyes. It was reported to me that while Holly was distracted cleaning up their table after class, Joshua took one of the specimens and hid it in her purse. The eyeball was later discovered by Holly as she reached for a tissue in the lady's room and it scared her terribly. Can you please have a word with Joshua regarding this matter and between you and I, Mrs. Ladd, that lamb was really looking out for Holly that day!'

She opened up another box and an immediate wave of sadness overcame her as she pulled out Josh's favorite bedtime stuffed toy. Her mother gave him the Elmo doll when he was six months old, and he slept with it until the puppy came into their world. On occasion, Lynne would tease him and ask if Elmo was hogging the bed but Joshua's stubbornness (which he inherited from her) refused to let any of her jokes sway him from keeping the stuffed character. Lynne stood up too soon and her head began to spin; a snowy haze filled her vision and as she sat on the edge of the bed, the sunlight burst through the clouds that had been holding it prisoner. A sheer and blinding white glare illuminated her face and suddenly the figure of a man stood between her and the window pane. His right hand reached down to her and she struggled to find the words to speak.

"I didn't go to the store." Lynne said, after a loud cracking sound resounded from somewhere inside her head.

"You did better Lynne, you found yourself again." He replied softly.

"Honey, wake up now." Ben whispered, his voice sounded as if it was coming from off in the distance.

"Ben?" She responded dreamily. "Were you just standing there in front of the window?"

"No baby, I just got home." He answered, gently touching her face.

"You didn't hold out your hand to me?"

"No, you must have been dreaming." Ben said, trying to assure her that all was well.

"No Ben, I wasn't dreaming. I think I saw the Lord." She petted Hexe's head that was resting on her chest then pointed. "He was right there in front of the window, and just before He appeared the clouds opened up and a beautiful ray of sunlight came into the bedroom."

"Are you sure?" Ben inquired, placing his hand on her forehead.

"I don't have a fever Ben, stop that." She ordered, whisking his hand away. "It was Him, please believe me."

"I do believe you Lynne." He stated, smiling at her.

"I admitted not going to the grocery store and He said that I did better than that." Lynne mentioned, propping herself up against the headboard. "Guess what He said after that?"

"What?" Ben asked, laying his head down next to Hexe's on Lynne's body.

"He said that I found myself again."

They napped in Joshua's bed until Hexe decided that she needed to go outside, and after looking at the clock on the nightstand, were amazed at the hour.

"It's ten o'clock Lynne, do you want to order a pizza?" Ben asked, with his head buried in the refrigerator.

"I can make a salad?" She offered with a smile

"It's ten o'clock Lynne, do you want to order a pizza?" He repeated, looking back over his shoulder with his smartass grin.

"I get it Ben, you want Dominos!" Lynne exclaimed with a laugh.

"No, I just don't want your yucky salad!" He teased back.

They sat next to each other on the couch in the cozy family room, and the small wood stove that had just been stoked kept the back part of the house nice and warm. They shared a large pepperoni pizza and while Lynne was distracted watching a commercial, Ben would hand Hexe a piece of crust that he had saved.

"Your never going to stop spoiling her are you?" She asked, taking a sip of her Pepsi.

"Nope, and I'll never stop spoiling you either." He winked.

"What did the insurance adjuster say?" Lynne inquired.

She motioned over to a trash bag on the floor while holding a wedge of pizza, Ben had filled it with her personal belongings that had been left in the car.

"He said that it was smart of you to get the gap coverage, and that the check was as good as in the mail."

"Wow, cool!" She exclaimed with excitement.

"Yeah, and I found your lost white wool mitten under the driver's seat too." Ben said nonchalantly. "And about a thousand stray Gummy Bears!"

Lynne let out a laugh and blushed. "What, you like Lemonheads and I like the bears!"

"When does shit this stop?" He suddenly cut in.

Lynne shot him a look of disappointment. "Your supposed to be watching your language!" She exclaimed, wiping her lips with a paper towel and patiently awaiting an apology. Instead, she noticed that his focus was on the news report being aired.

"The victim was sitting in his car and stopped for the red light, here behind me on Luzerne and North 7th streets this morning around 8:30 a.m. A lone gunman approached his vehicle dressed in black and posing as a windshield washer." Katie Katro announced into her microphone with an air of discontent.

"All reports indicate that the driver of the car was shot through a bag that the gunman was carrying, and robbery doesn't seem to be a motive. We have a few eyewitnesses who stated seeing a man raise and point his left arm before they heard shots being fired." Detective Richards stated, looking directly into the camera.

"Unfortunately, there are no further details available at this time and police are asking for the public's assistance. If you or anyone you know has any information about this crime, please call Detective Richards at East Police Division Headquarters." Katie said, briefly looking at the taped off intersection. "Reporting live from Kennsington, I'm Katie Katro with Channel 6 Action News."

Chapter Nineteen

"The cat that got hit by the window washer down on Luzerne today, was none other than Agent Moss." Richards' tired, raspy voice came through Clayton's phone.

"No shit?!" He asked, with a surprised tone. "I'll be honest George, I did see it on the news at 5:00, but didn't pay that much attention. I played Mr. Mom all day and napped with Corey."

"You had off Chris, and I just found out myself about an hour ago." Richards claimed, concealing the white lie.

He had seen the aftermath of the shooting of course, and knew almost immediately who the victim was. Moss was discovered laying on his right side while his legs remained under the steering column. His head was laying on a large blood soaked area of the passenger's seat and the tan fabric had turned to dark red. The two .38 rounds that penetrated Moss's forehead were placed so close together that one would think that he had been hit with a single bullet. Moss's face was frozen in terror and his eyes were set in a moment of permanent surprise.

"They want to meet." Richards said under his breath, rubbing the back of his neck.

"When?" Clayton asked, as he quietly got out of bed.

"Now, I'm out front."

"Who's all going to be there?" Clayton wanted to know, slipping on a pair of gray sweats and lifting a slat from the bedroom window blind before kissing Alicia on the cheek.

"Everybody." Richards replied dryly.

"What's going on Chris?" She asked, half asleep.

"Boss is outside baby, we have to go meet up with some people. I'll be back in a little while, now go back to sleep." He answered, sitting down next to her.

She was gone by the time he had finished explaining the situation and Clayton had to smile to himself as he rubbed her shoulder. The woman could sleep through anything. When it was bedtime, it was bedtime, and when her brain shut off, that was it, lights out. Clayton used to harass the hell out of her in the mornings, after Corey would have his nightfits. "Why am I the one getting up for the baby every night woman, I ain't got no tits?!" He'd ask mockingly, using a gruff old black man's voice.

"Because you don't sleep, and besides, I'm the one that pushed his ass out!" She would respond sarcastically.

Clayton fastened the velcro straps to his concealed chest holster and slid the Glock 21 Gen. 4 inside. It was one of his personal weapons and by far his favorite caliber, .45; because as they say in the Army, nothing knocks a man down like an ACP! Lastly, he grabbed the quilted diamond patterned stitched North Face, or the 'black marshmello' as he liked to call it, and walked out into the windy cold night.

"Hey Chris." Richards said, after Clayton got in his old Buick. He had purchased the 2010 Regal new and after driving it for six months swore that it would be the last car he would buy before retiring. The gang at the office simply referred to it as pop-pop's whip.

"Follow the road back to the loop, they're waiting for you now." The young park ranger said with a smile. He was wearing civilian clothes and pointing a flashlight at the ground.

"Thank you." Richards replied with a wave before slowly pulling away. In his rearview mirror he could see the ranger getting into a small pickup and flashing his headlights.

The John Heinz National Wildlife Refuge, is located off of Lindbergh boulevard just West of the Philadelphia international airport at Tinicum in South Philadelphia. The twelve hundred acre wildlife refuge is the largest remaining estuary in Pennsylvania and brings a touch of natural beauty to the doorstep of the city. It boasts over ten miles of trails that wind throughout the area and boardwalks that cross the tidal wetland and the main focal point of the park, Tinicum Marsh. Birdwatchers have charted over three hundred species, and deer, red foxes, river otters and mink are but a few of the protected variety of wildlife that reside there.

Richards cut his lights after rolling up close and parking behind a black Chevrolet Suburban; almost immediately afterwards a silver Impala pulled in behind him. He and Clayton got out of the Regal without saying a word to one another and walked over to a man standing alone in the middle of the loop smoking a cigarette.

"Gentlemen." Timmons called over after exiting her car and putting on a gray London Fog raincoat.

"Hey." Richards and Clayton responded almost simultaneously.

"This is Agent Dreyer with the DEA, he runs field ops over there. Tom, this is Detectives Richards and Clayton with the Philadelphia Detective Division." Timmons introduced the men in a professional manner. "And thank you both for coming on such short notice."

"No problem." Clayton said with a nod as both he and Richards reached out to shake Dreyer's hand.

"Tom, is fine." Dreyer stated, shaking their hand.

"I'm George, and this here is Chris." Richards exclaimed trying to be as courteous as he could be, considering the fact he was starved out of his mind and hadn't slept in two days.

"As you all know, I'm just plain old Timmons, the white 'Dragon Lady!'" She joked in an attempt to lighten the atmosphere. She had just lit a cigarette as an inbound heavy airliner on approach to PHL flew directly over the refuge's observation tower. The structure sat dark and ominous off to the right of Darby Creek, and its silhouette blocked everything that could possibly exist behind it.

"Let me get this straight, you want to borrow a Philadelphia cop and have him work as a surveillance operative?" Dreyer asked sharply. The steam from his breath was one beat ahead of his words.

"He has eyes wide open on the subject." Timmons explained, exhaling smoke from her nostrils and throwing Clayton a secret wink.

"Oh, really?" Dreyer asked, looking up at the cold night sky.

"That's right, and there's a very high trust level between us. It's very personal and sensitive in nature." Clayton added as diplomatically as he could under the present circumstance.

"Look, I'm only here for moral support. I'm his boss, but I'm also his friend." Richards added, nodding over to Clayton. "Think about it, what the hell do we have on him?"

"That's right." Clayton agreed under his breath.

"We got nothing to book Blaze on! I'm not trying to brag here, but in another six months I'm going fishing down in Florida." Richards exclaimed to Agent Dreyer, his tired eyes having the glint of a kid awaiting his birthday party. "I've been doing this shit since you were in grade school, you too Chris, and I'm telling you there is nothing that could bring an indictment. There are no witnesses to any of the murders, there is no DNA evidence tying him to any of the crime scenes, there is no weapon that can be traced back to him and just as important, there is no motive. Now ask yourselves this, don't you think that a lawyer wouldn't tear your asses up? Are you fucking serious?! Fed or not, it would never fly, not in this town it wouldn't."

"I agree." Timmons acknowledged, looking down at the pavement.

"Everything your op's touched turned to shit. Okay?" Richards stated in a serious tone, raising an eyebrow.

"What's that?" Dreyer asked defensively, moving in closer to Richards.

"I know it stings." Clayton whispered.

"You don't know jack shit! Dwayne was a good dude, he and me were tight!" Agent Dreyer shouted while pointing at Clayton. "He volunteered for the GSM assignment right out of the gate!"

"And I lost Moss." Timmons added abruptly.

"He was a bum next to Dwayne and you motherfuckers know it!" Dreyer snapped at her, shifting his anger. "My boy told me about Moss's whores and all his bullshit!"

"I grew up on those very same streets and in that same fucking 'hood man, so I'd say I know a little more than jack shit!" Clayton fired back.

"Alright fellas, knock it off!" Richards ordered, stepping in between the two men.

"Timmons, you're at bat so let's hear it." Dreyer said, pointing at her with a cigarette in his hand.

"First, Detective Clayton served three tours as an Army Airborne Ranger in Afghanistan, so my people think that he meets the qualifications for this kind of work." Timmons exclaimed, raising her chin.

"Go on, I'm all ears." Dreyer prodded, this time nodding over to Richards and Clayton.

"Secondly, as we discussed before, he has a contact that's a spit away from Blaze." She mentioned with a nod. "This girl is a familiar of Clayton's, and Blaze has never indicated in any way that he's suspicious of her, and as we all know in this business that's paramount."

"A girl, as in a teen?" Dreyer asked Clayton.

"She's a bit older." He responded, Timmons nodded again with narrowed eyes.

The kid can play ball, she thought to herself, as she studied Clayton's mannerisms and body language.

"We can get Clayton a couple doors up from Blaze, maybe even a cover job with sanitation…"

"Kind of like what I do now!" Clayton cut Timmons off with a joke.

"His informant will provide us, through Clayton of course, with all the intricacies such as who Blaze is with, what's he doing and are there any new players hanging around." Timmons offered with her hands up as if introducing a desert menu.

"We all have people in our respective clubs that monitor criminals, Timmons, c'mon." Dreyer mentioned with a grin, referring to the personnel in their agencies that were used at times like these.

"Not this cat." Richards warned while he stood off to the side of the conversation with his hands crammed deep into his black Vinci full length wool coat.

"We talked about that a little while ago." Clayton agreed softly, so as not to stir up Dreyer's passion again.

"Look, as we're all more than aware, Andre' Pelts is twenty one years old and has no criminal record, not even a parking ticket, therefore we don't have his prints or mug on file anywhere. The prints lifted in the Acura the day your boy got hit is really the only thing we have to compare anything to in the future. Also, his uncle, Aaron Pelts, aka 'Breach' is GSM's top man and a graduate of Maryland." Timmons reasoned, searching for more things to say.

"Things aint the same as they used to be. These guys are educated and have learned to communicate by code. Sometimes they use hand signals or imagery, and believe it or not we've even found notes that have a mathematical language, a type of encrypted message within the numbers. One of the oldest used is an ancient Hebrew formula, the number '1' representing the letter 'A' and so on through the alphabet. That is of course, a very basic code. They also use stolen or burner phones, sometimes friends of friends sell them; so any positive ID is almost impossible to establish in order to attain a correlation with a gang member." Richards explained, using the most rational tone that he could muster.

"We have a ton of surveillance footage and body wire threads." Dreyer added.

"Which all adds up to about nothing." Richards explained, pinching the cherry off his Newport.

"And in the future, what the hell is that supposed to mean?" Dreyer asked in an angry tone. "So what, you want to play hide and seek and then when he's out of earshot doing business, collect some information after he surfaces again?"

"Absolutely not." Timmons assured.

"Well how about we just pass a little message along to Joshua Ladd's daddy? I'm sure the Sworn would have a few creative ideas on how to handle this nigger!" Dreyer exclaimed, using street language.

"Yeah, that's a great idea." Clayton agreed sarcastically. "We'll just sit back and watch an outlaw motorcycle club roll into Kensington, drag everyone out in the street and burn the whole fucking town down!"

"Plant his ass then." Dreyer hissed, looking at the ground.

"Stop!" Timmons interjected sternly.

"Yeah, just stop." Richards agreed, pointing a finger at Dreyer.

"My head is swimming and I can't feel my feet." Dreyer stated before letting out a loud groan and gazing up at another airliner on final approach.

"Me too!" Richards said loudly over the fan jets that were spooling down as they throttled back.

"Okay guys, let's mull it around some more and regroup in a couple of days. If we're going to do this, then let's do it." Timmons suggested in true FBI fashion. It was her way of saying: 'Shit or get off the pot.'

"Agreed." Clayton reasoned, rubbing his bare hands together in an attempt to generate warmth.

"Jelly, listen to me young brother. If you see me out there, act like you don't know me understand? Just keep on walking and act natural." Clayton instructed in a low voice.

"What's going on Clay, how are we supposed to talk?" The teen asked with concern.

"The Feds asked me to work surveillance and I refused to give you up as my operator, I told you before that I'm going to look out for you." He responded, giving Jelly a position of importance and endorsing their trusted bond. "We can still communicate via our phones but make sure you get a hold of a loaner, and I'll do the same. As usual, I'll text you with three stars before my message so you'll know it's me."

"Because if we keep using these phones, they'll tap us?" Jelly asked, holding his phone up to the kitchen ceiling light as if trying to see inside it.

"You better believe it man, in a fucking second." Clayton guaranteed.

"If I have to give you anything, I'll text you the location or a hiding spot in code." Jelly advised, causing Clayton to smile.

"Something?" Clay asked.

"You never know Clay." The boy teased.

"That's right you're a smart man, remember that, and just keep doing what your doing." Clayton offered encouragingly.

"Low key, and it ain't me!" Jelly laughed into his phone.

"It definitely ain't you man!" Clayton agreed, joining in the laughter.

Chapter Twenty

"How have things been the last couple of months, Towers?" Lucy asked in a low voice.

"Sometimes it's rough, but little by little." Ben answered his old friend while leaning against the back deck rail.

"I thought I'd give you a call and check in, see how you're doing."

"Thanks man, I appreciate it. How have you been Lucy?" Ben inquired, hearing the sliding glass door opening behind him.

"Same shit, a little bored these days if you catch my drift!" Lucy joked.

"If you're ever in the area again stop by and visit. Especially on Sunday morning, Lighthouse church has a great turnout and Mickey's been showing up too!"

"I'm flattered brother, believe me, but I ain't the church going kind. I'm glad you found a good life though." Lucy said with sincerity.

"Thanks man, and yes I have." Ben responded, keeping an eye on Lynne.

"Listen Towers, can you talk right now?" His old clubmate asked in a serious tone.

"Kind of." Ben replied, in a way that indicated that the answer was no.

"Okay, listen to me then?" Lucy asked, as if he was addressing his senior.

"Go ahead." Ben waited for him to speak while thanking Lynne for bringing out a cup of coffee. She was in the process of watering the house plants that were hanging from hooks under the wide and low eaves.

"Jocko's got a boy up in Philly who drives for FedEx. He told Jocko that a dude he was delivering packages to last week, has a neighbor who knows who shot Joshua." Lucy's voice was calm, deliberate and monotone.

There was a long pause before Ben was able to process the information that his old friend had just given him. A multitude of scenarios entered his mind and he needed a moment to clarify what he had just heard.

"That's good news man! Yeah, you can give him my name, I'd love to meet him!" Ben exclaimed, glancing over at Lynne with a smile..

"I was thinking." Lynne said, sitting the vintage No. 6 galvanized water can on the round glass top table.

"What's that?" Ben asked.

"About the baby's name." She walked over to him and placed her arms around his waist then looked up into his eyes. "I was thinking that if it's a boy, we should name him after you."

"Me?" He responded with a curious look.

"Yeah, and if it's a girl, maybe give her my mom's name." Lynne beamed.

"Broom Hilda?" He exclaimed, bursting into laughter.

"Ben, stop being an asshole!" She scolded, slapping his leg.

"Watch your language young lady!" He warned, flashing his ornery smile.

"Let's go inside honey, it's cold out here." Lynne suggested, blowing warm air into her cupped hands. "I'll cook breakfast for a change?"

"If you insist." Ben answered, opening the slider and motioning for her to enter the house ahead of him.

She was about to flip one of the over cooked eggs that had started out being over easy, when a message alarm chimed on her phone.

"It's Amanda, and she told me that Mickey just asked her out!" Lynne squealed with excitement.

"Poor girl has no idea what she's getting herself into!" Ben replied with a wink.

"She wants me to ask you, what he's really like?"

"I would really like to know when you're going to turn around and take those rock eggs off the heat!" He joked back.

"Oh, dammit!" She yelled aloud, seeing the result of high heat and inattentiveness. "Honey, can you whip us up some pancakes?"

"Of course, it just so happens that I have some premade in the fridge. Step aside, wench!"

They sat where they usually did at the small, round oak kitchen table and Lynne occasionally glanced out through the low bay window.

"You're still seeing him out there on that old tractor aren't you?" Ben asked, taking another large bite of his famous buttermilk pancakes.

"Yeah, sometimes. At other times, I see him trying to sneak that damned rooster into the house to scare the crap out of me!" She replied, nodding in the direction of the free range chickens that were wandering around the property aimlessly.

"So back to Mickey, what's he really like?" She asked with an innocent and inquisitive look upon her face.

"You're too damned cute, now stop that!" He answered in a tone that indicated that he wasn't going to get involved.

"Oh, c'mon!" Lynne protested, taking the last slice of bacon off of the serving plate.

"Lynne… okay!" He said, shaking his head in protest. "Mickey's a good brother, he hasn't drank in twenty some odd years, was never really into drugs and pretty much gets along with everybody. He was a lot like me back in the day, I suppose. He's never been married and never had any kids, just a stand up guy. A biker, ya know?"

"C'mon, c'mon let's go, hurry it up!" Mickey shouted through his black ski mask while pointing the Winchester 1300 Defender 12 gauge at the Brooks armored car rear rider. The four upper management Sworn members had taken advantage of the opportunity to heist a Brooks armored car cash pickup at the CityCenterDC shopping mall, in NorthWest Washington DC at the peak of the Christmas holiday shopping season.

"Last one!" Jocko exclaimed, looking up at him with a smile.

"We got forty seconds and counting!" Bones called back from the driver's seat of the stolen Crown Victoria while glancing down at a digital egg timer.

"I hear ya, Billy!" Mickey acknowledged with a wink. They had their cover names down pat and not one of them broke a bead of sweat.

"Yeah, that's it!" Lucy yelled to the driver. "Put that motherfucker in gear and watch this Desert Eagle blow your head off, genius!" Through the slightly tinted cab widow the driver could be seen holding his hands up.

"You good up there?!" Mickey inquired, craning his head from around the left side of the rear doors.

"I'm good Larry, how about you toots, you good?!" Lucy asked the driver sarcastically.

"Let's roll baby, we're out!" Mickey ordered, after he and Jocko had thrown the last of the four large cash bags into the Ford's trunk..

"I liked him right away too." She said softly.

"Well, that's what you need to tell Ms. Prissy pants!" Ben exclaimed.

"Honey!" She scolded.

"Oh c'mon Lynne, you can see it a mile away!" He said with a narrowed gaze. "She's worse than Nellie Oleson on 'Little House.'"

"Oh my God!" She screamed in a high pitched voice before bursting into laughter. "Nellie Oleson?!"

"Yup, a real female puppy!" He guaranteed with a quick nod.

"Anyway, they have a lunch date set for this coming Sunday after church." She nodded.

"Well, I'll pray for him." Ben added with a smile.

"Oh, hang on…" Lynne said after picking up her phone. "I forgot to tell you about the young man who sent me a 'Friend Request'. He was at Josh's prayer vigil after the toy run, his name is Jelly."

"Really?" He asked, reaching across the table. "May, I?"

"That's him!" She stated, pointing down at the photograph of the boy's smiling face.

"Why does he go by, 'Sky Dancer?'" Ben asked, looking through the rest of Jelly's profile.

"Not sure, maybe it's an inner city thing or maybe to protect his identity or something?" Lynne replied with a shrug. "Are you ready for this though? He's thirteen years old and passed an SAT practice test with a 1220 score!"

"Is that good?" He asked innocently.

"You better believe it! It puts him in the top twenty percentile of all those who test, and he's thirteen Ben! Think about it." She explained, with a look of awe.

"Very cool!" Ben approved with a smile.

"I don't know if you remember him from the morning we were all up there, but I saw him standing across the street all by himself, before calling him over to get a present."

"Lynne, you really are the woman that I wanted to be with all my life." He whispered, reaching across the table and taking her hand in his.

He took one last look at the photograph of Jelly standing on a street corner before handing Lynne back her phone. Ben made a mental note of the exact location by remembering the names on the street signs which could be seen in the background. Kensington avenue and East Cambria street.

Chapter Twenty One

Clayton was the first to arrive at the meeting place that he and Timmons had agreed to a few days prior. He was sitting on a bench at East Fairmount Park watching the early morning joggers chug along the footpath that was directly in front of him. His twenty ounce Dunkin' Donuts coffee cup sat between his thighs, and as he lit a cigarette a pretty young blonde ran past him.

"Those will kill you, ya know!" She yelled over with a smile.

"So would you, honey!" Clayton joked back with a wave.

"Good morning, Chris." Timmons announced from behind.

"Good morning to you." He replied, squeezing the cherry off of his cigarette and placing the butt in the pack.

She sat a blue, soft Igloo lunch cooler next to Clayton then removed her leather gloves and reached for a tissue in her purse. "I can't keep these damned sunglasses clean from all the dust in the air around here."

"It's a regional curse." He replied, keeping his gaze upon the joggers. "Where are you from, may I ask?"

"Aspen, Colorado." Timmons answered, patting the cooler with her left hand.

"Let me guess, my kit?" Clayton asked playfully, looking over at her.

"Yup, everything you need is inside." She explained.

He looked down at the bag, and just for a second the thought of backing out crossed his mind. Instead, Clayton picked it up and sat it on his lap before unzipping the main compartment.

"The whole shabang Chris." She said, pointing at the items inside. "Your Pennsylvania driver's license, Philadelphia Department of Streets photo ID badge, Social Security card and three credit cards, all in your cover name."

"Colton Amos Bellows." Clayton whispered to himself. "I kind of like that."

"Yeah, we try to simplify all of this as much as possible." Timmons replied, waving at a young runner. "She's cute!"

"You had me fooled Timmons, I thought you were the married, dedicated and all consumed Fed." He quipped with a smirk.

"Sometimes, but once in a while I like the girls." She winked. "So, how did the Missus take the news?"

"As long as this doesn't turn into a career move and it's wrapped up within ninety days, she's good." Clayton assured her, taking another sip of his coffee. "Well, that and… nevermind."

"Well, that and never mind what, Chris?" Timmons inquired, looking at him over her Tom Ford designer sunglasses.

"That we have another baby." He explained, rolling his eyes.

"They want you to do what?" Alicia asked from the bathroom sink.

She was in the middle of brushing her teeth before bed when Chris dropped the bomb on her. Men have a way of waiting for such an opportune moment to announce important things, it's as if they're hoping that their better halves are too distracted or preoccupied to respond.

"Well, I did accept the assignment Alicia…" He began to say with his arms held up.

"Have you lost your fucking mind boy?!" She shouted, exiting the bathroom with toothpaste on her lips.

"Honey, Corey's sleeping." Clayton said calmly, attempting to calm her down.

"I love the way you bring this shit up before bedtime Chris, thanks." She said in disgust.

"Honey, they need me. Everyone, including us in the division, dropped the ball." He walked over to her and put his arms around her warm, soft body. "I love you baby and believe me, if I didn't think that I could do it…"

"I don't want my husband ending up in a box." She frowned, looking up into his eyes.

"And I can't let that scumbag get away with murder, and Lord knows how many lives ruined because of the drugs he's pushing."

"Ninety days Chris, that's it. Ninety days and you're out." She said adamantly, giving him an ultimatum while pointing.

They made love on the edge of the bed the way they always did, with a hunger that could not be mistaken and a passion that was true and hard. Neither of them cared for what some referred to as 'quickies' and their sexual energy could not be satisfied by anything less than time. Afterwards, Alicia kissed his neck and whispered into his ear. "I have an add-on to the ninety day allowance, Chris."

"Of course you do babe, what is it?" He answered, staring into her smiling eyes.

"We're going to make another baby." She said, letting out a large exhale as he reentered her.

"Under the first floor stairs of your new residence there's a small utility closet, and along the wall that divides the kitchen you'll find a section that can be lifted away, revealing a narrow compartment." Timmons said, with a serious tone in her voice.

"Goodies?" Clayton responded, narrowing his gaze.

"Yes, there's a 30-06 Springfield with fifty rounds, and an M4, with five hundred." She said with a nod. "Also, a PVS14 (night vision optics) and a dedicated radio channel that's as safe as the Pope's pooper."

"That is a safe channel." He answered, smiling up at the sky.

"If you ever need the cavalry, the emergency call sign is, 'Big Bird.'"

"Got it." Clayton acknowledged, holding up a small envelope that had been in one of the side pockets of the cooler.

"We'll be there in a second, you can believe that." She promised, giving him a nod. "Oh, and that's your house key and the keys to your '15 Chevrolet Silverado."

"Wow-wee, a cool truck too?!" He asked jokingly. "But it's good to know that you're there if I need your help." Clayton replied.

"One last question Chris." Timmons said, Looking directly into his eyes, making sure that he was listening. "If I give you the green light on Blaze…"

"I've gotten the green light a few times, Timmons, and the answer is yes, I'll take him."

Ben walked over to the KR655 Snap-On roll away tool chest and opened each of the eight drawers, spraying a fine mist of WD-40 on the surfaces of the tools inside. Likewise, he did the same to the twelve drawers of the large matching tool box that sat atop it, occasionally pulling out one of his favorite wrenches for inspection and wiping it down. The prized tool chest was the envy of many mechanics that he had known over the years and the crown jewel of his collection; for it had come by way of the misfortune of a rival club member who had been caught trespassing on Sworn turf while wearing his colors. The young man was given a choice, either a beat down, the likes of which could potentially kill him or the loss of every item in his garage. Ben's attention then shifted to spending most of the afternoon tinkering in his shop, he emptied the fifty gallon drum that was used as a trash can and swept the floor a half dozen times until his angst got the better of him. He turned around and navigated his way through his Road King, Joshua's Low Rider and a pneumatic motorcycle lift before stopping to look down at the refinished vintage French/English Steamer trunk. After unlocking the large, Yale brass lock and lifting the creaking lid he unfolded the linen cover inside. Staring back at him was his old Sworn club colors.

He hadn't laid eyes on the faded dungaree cuts (a denim jacket with the sleeves removed) in a decade. The back of the vest proudly displayed the black and white Sworn logo of a Viking warrior in battle armor charging at the viewer with a broadsword. The arched name plate also had a black background and the old English font with the club's name was in white. A four inch rocker (the patch at the bottom of the vest that curved upward on each end) simply read 'Nation.' Putting on his old vest made him realize just how much time had passed since he last wore it, as he could barely get the garment on, due of course to his belly that protruded from the front section.

About twenty patches were stitched on the front of the vest; the high ranking diamond insignia with the initials 'NP' (National President) along with the Viking horns with oak leaf clusters (Sworn inner circle) and another that was coveted by all outlaw club members everywhere, the diamond shaped one percent. He touched the newest looking patch and smiled to himself, 'In Memory Of The General, SFFS, 5/10/2013' (Sworn Forever, Forever Sworn). After gently folding the vest and wrapping the linen sheet around it, Ben placed it back in the truck and locked the lid. His head began to swim and anxious thoughts overtook him as he reached for the large hardback Chevrolet Chiltons repair manual that was up on the shelf over the workbench and opened it. Inside the thick bound book, a 7"x 9" oblong section had been neatly cut out which created a deep recessed compartment. Ben removed the Smith & Wesson .44 caliber Model 29 from the book, gripped it in his hand and gazed down its four inch barrel. He closed his eyes and slowly shook his head.

"What are you thinking about honey?" Lynne asked softly, standing just inside the doorway.

He hadn't heard her enter of course, as women had a way of magically appearing when their men were up to something they shouldn't be, or checking to see if the coast is clear before bringing the booty home from a secret shoe shopping trip.

"I don't know Lynne, but I know I don't want this." Ben said with a sad look.

"What would the, 'I don't know' part be?" She asked, hugging him from behind.

"Murder." He simply replied.

"What brought you to this place, have you been harboring that thought?" She inquired, with a concerned look.

"It was seeing that kid, what's his name, Jelly?" Ben asked, turning around to hold her.

"Yeah that's his name, but why would seeing his message trigger all of this?" Lynne wanted to know, pointing down at the gun.

"He knows something Lynne, I can feel it. There's no other way to describe it and no other way to explain how I know." He stated, momentarily looking away from her.

"Are you thinking that maybe Jelly 'Friend Requested' me because he knows who Joshua's killer is?" Lynne asked, placing her hands on his face and making him look into her eyes.

"Yes, that's exactly what I think." Ben replied under his breath.

"Go on." She requested.

"You said that he 'Friend Requested' you and then messaged about being at Josh's prayer vigil right?" He explained with a frown.

"Yeah Ben, that's right, I told you that."

"Okay, Jelly also mentioned that he was across the street from Pastor Walts trailer, when you were handing out the Christmas toys…"

"Ben, there were a lot of kids there that day. It was also the annual toy run honey, c'mon!" Lynne explained, trying to sound reasonable.

"No wait, hang on, let me finish." Ben interjected, holding up a finger. "He introduced himself as 'Jelly' yet his profile picture is of a SpaceX rocket with the User Name: 'Sky Dancer.'" He reasoned, nodding down to her.

"He also told me that his real name was Jerome Wilts, and I thought we already covered that honey. You know, maybe Jelly is protecting his real identity?"

"My point exactly. Why would an innocent thirteen year old kid have to go through all that trouble, and why doesn't he have any friends or followers in his profile?" Ben asked with a sincere look.

"Could you be making more out of this, than there really is?" Lynne wanted to know, touching his cheek.

"Lynne, the street signs in the background of Jelly's profile picture are approximately three blocks from where the prayer vigil was, three blocks from where Joshua was murdered." He said, narrowing his eyes.

"Jelly is not the only…" She began to say.

"Lynne, I'm the ex-president of the second largest outlaw motorcycle club in the country. Don't you think that there was ever a time when I received information on people and had to have them hunted down?" Ben asked with a slight grin.

"I'm sure that you've seen dark days, my love." Lynne whispered into his chest.

"In any subculture, the easiest way to conceal something is to make it appear that it belongs there. That includes people and who they are pretending to be." He spoke to her in layman's terms as if she were his daughter or kid sister.

"Then what, I mean what would happen next?" She asked as if waiting for the surprise part of a scary movie.

"You never, ever act like you know who they are and what they're doing; that's rule number one, the idea being that you want them to feel comfortable. Then, when enough information has been gathered and when the time is right, you either force their hand through muscle or just simply…"

"Take them." Lynne whispered as she looked into Ben's eyes.

"I'm sure you've heard the saying: 'Every dog has his day.' People are people, honey and they always get caught out." Ben assured, giving her a squeeze.

"Who would've been messing around with my old man's club?" She asked in a deep voice and a frown, accompanied with a giggle before slapping his butt.

"Ouch!" He playfully yelled. "Mostly Feds or local cops but a lot of times it would be other clubs trying to gain information."

"It must have been crazy."

"Well, ya get what ya ask for in this world right?" He asked hypothetically. "There's another part of me saying that Jelly is trying to tell you something, he's trying to communicate with you. First, by placing himself in close proximity while you handed out the toys, then by 'Friend Requesting' you, and finally through the street signs on his profile photo."

She had the look of someone who was trying to figure out a difficult crossword puzzle, before shaking her head slowly.

"Maybe he's doing it subconsciously?" Lynne reasoned.

"Possibly, but my experience tells me that in situations like these, there is no such thing as coincidence. Whether Jelly is being indirect because he may feel a sense of guilt, or he's unaware that he's bleeding out information, is irrelevant. I know that he knows something, Lynne."

"That thought would have never crossed my mind." She pondered, squinting her eyes.

"That's probably not a bad thing, because that means that you're on the better side of suspicion which is normal in the everyday world." Ben grinned.

"That's me, innocent little Lynne." She teased.

"I think you should contact him and see if he'd like to meet us for pizza after school one day."

Chapter Twenty Two

Blaze gazed at the top of the girl's head as it slowly bobbed up and down, and it was painfully obvious that she had no idea how to give head.

"Watch your damned teeth!" He shouted, nervously jerking his hips back and away from the action.

"Sorry, baby." She replied, looking up at him with a pouty expression.

"And stop that baby shit, I aint yo man bitch, I'm your customer!" Blaze ordered with a growl.

"You need to relax and let me do my fucking job then!" The young woman yelled back at him with an attitude.

"My weenie ain't no damned Slim Jim ho, and all you been doin' is crunchin' my shit!" He said, lifting her head up.

"Hell it ain't no Slim Jim!" She giggled, attempting to piss him off.

"You know what Shakira, take the fifty dollars and get the fuck outta my crib!" Blaze suggested with a stern voice and pointing at the bedroom door.

In all outward appearances the duplex that sat amongst the others in the middle of a row of old brick homes looked placid and ordinary. These were by no stretch of the imagination nice homes, and like the majority of the neighborhoods that clustered NorthEast Philadelphia they hadn't seen the brighter side of life since the mid 1960's.

Blaze had purchased the property on the 900 block of Anchor street, three years earlier (with the help of Breach and some GSM startup money) and retained Ms. Styles, the nice elderly woman next door as a tenant. He prided himself on keeping as much of a low profile as possible (unless some punk like Moss, who was posing as a gangbanger decided to start some shit) and demanded that all his gang members do the same; especially if they had to stop over for some quick business.

"How many times do I got to tell your dumbass not to bring that fucking pimp whip over here Sloan?!" Blaze shouted to a new GSM member after he stepped out of his gold and white, 2014 Cadillac XTS. "I can't have that bullshit 'round here!"

"Okay Blaze, I'm sorry, I won't drive it over no more." The skinny dark skinned kid who was wearing a New York Nicks hat sideways promised.

"That bitch got gangsta all over it, low profile red and chrome wheels and shit. You aint no damned Rican anyhow, boy!" Blaze laughed.

"Yeah, I feel ya." He replied, breaking his eye in shame.

"You never shit where you sleep boy, understand?" Blazed asked, glaring at the kid.

A vanilla lambskin couch and loveseat sat in one corner to a right angle and within the section where the two pieces joined, a chocolate and bronze patterned ottoman created a wide and comfortable diamond. Mounted on the wall across from the couch was a 79" LED TV and underneath, a black lacquer floating stand held all of Blaze's entertainment gadgetry, including his prized Limited Edition Gucci Xbox.

Blaze lifted one of the two inch wood slats from the Levolor blind that covered the front window and peered outside. He immediately noticed Ms. Styles getting ready to take her trash to the curb. She had given him permission a thousand times to call her by her first name Thelma, but he refused to break his culture's traditional code of respect. The eighty four year old was wearing black rubber galoshes (even though there wasn't any snow on the ground) and an ancient long brown wool dress coat with a mink collar. On top of her head was a blue scarf that lifted occasionally from a gust of wind, revealing her thinning white hair, and to Blaze she looked like ET ambling along and talking to the birds while humming gospel songs.

"Good morning Ms. Styles, do you have your grocery list yet?" Blaze asked, as if he were talking to a child.

"Oh Lawdy no peanut, now you know it won't be ready 'till noon time!" The elderly woman answered with joy in her voice.

"Yes ma'am, you just give me a holler then." He replied with a boyish smile. It was the good natured and innocent elderly folk of this world who earned their way through, that could make any man feel like a youngster.

"Look at this here!" Ms. Styles called over to Blaze, just as he was about to go back into the house. "Got pigeon shit all over my pots. Oh, Laaawd forgive me!"

"Yup, they been sittin' on your porch rail again." He agreed, pointing at more of the dried avian poop that clustered her planked floor.

"Devil be gone! I know he comes 'round here sometimes!" She cackled aloud.

"Yes Ms. Styles, I know he does." Blaze answered, looking down at her with a smile.

"I'm gonna have to start feedin' the cats again I suppose, keep these damned boids off my porch!" The old woman screeched in a threatening tone as if warning the pigeons.

"Now please don't do that ma'am, it started out with a small bowl full and the next thing you know, we had the whole damned cat crew over here. They was all over the place Ms. Styles!" He joked back wagging his finger at her.

"I'm putting cat food on my list then Andre, ya here?" She asked, through the black mink collar that covered most of her small face.

Blaze laughed and pointed at her head scarf. "You gonna lose yo dew rag, Ms. Styles!"

"Boy, I ain't too old to whoop that butt, now stop being smart!" She said, giving him a cute girlish smile.

"Oh, I know dats right!" Blaze teased back with a wink.

"Did you see we gotta a new neighbor moving in across the way?" Ms. Styles asked, pointing the end of her broom handle in the general direction.

"No." He replied under his breath.

Sitting across the street and parked in front of a first floor unit (that up until recently had a for rent sign in one of the front windows) was a white Chevrolet Silverado pickup. In its bed was a boat load of brown boxes and large green plastic leaf bags. The doors were opened and sitting on the cab's seat was a pile of clothes and folded towels.

"He seems nice." Ms. Styles said softly. "Works for city sanitation."

"You met him?" Blaze asked curiously.

"No, but Bee down from him has, and she said so." She replied, with an assuring glance.

"I see." Was all he could manage to say. "Ms. Styles, I gotta get back inside now and finish my classwork." He had lied to her about attending Temple and majoring in finance.

"Alright now, and I'll have that shopping list ready by lunchtime."

"Yes ma'am, I'll get one of my friends to go for you." Blaze said with a sharp nod before opening his creaky front door.

Clayton sat the used Banker's box on the tiled floor of the small entryway just inside the front door. The FBI was so astute in their craftwork that everything Clayton had in his possession appeared natural and plausible to the outside world. This form of natural distinction by way of the use of everyday and ordinary items, in order to cloak an operative was honed in the early 1950's by CIA and used by both agencies domestically and abroad at the height of cold war. He immediately noticed the new beige wall-to-wall carpet and freshly painted walls and ceiling.

"Damned Timmons, you're alright for a white girl." He whispered to himself.

After bringing in the rest of his stuff from the truck, he locked the front door behind him and did an entire walk through of the place. Clayton was pleased to see that all of the first floor windows had steel guards on their exterior, and that the appliances had been upgraded. He opened the door underneath the first floor stairs and after entering into the utility closet shook his phone, turning the flashlight on. He placed his hands gently on the surface of the wall that separated him from the kitchen, then began tapping around its parameter. The wall felt completely solid except for the vertical seam that joined the two halves of drywall, and the furthest edge to the far right that ran from the floor to the underside of the steps. Clayton pressed this section with his palm, and in one quick motion the right half of the drywall popped open from a spring loaded magnet lock, the likes of which are used in refrigerators and higher end pneumatic kitchen cabinets. The sheetrock was made rigid by a frame made up of fir strips that was affixed to the wall's interior.

"Yeah, that's nice." Clayton whispered, while looking at the firepower that was well racked and secure within their individual slats. A separate shelf that ran horizontally above the stored rifles was lined with plain brown cartons of ammunition. Four, thirty round NATO magazines for the M4 sat just to the left of them and next to those was a Leupold Mark 4 spotting scope. His text alert went off on his phone, and he let out a roar of laughter after reading the message.

'You're alright for a black man, and I'm happy to hear that you like what you see in the closet! lol.' -Mom.

'Thank you, and yes, I guess I'll have to get used to the new radio station!' -Jr. He replied back to Timmons.

'No worries, our people say crazy shit all the time, it helps break up the monotony.' -Mom. She assured him.

'Roger that and ttyl.' -Jr. Clayton texted with a smile on his face after realizing just how tuned in they were.

'K and behave.' -Mom. Timmons teased, signing off.

He removed the M4 from its secured position and pulled back on the charging handle which in turn retracted the bolt; this simple action allowed him to see that the weapon was unloaded. Clayton then fed thirty rounds into one of the magazines, snapped it into the feed and after pressing the magazine release button and dropping it into the palm of his right hand, he checked to see if the left and right staggered position of the rounds at the top of the magazine had changed. They had, which indicated that a round had automatically been chambered after pulling back on the charging handle and ejecting the loaded round; he reinserted a full magazine and snapped it back into the feed. His spot check was now complete and the weapon was cocked and locked. "Hoy." Clayton said proudly.

He gently sat the rifle back into its slot and was about to lift out the 30-06 Springfield when a mark on the furthest 2 x 4 framing stud to his left caught his eye. Peering around it to get a better look at the other side, he noticed that an arrow pointing to his left had been drawn with a thin black magic marker. Clayton tapped on the 2 x 4 (that the arrow pointed to) and noticed immediately that it wasn't nailed into the footer or header. He then carefully removed the snug fitting piece which revealed another set of hidden shelves (these of course being deep, as they ran horizontally along the inside of the wall). He reached inside and pulled out the night vision optics, a medium sized manila envelope (which contained ten thousand dollars in marked, one hundred dollar bills) and a Motorola R7 UHF two way radio, the channel of which was preset. Clayton jumped a little when he heard the front door bell ring.

"Be right there!" He shouted, craning his head around toward the direction of the living room.

The cop in him instinctively kicked in, and he reached around his waist and felt the security of his Glock 21 Gen 4, which was against the small of his back in a concealed weapons holster. Clayton made it halfway through the room when he heard a woman's high pitched voice, the kind you hear when they sound like they're singing.

"Yoo-hoo! I know you're in there Mr. Colton!" Ms. Bee, from down the way, sang out.

He gently moved aside a section of the sheer white linen window shades and peeked out. There standing on the stoop was the three hundred pound Ms. Bee, wearing a long yellow puffy coat (which added another two hundred pounds to her mass) a pair of red yoga pants that exploded at the calves, fuzzy white open toed slippers and hot pink lipstick that wrapped around her perfect white teeth.

"I can see you, Colton!" Ms. Bee warned with a flirtatious stare, holding a box of Entenmann's chocolate chip cookies under her arm.

She looked like the runway model version of Jabba the Hutt, but Ms. Bee was the purest and nicest person that Clayton had met since he moved in.

"Oh ma'am, now you know you didn't have to go and get those!" He exclaimed, after opening the front door.

"Nonsense, they was on sale anyways and you're my new neighbor!" She announced, beamng up at him.

Well, I must say you look all percolatin' today Ms. Bee, and as soon as I'm all moved in up in here, I'll have you over for coffee." Clayton said, giving her one of his cute winks.

"Oh now you better stop right there Colton, Oh my Lord!" She replied, throwing her head back and letting out a squeal.

Ms. Bee handed him the cookies and waddled off down the sidewalk with a laugh, before breaking into a beautiful humming of, 'Ringing In The Sheep.'

"Yo Tubby, I gotta new nigga movin' in across the way and I need you to check his ass out, ya hear?" Blaze ordered into his phone while looking through a pair of binoculars. "Write this down blood. White, mid teens Siverado, Pennsylvania TLA1217, ya got that?"

"Yeah Blaze, got it, and on it." His senior street soldier replied.

"Alright and don't forget, we all meeting this Friday night, and that means all the middle management too."

"I got that down too, boss." Tubby assured him.

Blaze hung up, went to the XBox and popped in his new favorite game Mafia III but before he sat down, noticed that he had left the binoculars on the coffee table. He was a methodical young man by nature and raised in a home where everything has its proper place and the proper place for all his gear was in a black Nike Brasilla gym bag that was stashed behind a HVAC return vent located at the end of the upstairs hallway. Blaze sat crossed-legged on the floor and removed the 13" x 16" pressed steel vent cover and instinctively looked around making sure that he was indeed alone before reaching in and pulling out the bag. After unzipping and opening up the duffle, he stared down and took a quick visual inventory of its contents. He then removed the four, fifty round Magtech boxes of 9mm ammunition and set them by his side along with a custom made silencer. He then pulled out one of his favorite guns, a Glock 26 Gen3 followed by the removal of a stainless steel Ruger P95 and for each he had two extended magazines. Digging further into the far right corner at the bottom of the bag his hand felt what he was seeking, six M67 fragmentation hand grenades that were individually placed into thick white gym socks. They made a soft dull metallic clicking noise as he shuffled them about counting them by hand, but Blaze's checklist immediately screeched to a halt like a virgin who had just shut down a runner attempting to steal home. His hand desperately fumbled throughout the entire bottom of the Nike bag in vain, until giving up the ghost.

"What the fuck?!" He shouted at the top of his lungs.

Blaze was filled with fear and frustration as he picked up the duffle and upended it, spilling its contents on the hallway carpet. He slowly looked around and narrowed his eyes trying to remember if this was the last place that he had hid the gun that killed Joshua Ladd.

Chapter Twenty Three

"Listen to that rain." Ben said, not taking his eyes off of the Philadelphia Flyers - Tampa Bay Lightning game. John Tortorella (the Flyers head coach) was ejected just ten minutes after the start of the match and the Flyers fell into an early 4-0 abyss. With five minutes and forty seconds left in the third period and Tampa beating Philadelphia with a score of 7-0, Ben shook his head and gave Lynne a look of disgust.

"Broad Street bums!" He cried out, covering his face with a throw pillow.

"Oh my God, you're such a brat!" Lynne giggled, tugging on the pillow and yanking it out of his hands.

A strong howling gust of wind accompanied with a deluge of water slammed into the double bedroom window, causing them to jump with excitement. The blast of air continued along the NorthWestern edge of the house creating a vortex, which reduced the air pressure along the backside of the home but increased the pressure of drag. Eventually everything that wasn't nailed down was carried away and sucked into an invisible vacuum cleaner.

"Oh my, Ben!" Lynne shouted with fright.

"Hang on now Lynne, let's go see." He replied, throwing off the comforter and getting up off the bed.

They had established this Saturday, early evening routine shortly after they were married; both would change into sweats or pajamas (sometimes making love in the process) before bringing a two litre bottle of Canada Dry ginger ale, glasses, a bucket of ice and Fritos to the cuddle spot. It mattered not whether it was a ball game, (the Eagles being their favorite) a cool old black-and-white movie, (that they sometimes bickered over before agreeing on which one to watch) or a comfort show, (as Lynne fondly called them) on PBS.

"Everything but the grill is gone off the rear deck!" Ben shouted from outside the house.

"My hanging plants too?!" She asked, gazing down at him from the opened upstairs bedroom window.

"Everything but the grill is gone off the rear deck!" He repeated in typical Ben Ladd fashion, shaking his head. 'What don't you understand about that?' He thought.

"Dammit!" She exclaimed, slamming the window shut and grabbing her black, puffy North Face hooded jacket.

"Ahhh!" She screeched, as a cold blast of rainy air blew open her unzipped coat and lifted the hoodie off her soaking wet head.

"Lynne, let's grab what we can for now and place it there in the corner!" Ben suggested, pointing to the only spot on the deck that was out of the weather.

The pair looked like two test subjects trying to clean up a mess in a wind tunnel, their clothes becoming wringing wet in a matter of seconds, and the cold water soaking their skin. As if all of this wasn't enough action, Hexe had overheard her parents outback and decided to come out of hiding (she hated bad weather especially if it was accompanied with thunder boomers) to rescue them.

"Hexe, go inside!" Lynne ordered, but it was too late as the dog became fixated on the potential threat of a piece of tumbleweed-like shrub that was being lifted by the air current and heading over the deck rail. A crashing noise followed by the sound of shattering glass echoed from inside the house which captured their attention momentarily before they stopped and stared at one another.

"Okay, that's it!" Ben shouted over the deluge. "Put that shit over here and go inside, I'll grab her!"

Once they were back in the house (and Hexe had shaken off the water that drenched her coat) they began removing their wet clothes and placing them on top of the laundry hamper that seemed to permanently remain in the mud room. Ben was about to take a towel to his head when he heard Lynne crying.

"Oh no, Ben!" She wailed.

"What, honey?" He asked with concern.

"I can't believe it!" Lynne hollered, breaking into tears.

"Lynne, I'm so sorry." Ben said, craning his head around and seeing her holding the broken picture frame.

Lynne's hands held the wood molding and fractured glazing together in an awkward fashion, slightly moving and rotating her grip position in a futile attempt at reconstruction. Within the broken and jagged shards of glass and haphazardly shifted mat board was Joshua's very first work of art. The bright multi-colored, very sloppy and beautiful finger paint had been created for his mother when he was just ten months old. Ben grabbed a dustpan and broom before sweeping the smaller pieces of glass and wood from the frame that had scattered across the kitchen floor. As Lynne wept while hugging the broken picture, he remained silent allowing her to grieve and process the loss of this priceless gift, and as usual (especially during these emotional moments) Hexe stayed by Lynne's side consoling her with constant nuzzles and whines.

"I'll get it remounted honey." Ben said softly, reaching down and offering his hand for her to rise up off the floor.

"That's not the point. The whole afternoon just went to hell as soon as we went outside to pick up the mess…" She tried to explain, before breaking down again.

"Come on woman, get up now." He insisted, crouching down and lifting her into his arms.

"No good deed goes unpunished." Lynne scowled at him, looking up from underneath his bear hug.

"Nonsense, sometimes situations bleed into other situations and mistakes are often made from oversight." Ben whispered with a wink.

"Oversight?" She asked sharply and indirectly, informing her husband to walk softly with his reply.

"Well, *we* were in such a hurry to see what was going on outside that *we* left the sliding glass door open, right?" He explained, flashing his pirate's smile.

"Asshole." Lynne said with narrowed eyes and a crunchy, pouty wrinkled forehead. "I left the door open."

"I'll settle for *we*." Ben said sweetly. "What does the bible say about God testing us?"

"Well, in 1 Corinthians 10:13. 'God is faithful and won't let you be tested beyond your ability. Along with the testing, He will provide the way of escape, so that you can bear it.'" She quoted with a nod of certainty.

"Amen." He whispered, looking up at the ceiling. "God doesn't put us through anything that we can't handle, or give us what He hasn't already instilled in us."

"Yes, I believe that too." Lynne agreed, holding him tightly.

Time seemed to stand still, almost to the point of irrelevance until Lynne's phone chimed indicating that she had received a message.

'Hey, it's Jelly, just wondering what's up?' - Jelly.

"You're not going to believe this, but it's Jelly and he wants to know how things have been lately!" She exclaimed, smiling down at her phone.

"They say that everything happens for a reason." Ben said as he began to remove the fingerpainting from what was left of the picture frame.

"Please be careful with it, Ben?" Lynne asked pleadingly.

"Yes, dear." He answered gently with a smile.

'Well Jelly, I can't say that I'm having a great day. The rain and wind is so strong, that a picture that my son made for me when he was a baby blew off the wall and smashed onto the kitchen floor. Of course, it's totally my fault for leaving the back slider open. How have you been and I hope you're not getting the high winds and heavy rain that we are out here in the country?'

'Sorry to hear about the picture and hope that the painting or drawing can be reframed? Yes, it's very windy and rainy here also. I was thinking about you earlier and thought I'd see how things were going.'

'I'm a lot better than I was a few weeks ago, thanks to the Lord, but I still have my moments. I miss Joshua very much and pray that he's at peace.'

'Amen, and I know that he is ma'am. I feel very sad for anyone who loses a loved one. I don't think that I mentioned this before, but my mom died when I was young. It gets easier to deal with, but I'll always miss her.'

'I'm so sorry Jelly, I'll say an extra prayer for you tonight.'

She momentarily thought about asking the teen what happened to her, or maybe inquiring as to how she died, but Lynne could read between the lines. Jelly was sounding more apologetic toward her losing Joshua than he, himself wanting to relive a bad time in his life.

'Oh, I almost forgot to mention the good news!' - Lynne.

'What's that?'

'I'm pregnant!'

'What?! Are you kidding?! lol.'

'Nope! I'm preggo! lol.'

'LMAO! CONGRATULATIONS!!!' Jelly wrote back excitedly.

"Lynne, don't forget to ask him about meeting up for pizza?" Ben whispered to her, as if hinting around about a secret. She looked up from her text and gave him a frown before waving off his prompt.

"I'm serious." He said directly.

"Okay Ben, I remember what we talked about, give me a second." Lynne answered him as if she was a busy waitress in a restaurant full of hungry patrons.

'Jelly, I just got the coolest idea. My husband Ben and I would love to meet you and maybe the three of us could get together and go out for pizza (our treat) or even meet up somewhere if you would feel more comfortable doing that?'

Jelly looked up at the ancient, cracked and peeling ceiling paint in his living room and closed his eyes. He wasn't expecting the dialogue to take such a sudden and unforeseen direction, and no matter how sincere the offer, (which Jelly was sure that it was) a red flag of caution gripped his receptiveness. This proposed meeting could possibly lead to a very dangerous or even worse situation. Surely, if any GSM reported back to Blaze (in the likelihood that they would be seen) it wouldn't be long before Jelly was taken to a dark place for questioning. He shook his head in disgust, realizing that under any other circumstance or in another time and place, Lynne's proposal would be awesome.

"Fuck it." Jelly whispered. "Let's do it."

'That sounds like a great idea Lynne, let's figure out a time and date?'

'Okay, we're usually free everyday except for Sundays, so just let me know what works for you?'

'Lighthouse, that day?'

'Yes, and this week I'll be sending up a prayer for you!'

'Aweee… Thank you Lynne, and likewise!'

"Are you sure this isn't going to interrupt your schedule Mickey?" Ben asked, walking down the stairs so he could hear him better. Hexe was in their bedroom yelping her head off as Lynne relentlessly teased the dog (as she did since she was a puppy) by throwing sheets over her head.

"Are you kidding me brother? No way, I'll be right where you need me to be." Mickey replied with a serious tone. "The same spot you talked about yesterday?"

"Yeah Mick, Angie's Pizza on the corner of 9th and Fitzwater." Ben said in a low voice.

He was looking through the front glass storm door and could hear Lynne walking up from behind in her stocking feet. "What's that Mickey? You made it to home plate with Amanda? First date too?!"

"Ben Ladd!" Lynne squealed out loud, slapping his arm.

"Nice man, thanks!" Mickey howled through the phone. "What a guy!"

The drive up to Philadelphia was uneventful except for the occasional gust of cross wind that pushed against Lynne's new Hyundai Tucson. She absolutely loved the popular white colored car and all it's features but Ben on the other hand hated it.

"It looks weird." He said in a low voice while playing with the electric seat.

"It does not, and it's very highly rated." Lynne scolded from the driver's seat.

"Highly rated from outer space aliens." Ben grumbled, turning his attention to the controls on the door. "Aaand it's Jap!"

"It's Korean, biker boy." She giggled.

"Same thing, it's Asian." Ben complained.

"Honey, I feel kind of strange about all this." Lynne began to explain with guilt in her eyes. "It's as though we're baiting the kid or something."

"As I said before Lynne, there's something else here, I can sense it. All I want to do is feel him out a little and read his movements, that's all." Ben explained with a smile. "You have absolutely nothing to worry about." He finished, patting her hand.

"Maybe we should have contacted Mark." She exclaimed, with a questioning look.

"For what Lynne, because I have a suspicion, a hunch? No, and the worst case scenario is that Mark would only contact Philly PD and they'd hound the crap out of him." Ben explained, like a man who knew from experience.

"Well, if they really thought that Jelly had information about Joshua's murder, I would think they'd want to talk to him, Ben." She reasoned.

"Lynne, number one, cops think they know everything and two, they move too quickly." He said in an attempt to get his wife to see the reality of the situation. "They tend to have sensitive egos and they could potentially put the boy in harm's way."

"Harm's way, how?" Lynne asked with concern.

"If Joshua's murder was really a direct result of gang activity, the cops could inadvertently expose Jelly by picking him up or even cruising past his house. In gangland terms, those are telltale signs that one is being watched or is considered suspect by the law. If this kid knows something, then you can bet that someone else knows it too, and that's not a good position to be in honey." Ben explained, raising his index finger. "Just a small piece of schooling Lynne, you can call it, the unwritten code of being low key."

"Did you ever have to deal with…" She started to ask.

"Yes, several times, and here's another piece of information. It was The General who mandated the law; that any member who had 'paper' (a club member of any rank, who had a court document stating they were awaiting arraignment or trial, and or recently sentenced to probation) was to be outcast and no contact was permitted with that individual until their legalities were finished, and they had been approved after a reinstatement interview." Ben replied, as if reciting constitutional law.

"What if the club found out that the guy was a rat?" Lynne asked, taking her eyes off the highway momentarily in order to see his expression.

"That guy had better be blasting off from Cape Canaveral and on his way to the moon." He said with a wink.

"Seriously?" She asked, wanting confirmation.

"Yeah, and believe me, it would be a lot more serious than that." Ben assured her, looking out the passenger window.

"Do you remember the summer we took Joshua to see the USS New Jersey?" Lynne asked, pointing over to the battleship that had been towed from her permanent berth in Camden, New Jersey.

She was dry docked and undergoing extensive maintenance work at the Philadelphia naval yard, which could easily be seen (even on this gray March day) from the I-95 Delaware Expressway bridge that crossed over the Schuylkill river. The Iowa class battleship's keel was laid down on September 16, 1940 at the Philadelphia Naval Shipyard and she was launched exactly a year after the Japanese attack on Pearl Harbor, December 7th. 1941. "Big J" (as the ship is so fondly called) is 887 feet long and has a beam of 108 feet; she weighs in at an astounding 49.700 long tons (standard) and drafts 38 feet with a full load. The ship is powered by four massive 53.000 hp steam turbines and offered a top speed of 33 knots; the largest gun in her arsenal is the sixteen inch Mark 7 (there are nine of them that are staggered in three gun turrets) that fired a 2.700 pound shell some twenty miles. The broad beam ship was state of the art for her time, and is truly a beautiful living piece of American history.

Jelly was standing where he said he would be, right out in front of Angie's Pizzeria on South 9th street. He was wearing a black Columbia Pike Lake II hooded jacket, a new pair of Levi's dungarees, and on his feet were his good pair of unlaced nubuck Timberlands (Jelly owned several but kept these fresh ones for special occasions) that still had the logo fob attached to the eyelets. A gold cross hung from his recently purchased Harley Davidson hoodie and on his head was a pair of blue glazed Oakly sunglasses.

"My man!" Ben exclaimed with boyish excitement as if teasing a little kid. "I'm digging his style!"

"Awe, he looks cute Ben!" Lynne cooed, giving her husband a 'shame on you' look.

"No, I'm serious Lynne, this kid's got vibe."

"I think he's very handsome." Lynne added, taking a left onto Fitzwater street.

Ben squinted his eyes into the passenger side rear view mirror until his vision focused on what he had been looking for. He shot Lynne a quick glance and was happy to see that she was preoccupied parking her new, self parking car. Mickey's truck sat on the right hand side of Fitzwater, a block behind them. Just as Ben was about to inform Lynne of a parking spot he had noticed, (because she never noticed them) he saw Mickey flash his head lights.

"Please don't tease him Ben?" Lynne asked pleadingly.

"About what, I just said that I like his style!" He replied with a smile.

"Well, about him wearing sunglasses on a cloudy day like Joshua used to, it's just cool kid fashion." She explained, nodding over at him.

"Clearly!" Ben said before letting out a laugh.

"Hi Jelly!" Lynne yelled over to the boy after shutting her car door.

It took a second for the teen to realize just where the woman's voice was coming from as he had been staring down at his phone waiting for her to text.

"Lynne!" He responded with excitement, while making his way up the block to meet her.

Ben exited the passenger's side door and smiled while waving over to him, and Jelly was amazed at how tall and solid he looked, even from twenty feet away. Lynne walked slowly and deliberately towards Jelly until her maternal instincts and emotions sprang forth.

"Come here honey, it's alright!" She invited, with genuine warmth in her voice.

"Lynne!" He called out again, his slow gait turning into a walk-run.

"You look very handsome, Jelly!" Lynne exclaimed, embracing him.

"Thank you ma'am!" Jelly responded, his voice cracking with a mix of pubescent change and charged feelings.

"My name's Ben and I'm her husband, it's nice meeting you." Ben said, extending his right hand.

"Pleased to meet you too Ben, I'm Jerome but everybody calls me Jelly!" He replied, as his hand was swallowed gently into Ben's grip.

The three proceeded to walk to the entrance of Angie's Pizzeria and were completely unaware of the dark red Mazda CX-5 Sport that was slowly cruising toward them, heading down Fitzwater street. Mickey looked over and into his driver's side mirror and watched with vigilance until the Mazda crept past. He momentarily broke eye contact with the vehicle and pretended to be distracted on his phone.

'Blood red Mazda Sport heading to you.' Mickey keyed into his phone.

Ben glanced down at his screen, read the message and intentionally acted as if everything was normal.

'Got it.' He texted back.

Ben opened the door for Lynne and Jelly hesitated momentarily before following her into the restaurant. He wasn't used to the open display of courtesy, especially from such a large figure of a man, "Go ahead son, it's alright." He said with a smile.

"Thank you, sir." Jelly replied with a nod.

The three were immediately engulfed by a warm blast of air that was filled with the aroma of garlic, onions, and freshly baked pizza. A young petite raven haired girl flew around the main dining area maneuvering through the clusters of tables and chairs with the grace and poise of a ballerina, and the precision and speed of a grand prix race car driver.

"Give me just a sec, be right there!" She hollered over to them, before disappearing through the double kitchen doors.

"Nice retro Harley hoodie by the way." Ben said, attempting to break the ice by paying the kid a compliment after they had been seated. "When did they start reissuing those again?"

"Thanks. I was just about to mention how much I like your bear sweater Lynne." Jelly beamed. "I got it through the online catalog Ben. The ad said that they were a limited edition and only available through this coming summer." He took his jacket off and held the front of the sweat shirt wide so Ben could get a better look.

"Thank you Jelly, I knit them myself." Lynne replied, giving him a nod of approval while pointing at his sweatshirt.

"Yeah man, that's nice, huh Lynne? I want one!" He jokingly ordered. "She's my sugar mama." Jelly let out a giggle after noticing her roll her eyes and wave off Ben's poke.

"He's a big kid, Jelly." Lynne exclaimed, not looking up from her menu.

"She's made tons of sweaters, one for every holiday season, and every occasion in between." Ben stated, giving his wife a wink.

Chapter Twenty Four

"Ma'am, I've got something you should see." The young studious looking man who was dressed casually announced after popping his head into Timmons office door.

She looked up from her laptop and could see the urgency on his face. "Okay, Barron lead the way."

They walked through the crowded busy open office that took up an entire floor of the building, and he led her down a narrow hallway eventually coming to a nondescript door; the likes of which could be seen in any office building or public facility anywhere. Barron took a quick look around before the two entered into what was once a small utility room. Rows of monitors revealed real time, live footage that was being provided by traffic street cameras. At the flick of a switch or by pressing a button, Barron could patch into any metropolitan surveillance system in the country, all in a matter of seconds.

"Whatcha got kiddo?" Timmons fondly asked.

"Hang on…" Barron replied, the buttons on a keypad clicked as he typed.

"Right there." He said softly, pointing at one of the many monitors.

"Let me see." She said, lifting her magnifiers up from a neck leash, "The Ladds, I presume?"

"Yes ma'am and it looks like they have a friend at the caboose." Barron informed her, pointing at the pickup truck that had just flashed its lights.

"Who is it?" Timmons inquired, narrowing her gaze.

"No idea, unfortunately the cam on Fitzwater, the one just behind him shit the bed." He remarked, tapping the image of the street lamp pole that the camera is mounted on with a pencil.

"Hmmm… I wonder if old Ben and his boys are doing a little investigation themselves?" Timmons asked, touching her chin.

"Not sure, but wait until you see this part." Barron said, queuing up the scene that he really wanted her to see. "Right there, the Mazda SUV. Notice how it slows down approaching them and wait… right there he hooks a left off of Fitzwater onto South 10th street, cruises down Christian street and heads back to Fitzwater eventually parking about thirty yards up from Angie's, next to Palumbo Recreation Center."

"GSM for sure." She stated flatly, removing her readers and touching Barron's elbow.

"I'll go to real time now, see there? The Mazda hasn't moved and no one's gotten out of it." He explained, pointing at the screen.

"Stay on this like a whore on her baby daddy, I'm going to call our guy and see if we can get a couple of locals to check him out." Timmons ordered with a wink. "Good job too, Barron. I like that."

"Yes ma'am and thank you." He blushed, with a genuine smile.

"He's with an older white couple and they just walked into Angie's off of Fitzwater a couple minutes ago."

"What do they look like?" Blaze asked softly, peering through his living room window.

"The dude is older, really big and tall, the woman is smaller, middle aged and they both look country." The raspy voice informed him and sounded as if he had just exhaled from a blunt.

"They see you, Pearl?"

"Naw man, you know I got this Blaze, c'mon." Blaze's spy answered with confidence.

"That's good, because if this cat is who I think he is, you don't want him banging on your door." Blaze warned him.

"One thing though. There's a red Dodge pickup with a white cap, that's been down the way since I drove past following them in, and he's been there for a minute. I can't get back around without him seeing me though. You said you wanted to know everything, so that's why I'm telling you." Pearl explained, looking into his rearview.

Blaze nodded his head and smiled to himself knowing that Pearl was the right choice in replacing Marcus as his lieutenant. He came from a long line of gangbangers and even had kin down in DC (a fact that Breach also appreciated) who were not only standup villains but also trusted trigger men. At the age of sixteen, Julius Prell, aka Pearl and another GSM member got caught out exciting a club in Baltimore and when the smoke cleared he was the only one left standing in the street. The other five were not so lucky and Pearl served a ten year bit, but never opened his mouth once. Not one name was ever dropped, and it's rumored that the last thing he said in court on the day he was sentenced, when asked by the judge if there was anything else that he wanted to add, was simply: "Kiss my ass."

"Okay good, stay with the three and let me know what happens." Blaze instructed, before lifting the pair of binoculars to his eyes.

"Alright Boss." Pearl acknowledged, lighting up his vanilla Black & Mild wrapped blunt.

"If they split up, stay with the country folk, ya hear?" Blaze asked, a high pitch tone coming at the end of his question.

"I feel ya." Pearl replied, shaking his head.

"Alright, I'm snooping on this old head across from me now, get back when something happens." Was the last thing Blaze told him, before noticing his new neighbor getting into a white Honda Odyssey minivan.

"Motherfucker's straight up bat shit crazy." Pearl whispered to himself.

He looked over into his driver's side door mirror and could barely make out the red truck that was still parked two blocks behind him.

"Probably some damned redneck cowboy knowing my luck." He said under his breath before taking a large hit of his blunt.

"Available. 10 - 37, (suspicious vehicle). 10 - 40, (silent run - no light, no siren). Maroon Mazda SUV, Maryland 3DM783, 700 block, Fitzarwater." Dispatch suddenly announced.

"10 - 4, 726 and 890 responding." Corporeal Delano answered in his well practiced, soft mono toned voice.

"10 - 4, what's your 20?" The dispatcher asked.

"Market at Penn Square, ETA, three minutes." Delano replied, waving at his partner to take the lead.

"Let's hook a left when we get down to Fitzwater, sounds like he's close to the intersection." Corporal Dane suggested, both men knowing that they'd have to run up a one way street.

"Yeah, cool." Steve Delano replied with a grin.

As fate would have it (as it usually does concerning police work and familiar locales) on this cold and windy overcast afternoon, Corporals Delano and Dane were once again pressed into service by answering a call that could potentially be deadly. Both men had been briefed (as most officers had in every precinct in the country) on the particular attributes and the behavioral precursors of gang activity. What signs or markings (graffiti) to look for, that could potentially be a mark of claiming territory or an encrypted calling card left after a murder. Hand gestures were as en vogue as a Madonna hit single on MTV, and pimp flash went the way of the dime store hood. Silent but deadly, high tech, under the radar was where it was at, but if you got caught out, the code of the gun still answered the question as to who would walk away. A dead cop or a dead gangbanger was just that, dead.

With only their emergency stobe's pulsing, the pair blasted down South Broad street, slowing occasionally for pedestrians and thick traffic by downshifting their eight hundred and fifty pound Harley Davidson Road King, Police Specials. The incredible thrust response from the sensitive throttle was almost immediate as high octane was forced through fuel injection and sprayed directly into the intake valves. Half of the gears in the six speed gearbox were never used during the three minute, seven block, hot run. Dane downshifted into second and looked across the intersection before taking a wide left turn, heading up Fitzwater street the wrong way. Steve was right behind him and used the same technique, but only after noticing that his partner had made a mobile path for him.

"I see him!" Delano called over to his partner.

"Go ahead!" Dane replied, sweeping his hand with an invitation.

Pearl was distracted looking down at his phone while texting his girlfriend and didn't notice the two motor units until they were almost directly in front of him. Officer Dane backed his bike up close to the SUV and against the curb preventing any attempt of forward movement, while Delano shot ten feet past the Mazda, turned around in the middle of Fitzwater and put his kickstand down near the rear of the vehicle.

"Shit." Pearl whispered, looking through his windshield then glancing into the rearview mirror.

"You want it?" Dane asked, unstrapping his helmet.

"Yeah, why not?" Delano responded with a wink.

"Afternoon sir, I need to see your driver's license, registration and proof of insurance." Steve asked the young man who appeared to be high and not paying much attention.

"What's the problem officer?" Pearl asked, using the customary response to a traffic cop's initial introduction.

"No problem, we got a call about a suspicious vehicle and it matches the description of yours." Steve explained nonchalantly.

"You smoking weed man?" Craig asked, waving his hand in front of his nose while stepping in closer to the conversation. "Because it smells like skunk shit out here."

"Yeah, a little bit." Pearl replied, handing Steve his cards. "It's my girl's car…"

In the blink of an eye Corporal Delano saw the distinctive hourglass shaped GSM (with the initials, 'DC' underlined above it) gang member tattoo on the web of Pearl's left hand and their eyes met.

"I need you to put your hands on the steering wheel and look forward please." Steve ordered with a narrowed stare.

Corporal Dane moved in closer, but stayed just ahead of the driver's side mirror and off to Steve's left. "What's up?" He asked his partner, while keeping his eyes on Pearl.

"GSM, gangbanger."

"You got anything in the vehicle that we should know about?" Dane asked, stooping in lower so as to get a better look at the interior of the car.

"Like, what?" Pearl hissed out of the corner of his mouth.

"Guns, drugs, someone else's EBT card?" Steve quipped.

"Your girl's shorts..." Pearl snapped back sarcastically, beginning to show attitude.

"Don't you mean your bitch's shorts? What was her name? Marcus, yeah that was her name." Dane jabbed back sharply.

"Okay, we'll skip happy hour, now pop your trunk and get the fuck out of the car real slow." Steve ordered, stepping back from the driver's door.

"What for? I didn't do anything wrong, this is some cop racist bullshit!" Pearl mockingly protested with excitement.

"I don't really give a shit what you think, okay? Now I said pop the rear lid, and get the fuck outta the car!" Delano barked back.

Pearl opened his door slowly and Delano motioned for him to go to the front of the Mazda.

"Place your hands on the hood please." Craig asked professionally. "You got anything in your pockets, man?"

Detective Richards hooked a right off of South Mildred street and drove slowly down Fitzwater. His black, 2018 Dodge Charger blended into the cityscape so well that neither Delano or Dane noticed him approaching until Richards gave a quick siren blast and flipped on the cold white strobes that were recessed into the grill of the car. Delano leaned out from the front of Pearl's vehicle and gave Richards a wave as he slowly rolled up next to the scene.

"Afternoon gentleman!" Detective Richards said, stepping out of the Dodge.

"Sir." Corporal Delano replied, while Dane shot him a sharp nod of hello.

"What's going on Pearl?" Richards asked after he lit up a cigarette, and exhaled the smoke from his nostrils.

Officers Delano and Dane gave each other a curious glance. "You know this guy, sir?" Steve Delano asked.

"Oh, I'm getting familiar with all of them." Richards replied, winking at Pearl. "We're going to get real cozy."

"How much weed do you have on you?" Delano inquired, while putting on a pair of blue latex surgical gloves before searching Pearl's clothes.

"It's in the pack of 100's in the console." Pearl said under his breath with a head shake of disapproval. "That's all I got."

"Nothing else in here." Corporal Dane reported.

After the brief search of the Mazda he left all the doors and the glove compartment hatch open.

"Let me see, Steve." Richards asked, pointing to Pearl's cards that were in Delano's hand.

"You can stand up now." Craig told Pearl.

"What the hell are you doin'?" Pearl asked vehemently, looking over at Detective Richards taking a photograph of his drivers license.

"You can't do that!" He protested further still.

"Says who?! And watch how you talk to me son, understand?!" Richards warned, stepping in closer to Pearl's space.

"Sir, what about this?" Corporal Dane asked, holding up the eighth ounce of marajuana that was crumpled up in a baggy.

"Through it back in the car, we're not stooping that low." He ordered, smiling at the two motor unit officers.

"Here." Richards said, holding out the license to Pearl. "I know what the fuck you're doing here today, and I know that you're up from DC replacing Marcus. But what I don't think you realize is, Blaze went and fucked up your whole GSM schedule and got some good people killed."

"I don't owe you shit, cop." Pearl stated without so much as batting an eye. "And I sure as hell ain't listening to you run your mouth!"

"Your ass will be laying in a cooler at the morgue before summer working under Blaze. I guarantee it!" Detective Richards exclaimed, tapping the hood of the Mazda. "Cut him loose fellas."

"Grab your shit and go." Corporal Delano muttered with his smart-ass grin.

"See ya around." Pearl snapped back, after he got behind the wheel.

"Yeah, I'm Delano and this here is Dane, come on down to the 26th anytime and bring the rest of the girls!" Steve Delano cracked back, taunting him.

"Anytime, Pearl!" Dane added with a grin, fastening his helmet strap.

Ben's phone vibrated just as the waitress was bringing the beautiful large pepperoni pizza they had ordered. "Excuse me." he said before picking it up off the table. "Probably Mickey, texting about Amanda."

'There's about three cops around that red Mazda down the street, it seems he's been a bad boy.' Mickey texted.

'Whoever he is, he's here for a reason.' Ben texted back.

'No doubt, and I think the reason is, they're watching that kid.' Mickey surmised, looking up from his keypad at the action down the street.

'Yeah, that's what I was feeling walking down the sidewalk.'

'Has the kid dropped any hints yet?' Mickey asked, referring as to whether or not Jelly's behavior or body language suggested that he knew something about Joshua's murder.

'No, I haven't pitched anything yet, just keeping it real light for now.'

'Cool, all's quiet out here except for the punk in the Mazda and the cops are about to leave.'

'What's going on with Jocko?' Ben asked, glancing up over his phone at Jelly.

'Jocko said that everything is on schedule, and that the contact is with him.' Mickey texted back, assuring Ben that Jocko had managed to convince his neighbor to make this arrangement happen.

'Five hundred?' Ben inquired about the payment made to the contact for his effort.

'Free to you, my brother.' Mickey answered proudly.

'I'll text you when we're about to leave.'

'We'll be here.' Mickey promised, adding a thumbs up Emoji.

"Wow, this looks good huh?" Ben said with a broad smile. "C'mon man, let's have at it!" He exclaimed invitingly to his wife and young guest.

"Ben, I think he's waiting for you to cut the pieces." Lynne suggested, pointing at the gigantic wedge slices. "This flying saucer pizza probably wouldn't fit on the table if it wasn't for the center stand."

Jelly let out a giggle and pointed at the pie. "It's the biggest pizza I've ever seen in my life!"

Ben asked the waitress for a cutting wheel then proceeded to separate the individual pieces before serving them to the upheld plates.

"Lynne tells me you're a straight 'A' student genius!" He stated, taking a big bite of the perfectly baked pie. The cheese pulled long and slow off the top and almost melted in his mouth. "Lynne, we are coming back here again!" Ben growled, in his signature pirate's voice.

"Yeah, and I scored a 1220 on my SAT study guide test!" Jelly replied, beaming across the booth at him.

"Wow! Is that a good score?" Ben inquired with his ornery grin.

"Ben Ladd! Are you kidding me?! It's fantastic!" Lynne cried out, knowing damned right well that her husband knew it was a stellar score, especially for a thirteen year old.

"I know Jelly, I'm just teasing you. Congratulations brother, that is an excellent achievement!" Ben said with a wink. "What do you think you want to do after high school?"

"Thanks Ben. College and then I'm not sure, maybe the Army or law school." The teen answered while looking up at the ceiling.

"The Army or law school? We need to hang a little more Jelly, c'mon man with grades like that you can write your own ticket."

"Ben, maybe that's what he wants to do." Lynne said softly, with a tone that suggested that he should be more encouraging.

"Yeah, if I can get a college scholarship and join ROTC, I could go in as a lieutenant, then attend OTC and maybe start as a captain." Jelly mentioned proudly.

"Then what? I mean what do you want to do in the Army?" Ben inquired.

"I'm not sure, maybe Airborne Rangers, like my friend did." Jelly beamed proudly.

"Honey, grab your coat. Dwayne Johnson's gonna snap out and eat the whole pizzeria!" He exclaimed, pretending to get up from the table.

Lynne and Jelly roared laughter as Ben held up his finger pretending to request the check from the waitress. "And what if it's law school, what would you want to practice?" Ben asked after they settled down.

"I would want to be a litigator, and defend reformed outlaw bikers!" Jelly cracked back.

"Oh, a wise guy huh? Well, you'd probably be good at it too!" Ben exclaimed with a smile.

"Get me all the street cam footage as soon as you can." Timmons ordered after swiveling her chair around, and gazing through her office window at the overcast sky. "And stay with the Mazda as far as you can."

"Yes ma'am, tracking him now. He just turned right off Fitzwater and is heading up South 11th., street." Barron reported back to the boss lady assuring her that he was on it. He was obviously excited to finally be on a real assignment and working from his tech cave that was cloaked as a utility closet.

"Thank you, Baron," She said softly, before hanging up her office phone.

"Magpie, do you have the drone up yet?" Timmons asked into her Motorola two way radio.

"Yeah, Cody is off the roof and on the way now, ETA is three minutes." Magpie's voice answered with military precision.

"Loiter around Angie's, our guests will be leaving soon." Timmons instructed, placing the radio back into its docking station.

"!0 - 4 Dragon Lady." The operative replied.

'They tried jammin' me up, down off Fitzwater and I had to roll.' Pearl texted, knowing that his boss was probably going to flip his pancakes.

'Okay, you're hot. DO NOT COME HERE! Cruz and Junior are headed that way now.' Blaze informed him, stressing the fact that Pearl was most likely being tailed. 'Take em for a ride.'

'Gotcha, later on.' Pearl answered, looking back through his rear view mirror after a wave of paranoia struck.

"Aint gettin' me, ya Five-O nigga's!" He shouted out his open window, howling like a wolf.

'Jocko and the neighbor are parking two cars ahead of me now, they're in the white, Honda minivan.' Mickey texted, facing the passenger window.

'Outside in a couple of minutes.' Ben keyed back.

"Yeah Blaze, I'm here." Cruz announced, after his boss answered his call. "The Honda minivan just parked across from Angie's." (He was referring to Blaze's new neighbor from across the street who had been picked up by Jocko a little while earlier).

"I fucking knew it! Now listen up here?! That place could be crawling with Feds but hit that old nigga and Jelly, you are my star! " Blaze ordered excitedly. "And stay on the damned phone!"

"They coming out now. I'll hit the kid and Junior's got the old biker and your neighbor." Cruz said, pulling the hot Ruger P89 from under his crotch.

"You heard what I promised him, now hit that fucking Honda boy." He told his young partner.

"I'm on point." Junior replied, lifting his AR-22 and pressing the power window button. "I'm gonna fuck his ass up."

Cruz slowed the stolen Cadillac CT5 down to a crawl, lowered his window and pointed his gun at the three walking down the sidewalk.

Mickey was the first to notice that something horrible was about to occur and he laid on his horn just as the midnight blue Cadillac stopped parallel to Ben, Lynne and Jelly (who were on the sidewalk to its left) and Jocko's minivan (which was on its right). Ben looked in the direction of the warning but it was to late, as semi automatic gun fire erupted from inside the Cadillac. Incandescent muzzle flashes simultaneously mated with the clapping sound of discharged rounds; immediately afterwards, the buzz of ricocheting bullets whizzed through the air and punched into the sides of parked cars and smashed through building front windows.

"Get down Lynne!" Ben shouted, grabbing her and the boy in each arm before throwing them to the ground, engulfing them under his body.

Junior's AR-22 lit up, and in an instant all of the minivan's windows exploded into tiny crystals before disappearing into the rain drizzled air. Jocko and Clayton banged their heads together as they dove for cover but not before Jocko felt the hot sting of a round glancing off his left shoulder. The round tore through the deltoid muscle before blowing out a chunk of his shoulder ball; it continued and passed directly over the back of Clayton's head before striking the passenger door rear view mirror.

"Stay down man!" Clayton ordered, jumping out of the Honda and pulling his Glock 21 Gen 4 from his concealed weapons holster.

He stayed low until reaching the front of the minivan, popped up and shot five rounds into Junior's door. Clayton was always excellent under fire and found it easy to quell his excitement. Raising his pistol a little higher while controlling his breathing he found paydirt; squeezing another two rounds directly into the middle of Junior's face, killing him instantly. Shattered pieces of his cranium and brain exploded, splattering the right side of Cruz's head as blood mist covered the headliner and dash. Cruz then retrieved the AR-22 and turned his attention to Clayton. He managed to hit his target once in the lower right abdomen before the gun's magazine was expended.

"Shit!" Clayton screamed in agony, as he dropped to one knee on the wet street.

"Clay!" Jelly screamed in fear, after seeing what had just happened while peering through Ben's bent elbow.

"Go with them Jelly, go now!" Clayton replied, placing his hand over the wound and pushing himself back around the front corner of the minivan seeking cover.

Ben stood, lifting Lynne and the boy with him as Mickey's truck slammed into the rear of the Cadillac. The force of the impact was so brutal that the entire rear of the vehicle was punched in three feet, and Cruz was violently thrown backwards between the front seats as he reloaded the rifle.

"Go!" Mickey called out, backing his truck up so he could ram it again.

Ben picked Jelly up, holding him close and threw an arm around his wife before rushing away from danger.

"Get in!" He ordered after popping the passenger side rear door.

Cruz had just slapped another magazine into the AR-22 and was about to point it through the Cadillac's blown out rear window in an attempt at killing the pickup truck driver. But Mickey was faster in combat and was now reaching into Cruz's open window, grabbing him by his throat and hauling him out onto the street.

"Now ya did it!" Mickey shouted at the terrified gangbanger who was trying to break free from his death throttle. He gripped down tighter and turned Cruz's head slightly inward before slamming the side of his face into the Cadillac's door pillar.

"Mickey, over here brother!" Jocko yelled from across Fitzwater. His driver side door was ajar and he was holding what looked like a plastic shopping bag over his left shoulder. "The other dude's up front too!"

"You hit Jock?!" Mickey asked, gently laying Cruz's body on the sidewalk.

"Yeah, blew my shoulder out and it hurts like a bitch!" Jocko struggled to laugh. "They got him pretty bad, though!" He said, thumbing to the front of the minivan.

"I'm here brother." Mickey said gently, helping Jocko out of the Honda. "Now let's get the other guy some help."

Chapter Twenty Five

"Micheal Lewis Cook, aka Mickey, aka the past president of the state of Virginia, Sworn motorcycle club; allegedly retired from that life and now a born again christian." The young attractive blonde detective addressed him with a straight face. Her hair was pulled up tight into a bun and streaks of water ran down the length of her royal blue Ralph Lauren rain coat. They were sitting in the small waiting area of Angie's and the only people left inside after the melee were the manager and a few employees.

"That's right." Mickey replied dryly, staring through the double glass doors at all the activity taking place outside.

"What church do you go to?" She asked, softening up a little.

"Lighthouse, in Kennett Square."

"My husband and I attend Calvary Christian, over in Media. I'm Detective Hoovler by the way, but you can call me Holly." She said, offering him a handshake.

"Sorry we couldn't have met under better circumstances." Mickey replied, engulfing her right hand in his massive paw.

"You've had an interesting day." Holly said with a slight smile, nodding out to the taped off crime scene that lined the sidewalks and the blocked off street.

"Yeah, so far I suppose." He answered, squinting his eyes at her and waiting for the real questioning to begin. "How's Jocko and the other guy?"

"They were rushed to Penn and went straight into surgery." She stated with a nod guaranteeing him that they were in good hands. "However, the gangbanger's head you introduced to the Caddy's door jamb, well, he'll probably be eating through a straw for the next few months but..."

"Thank goodness, I thought we'd lose the other guy." Mickey said with concern, completely ignoring her cute remark about the punk he had handled.

"Yeah, he was in pretty bad shape, took one to the abdomen?" Holly asked, raising her eyebrows.

"Yes, he didn't go into shock but he almost lost consciousness. I kept pressure on the wound and Jocko kept talking to him, telling him to hang on."

"Were you and Jocko here today by coincidence or were you meeting up with someone?" She inquired, folding up the stat sheet on Mickey that had been printed out in her car.

"I think the three of us were going to grab a pizza." Mickey said, turning his attention back to the outside world. "Right in this place, too."

"And then a Caddy cruised by and started shooting?" Holly questioned, tilting her head to one side with look of concern.

"Something didn't look right, it didn't feel right to me either. Maybe some of my past experience with sticky situations kicked in, I don't know. There was definitely something up with those cats." He explained, pointing to the Cadillac CT5 that looked like it had just competed in a demolition derby.

"Sergeant?" A uniformed officer announced, popping his head into the front door.

"Yeah?" Holly answered, not turning around to face him.

"There's a 10-21 (phone radio dispatch) request for you."

"Thank you, I'll be right out." She replied.

"Excuse me, Mickey." Holly said as she got up from the cedar bench before reaching for her phone which was crammed into the rear pocket of her tight black Elle Slim Trousers. She turned and smiled, then walked out into the chilly air.

"Hey buddy, can I get you a beer or anything? It's on the house." The petite raven haired waitress asked him with a smile. "You really stepped up out there, man."

"Thanks doll, just a water please, if you don't mind."

"You're a hero, do you know that!?" A news man shouted through the large plate glass window, the large red neon light that beamed 'Angie's' in bold cursive lettering radiated onto Mickey's face.

"This is Sergeant Hoovler here, go ahead." Holly acknowledged, after dispatch answered.

"Just a moment please." A monotone older woman's voice from dispatch replied. "Okay, go ahead ma'am."

"Hello?" Holly asked, placing her index finger into her other ear so as to minimize the background noise.

"Hello Sergeant Hoovler, this is Agent Timmins, FBI. I'm the assistant field director here in Philadelphia and I'm in charge of field ops, can you hear me?" Timmons announced professionally.

"Yes, I can hear you just fine." She replied, while opening the door to her unmarked Charger.

"Can you keep what I'm about to tell you under your lid?" Timmons asked in a serious manner.

"Yes, I can." Holly assured.

"Good, I like hearing that." Timmons said softly, choosing her words carefully before continuing. "We're currently in the middle of an investigation regarding the increase of violence and narcotics distribution that is directly linked to the Gold Sheik Mob. They set up a shop here in Philly approximately three years ago and their ranks have increased tenfold since then." There was a brief pause which indicated to Holly that it was her turn to ask questions.

"GSM, yes, I'm very aware of the activity they're engaged in." She stated with agreement. "You want me to let Micheal Cook go don't you?" Holly asked suddenly and with finalility.

"Yes, Sergeant Hoovler, I would like you to cut Mickey loose." Timmons replied. "Besides, he's a local hero after fixing that ganbanger's ass right in front of the whole town!" She said, beginning to chuckle.

"That he did." Holly agreed. "You think that maybe those old Sworn boys were down here for something else?" Holly inquired, insinuating that Mickey and Jocko didn't just happen to be on Fitzwater by coincidence.

"I dont really give a shit what they were doing there at the time sergeant." Timmons quipped under her breath, knowing full well that she had to keep the fact that there was an undercover operative involved a secret. "We had a drone overhead and eyes through the street cams; we saw everything in real time and that footage will be shared with the appropriate personnel over at your division. Understand?"

"Yes ma'am, I get it." Holly acknowledged, as if she was a little girl and her mom had just told her to get ready for bed. "You've already contacted someone over at division then?"

"Sergeant Hoovler, this is Detective Richards with Division Headquarters. First, I'd like to say good job down there today, you'll be commended. Secondly, cut Mickey loose." He ordered in a low voice, turning his phone away from the others who were sitting in the waiting room at Penn Hospital.

"Yes, sir." Holly flinched a little, suddenly realizing that she was on a three way conference call. "Will do."

"I have the utmost faith that you'll keep this conversation to yourself?" Timmons added, reminding her of how sensitive in nature the situation was.

"Yes, ma'am, we never talked." Holly assured her.

"Excellent, and it's been good talking with you." Timmons said, before hanging up.

"Same here Hoovler, and I'm going to look you up as soon as I get free." Richards stated, guaranteeing that she was doing the right thing.

"Thank you sir, I appreciate it."

"Well Mickey, It's been nice meeting you and if you're ever up in Media on a Sunday, please stop by and see us at Cavalry." Holly exclaimed with a smile after walking back into Angie's.

"You know it, and thank you Holly." Mickey answered, lifting up the plastic water bottle that had been given to him.

"Can I ask you one last question? I mean, it's totally between you and me." She promised, holding up two fingers like a scout. "Honest."

"Shoot."

"Does the biker brotherhood, loyalty thing ever go away or is it something that stays with you guys until the end?" Holly sincerely asked.

"Psalm 133:1 "Behold, how good and how pleasant it is for brethren to dwell together in unity!""

"Amen, now go visit your brother." She insisted, holding out her hand once again.

"In the news this evening, yet another episode of gang related gun violence that left two men seriously wounded, a gunman dead and another suspect rendered unconscious. Brianna Smith has the story." Rick Williams, the well respected and loved Channel 6 Action News anchor announced with a frown.

"Yes, thank you Rick. This all unfolded today in front of Angie's Pizzeria, located here at the intersection of Fitzwater and South 9th street." The savvy Action News street reporter said, momentarily turning her head away from the traditional stick microphone, bearing the famous '6 ABC' logo board. Behind her, blue and white strobe lights intermittently popped on and off glazing the dark early evening with coldness and severity. The windows of parked cars and building fronts reflected the dancing lights which in turn revealed the aftermath of the day. Yellow crime scene tape lined both sides of Fitzwater and triangular numbered evidence markers sat next to the shell casings that were strewn arbitrarily on the street.

"We were inside Angie's and all of a sudden we heard, pop-pop-pop!" A young mother said from a previous interview, recorded earlier in the day.

"I had just brought out a boat load of food to a big round top and then all hell broke loose out on the street. This is just unbelievable." The petite raven haired waitress exclaimed. "They need to nail this shit (bleeped out) down now."

"This is the guy you saw stop the whole thing?" Brianna asked, while motioning for Mickey to come and introduce himself. "Please sir, come talk to us?"

"That's him!" The waitress squealed.

"Hi." Mickey humbly said, looking down at the two women. "What can I do for you?"

"This young lady tells us, that you single handedly stopped the shooting and prevented it from going any further." The reporter declared, looking up at the large smiling man.

"Sorry sir, I hope you don't mind, I couldn't help it!" The raven haired girl added.

"Well, you ain't no slouch yourself. From what I hear, you were the one inside Angie's that shouted for everyone to stay away from the windows and get down on the floor!" Mickey explained, patting her on the shoulder.

"Can you tell us what happened?" Brianna asked.

"I was meeting up with a couple of buddies for lunch, when this Cadillac drove past me real slow." Mickey explained, thumbing over his shoulder in the direction of the crunched Caddy. "The next thing you know, the windows came down and then they started shooting at both sides of the street!"

"That's when everybody inside the restaurant freaked out!" The waitress shouted dramatically.

"What did you do?" The reporter asked with a slight pout.

"The only thing I could think of at the time was just ram him!" Mickey said with a quick nod. "I didn't do what anyone else wouldn't do to save a friend." He finished, winking into the camera.

"Well, yes of course, but you also disarmed one of the shooters by putting yourself in harm's way." Brianna added, wanting him to tell more of his story.

"It was very necessary." Mickey admitted more to himself then to the reporter.

"We're back here live Rick, and word has it that the two men who were wounded while sitting in the parked minivan and rushed to Penn Presbyterian Medical Center, are both expected to make a full recovery. As for the two suspected gang members, one was shot and killed at the scene, while the other was rushed to Jefferson emergency, with nonlife threatening injuries."

"What a tragic scene indeed Brianna." Rick Williams mentioned, the disappointment in his distinctive broadcaster's voice could not be mistaken. "We'll try to have more details for you later on this evening, on Channel Six Actions News at eleven.

The only source of light in the dark living room came from Blaze's gigantic flat screen television. He sat alone in his sweats on the leather recliner, rolling a blunt and occasionally glancing up at it; until a news report about the shooting on Fitzwater street was aired. His phone vibrated on the coffee table just as he was about to light up, and for a split second the thought of ignoring it crossed his mind. Blaze picked up the phone and stared at the text and smiled to himself.

'5 Newark Road, Kennett, Pennsylvania. They're farmers.' -Tubby.

Chapter Twenty Six

"You're safe now Jelly, no one knows you're here or even where this place is." Lynne said, attempting to calm him down. "Just try to be still now, and we'll figure all of this out."

The drive back to Kennett had been stressful, especially for the boy who at times cried aloud and blamed himself for everything that had taken place. The three sat in front of the fireplace on the large couch sipping hot chocolate. They stared into the soothing flames becoming mesmerized, unable to pull their gaze away while listening to one another speak.

"Clay knows, he told me to go with you." Jelly mentioned softly, petting Hexe's head that was resting next to his thigh. The dog was worried and hadn't left his side since she noticed him crying upon entering the house. "Isn't there any way we can find out how he's doing Lynne?"

"I can make a call in a little bit." Ben assured him with a smile.

"I brought all of this on you, and almost got Clay killed." Jelly stated, his voice filled with emotion and his eyes ready to tear.

"Jelly, listen to me." Ben advised with a serious look. "What happened this afternoon was going to happen regardless. In my many years as a member of an outlaw motorcycle club, I can assure you one thing son, that piece of shit…"

"Benjamin Ladd!" Lynne scolded angrily.

"Let me finish Lynne! That piece of shit gangbanger up in Philly has been watching you for a while. My guess is, he either thinks you know something that you shouldn't or you have something of his that he wants back. Anyway you cut it, whether he gets what he wants, or not, his plan for you is nothing less than seeing you dead. It's that simple." Ben turned his head away and gazed back into the fire. "I'm sorry if I came off to rough Jelly, but that's the way it is."

Hexe lifted her head tilting it sideways before running out of the room; her claws clicked on the hardwood floor of the main hallway, sounding as if she was in a trot of curiosity before graduating to a continuous full burst run of excitement.

"That's Mickey." Ben explained, getting up slowly off the couch.

"C'mon in." Ben invited, commanding Hexe to go back into the living room and lay down. "How's Jocko?"

"His left shoulder is going to need reconstructive surgery but as it stands now they have him bandaged up pretty good, and he's feeling no pain." Mickey replied, taking off his Carhartt barn coat. "The cop on the other hand is in worse shape, he took one to the gut and lost a lot of blood. The last I heard though is he's going to make it."

"Yeah, that secret didn't last long after we hightailed it out of Philly." Ben said, nodding over in the direction of the living room. "That kid in there loves him like a father."

"It wasn't much of a secret to me either, especially after seeing a senior detective, and about six uniforms in the waiting room." Mickey explained with a chuckle. "How's the kid doing, has he said anything?"

"Bits and pieces. I think he knows that our little lunch date wasn't just for the three of us to get together." Ben whispered back, as they entered the living room.

"Jelly wanted to be honest, so he gave me this to hold onto while he's in our house." Lynne explained, pointing to the Ruger LC-9 laying on the coffee table. The magazine had been removed and the slide locked open, indicating that the weapon had been cleared and was safe. "I think that was a good thing to do, right honey?"

"Yes, I really appreciate that Jelly." Ben said, giving him a nod of approval. "Thank you."

"I'm sorry Ben." Jelly replied with guilt in his voice.

"That's it!" Ben barked in his playful pirate's voice. "Oiv had enough of the sad lad, an now ye gonna pay!"

In an instant Ben had Jelly up off the couch and screaming with laughter. With one fast hand he grabbed the boy by his wrists, and held his arms high in the air before tickling him relentlessly with the other.

"Are ye gonna stop with the sad sack shat now laddy, or is it more arm pit torture?!"

"Yes, yes, stooop!!!" Jelly squealed aloud.

Hexe couldn't take it anymore and decided to get into the spar, jumping playfully on Ben's back while yelping her high pitched, playful excited barks.

"Now, this is the nut house it used to be Mickey!" Lynne shouted with laughter. "Get him Hexe!"

"Hi, my name is Mickey and it's good meeting you." He said, introducing himself with an extended hand.

"Good to meet you too, Mickey." The teen replied, shaking his hand before sitting back down on the couch between Lynne and Ben. "You're a good friend of Ben's?"

"Yeah, we go back a long way." Mickey assured, with seriousness in his eyes.

"Jelly, Mickey was up the street from Angie's today and he noticed them cruising by just after the three of us met up. He's also the guy that distracted them by ramming their Caddy."

"You were the lookout." Jelly stated softly, looking over at the large man who by now had gained Hexe's trust and was petting her head.

"That's right, son." He confessed with a wink. "You'll be able to see the aftermath of today's events in living color on Channel Six Action News at eleven."

"Are you born again too?" Jelly asked, raising an eyebrow.

"I am, or at least I'm trying my very best." He answered, nodding his head.

"You're doing great, Mickey." Lynne added, smiling. "Does anyone want anything from the kitchen? I'm going to feed her and make us some more hot chocolate."

"That would be great Lynne!" Jelly exclaimed.

"Marshmallows?" Ben asked teasingly.

"Jelly, I have a few questions to ask you and I would appreciate it if your answers were truthful." Ben advised, as he leaned back and rested his head on a throw pillow.

Jelly looked down into his lap and shook his head. "I wouldn't know where to begin." He sounded exasperated and tired.

"The beginning is always the best place to start, bro." Mickey suggested. "Hey, look at me." Jelly glanced over at him as if he had been awakened from a trance.

"You're in a good place here, no one's going to hurt you, and this conversation won't leave this room."

"As God as my witness, you can believe that." Ben said with resolve.

Lynne fed Hexe then took the milk out to make the hot chocolate, it was a simple old family recipe that had been passed down generations. She was mixing the ingredients into the simmering pot when a photograph on the bookshelf (that was used to house her many treasured culinary recipe books) caught her eye, and she had to place a hand over her mouth to prevent an outburst. Joshua was sitting in his highchair and the only thing he was wearing was an oversized bib that had been tied around his neck. His entire face, hands, and torso was covered with strawberry icing (his favorite flavor) and what was left of the poor cake lay in a flattened state of mush. A huge smile projected through the pinkish red goo, and above the image was a message that simply read: "Today, I Turn One!"

She carried the silver German antique serving tray that held the four large mugs of hot chocolate into the living room, and upon sensing the serious nature of the conversation taking place, Lynne decided to add her maternal guidance.

"A thirteen year old boy shouldn't feel the need to carry a gun." She said, pointing at the Ruger on the coffee table. "He shouldn't have to live in fear, worrying about whether or not someone is going to take a shot at him. You should be able to go to school and get good grades so that your only thought is what university you'll attend after graduation. Jelly, you should be playing baseball or basketball, be involved with Boy Scouts, going to Sunday school and dances. Those are the things that are healthy for a young teenager such as yourself."

Jelly looked like a deer caught in the headlights of a fast approaching car. "Yes Lynne, you're right and believe me, I never wanted to be a part of that gangster lifestyle, ever."

"I know that son, you're a smart young man. I just think it's a damned shame that common sense isn't a part of raising children anymore. It makes me very upset when I see the total disregard of responsibility and the lack of accountability from these so-called mothers."

"My mom raised me the best she could, honestly she did. Until she was killed by a stray bullet out in front of our house." Jelly explained, looking down at his feet.

Ben and Mickey gave each other a quick look of surprise, and Lynne raised her head slowly and stared at the ceiling.

"My God." She whispered.

"Believe me Lynne, If I could have chosen to be born and live in a better place, I would have." Jelly said, looking at her with sincerity. "But I would have never chosen a different mother."

Lynne raised a napkin to dry the tears that were welling in her eyes. "I know you wouldn't honey." She said, putting an arm around the teen and giving him a squeeze.

"Imagine the countless, innocent lives that have been lost or altered for the worse due to the fact that they were a byproduct of a bad environment. A lot of talented, smart kids with potential that didn't stand a chance." She explained, shaking her head in disbelief.

"I'm ready to tell you guys everything now." Jelly said softly, taking a sip of his hot chocolate. "This might take a minute."

"I'll order a pizza." Ben replied with a nod.

"Ben, we had that for lunch!" Lynne exclaimed with a frown.

"I didn't!" Mickey joked. "I was a little busy and worked through lunch."

"Subs it is then." Ben said with finality. "Besides, it's the only other joint that delivers out here in the woods."

The four sat in silence at the small cozy table in the kitchen, and after they had devoured their Italian subs, Jelly began telling them how he became involved with GSM. He described in vivid detail how it all started his first day of seventh grade when he met Dante' Brooks. A few days later Jelly was invited to go over to his new friend's house after school and that's when he met Dante's older sister Trina, and her boyfriend Andre' Pelts, aka Blaze (the head of GSM in Philadelphia). Jelly spoke of the many occasions in which he witnessed Trina stepping on heroin with fentanyl, (adding other ingredients to add more weight and increase sales) that was given to her by Blaze. He also mentioned several times that Blaze had a ruthless and brutal way of dealing with fellow gang members who didn't follow his orders or if someone was a threat. One instance in particular stood out, and he reminisced about a rival gangbanger named Shey, who at times would drive past Blaze's representing his gang, and looking to start trouble.

"Just like that it stopped." Jelly said, looking at Ben. "Shey just vanished off the face of the earth!" He exclaimed.

"This happened after Joshua was murdered?" Mickey asked.

"Yeah." Jelly responded, shaking his head slowly.

"I kind of fell away after Blaze and Trina got into a big fight and he kicked Dante' out. That's how we ended up living together, I took him in." The teen smiled, remembering his friend. "That is, until they murdered her."

Lynne flashed Mickey a quick stare and shook her head, 'no.' They had informed him of their conversation with Mark, regarding the fact that a weapon found in a car where Trina's remains were found matched the gun that was used to kill a DEA agent. He was found shot to death inside the vehicle that the man who murdered Joshua fled from. Ben glanced over at his wife then nodded over to Mickey who was sitting with his leg crossed over, resting his large chin in the palm of his hand.

"How did you end up friends with an undercover cop, Jelly?" Ben asked, with a look of curiosity.

"I called him after I found one of his business cards on the sidewalk off Frankford avenue." Jelly replied with remorse.

"They were left behind in the hope that someone knew, or saw something that morning?" Lynne inquired, alluding to the location where Joshua was killed.

"Yes ma'am." He answered softly.

"Why would you call him, did you hear something about what happened?" Mickey asked, looking at Ben.

Lynne hadn't noticed his maneuver, as this technique of indirectly asking a question was their way of queuing the other to pay close attention to his body language and tone of voice.

"Yes." Jelly responded, looking down into his lap.

"What do you know, Jelly?" Ben asked, leaning in closer to the boy, assuring him that he was safe.

"It's okay honey." Lynne whispered.

Jelly looked up and tears began to streak down the sides of his face. "I know he killed your son and Trina!" He exclaimed with pain in his voice.

"How do you know that?" Ben asked with caution.

"Me and Dante were over Blaze and Trina's the afternoon of the shootings on Frankford. I was in the upstairs bathroom when Blaze came running into the house with blood on his pants."

"Trina! Get me some towels, I been shot!" Blaze shouted from the living room.

"What the hell happened baby?!" She shrieked back, with concern and fear.

"Just get me some fucking towels, girl!"

"Pull your pants off, let me see!" Trina cried, running over to him with an arm full of kitchen towels.

"They got Cleats, and then he shot me by accident!" He explained, wincing as Trina gently removed his sweat pants and underwear.

"Cleats dead?!" She asked excitedly.

"Fuck yeah, he dead as hell. I tried to grab a van but my gun went off!"

"I should have told Clay but I didn't, I was scared because I knew that Blaze was watching me like a hawk. I'm so scared that he's going to kill me!" Jelly exclaimed, the fear and pain in his teen voice could not be concealed.

His angst was too much for Lynne to bear, and in an instant she stood up and grabbed ahold of him. She looked over at Ben and Mickey while clutching onto Jelly's shoulders and his muffled sobs caused the three of them to choke up, suddenly Mickey shot Ben a stare requesting retribution.

"It's okay, son." Ben said, reaching over to rub his back. "Believe me, we understand."

"You thought you had some collective bargaining power with Blaze if he decided to come after you, huh?" Mickey asked gently.

"Yeah." He said, sounding as if he were talking into a pillow.

Everyone flinched and looked up as Hexe tore out of the room and ran down the hallway toward the front door.

"We have company." Ben announced, taking his concentration away from Jelly and getting up from the couch.

The dog's barks were a mix of anger and confusion, and occasionally she bore her teeth in a menacing sneer.

"Hexe, come here now!" Lynne shouted after her as Ben slowly approached the door.

"Go back!" He commanded with a quick snap and a point.

Mickey stood up and went to the front window and slightly moved the curtain aside. "Looks like Mark and a woman are out on the front porch." He said, squinting his eyes from the glare of the outside dome light.

"Who's, Mark?" Jelly asked, raising his head away from Lynne's body.

"It's fine Jelly, he's the chief of police here in town, and a good friend of ours from church." She replied assuringly.

"Please don't tell him anything, Lynne!" The teen pleaded with beckoning eyes.

"Everything we discussed stays in this room, Jelly, do you remember that?" Mickey answered, removing the Ruger from the coffee table and placing it in the drawer of the dining room sidebar.

"Ben, this is Agent Timmons, FBI. Timmons, this here is the one and only Benjamin Ladd." Mark introduced the two with a smile.

"Nice to meet you Ben, sounds like you got one helluva dog!" Timmons exclaimed, offering him her hand.

"We sure do, and it's good meeting you also." He replied with a smile.

"I'd like to see Jelly if you don't mind." Timmons said, slightly looking around him.

"Sure thing, let me just check to see that the dog's been put up." Ben responded, walking ahead of them and holding his hand back.

"It's okay, she's in the basement and I'm Lynne, Ben's wife." Lynne said, offering the well dressed woman a handshake.

"Believe me, I appreciate that and my name is Agent Timmons, but please call me Deb. I would like to have a few minutes with this brave young man here if you don't mind?" She asked kindly.

Ben intentionally bumped into the coffee table and as he bent over to rub his shin, shot Jelly, a nod and a wink. "I'm sorry Agent Timmons, this is my old friend Mickey." He mentioned, pointing over.

"Please call me Deb, and it's nice to meet you boys in person." Timmons said playfully. "And I'm glad to hear you're both well."

Subdued scratching noises could be heard coming from the closed cellar door that stood to the side of the kitchen, and every couple of seconds or so, a slight whine was added for begging effect.

"That's Hexe." Jelly added, looking up at Timmons with wide eyes.

"Yes, well it's good meeting her while she's behind that door." Timmons replied, nodding her head toward the direction of Hexe's whimpering.

"You two can talk in the family room if you like." Lynne suggested, noticing that Agent Timmons had offered Jelly a social que for them to exit the living room.

"Thank you Lynne." Timmons responded, waving her hand to Jelly. "Please Mark, if you don't mind I'd like a word with him alone."

"First, I would like to start out by saying that you are a very brave young man." She said, putting her hand softly on Jelly's shoulder as the two sat down. "Secondly, I can't tell you how happy I am to see that you're safe and in good company."

"Ma'am, please dont misunderstand me or think Im being rude, but who the fuck are you?" Jelly asked with a curious gaze, his eyebrows moved closer together as if he was looking for an answer.

Timmons burst out laughing and had to momentarily look away, as the look on his face was too much for her to be able to conduct any kind of formal conversation.

"I'm sorry Jelly, let's start over." Timmons suggested, after her howl had subsided to a giggle. "I'm Special Agent Timmons, FBI but please call me Deb."

"Jelly." He responded, offering a handshake.

"I'm the assistant field director in charge of operations out of the Philadelphia office." She informed him, her demeanor became more professional and stoic.

"Sounds important, but it also sounds like you're a cop manager." Jelly quipped.

"That, I am." Timmons agreed.

"You've been watching Blaze and GSM?" The teen inquired with narrowed eyes.

"Going on four years now son." She admitted, folding her hands in her lap while looking over at a Ladd family portrait on the end table. "And that's also how I became familiar with Jerome Wilts."

"I see." Jelly acknowledged, after hearing her use his proper name.

"And as things panned out, as they often do, we also came to meet and know Detective Chris Clayton."

Jelly looked up at Timmons wide eyed and surprised. "But he's a Philadelphia cop and he and me…"

"Have been like this." She mentioned, holding up her right hand with fingers crossed.

"Yeah, like that." Jelly agreed with a hint of suspicion in his voice. "I'm worried about him…"

"It's okay Jelly, he's going to make it." She assured him with a sharp nod. "Look, this is some real serious shit, as I'm sure you're already aware. I need to know everything that you know about Blaze and any GSM activity that occurred just prior to Joshua Ladd's death."

Jelly told her everything that he had just told his new friends out in the other room (except the part about seeing Blaze, after Cleats and Joshua were killed) and before Timmons and he finished their little meeting, she asked him if there was anything else that he could think of.

"When you see Clay, tell him I love him." Jelly's eyes beckoned.

"You know that I will, Jelly." Timmons assured, giving him a wink.

Jelly loved the spare bedroom that he was given and giggled as Lynne and Hexe put fresh sheets on the double bed. Every maneuver the woman made in an attempt to straighten out the sheets, the dog would trot around to the opposite side and tug them away from her.

"She has done this since she was a puppy, just helping me out you know?!" Lynne said jokingly, swatting Hexe's tail before the dog bolted from her to the foot of the bed.

"She's a kid!" Jelly exclaimed, trying to pet the dog while she was in motion.

"You should have seen her attack the laundry basket after I took your clothes out of the dryer!" Lynne mentioned, as if talking about a toddler.

"This is the first bedroom I've ever seen that has its own bathroom!" He said, pointing to the open door.

"Oh, that reminds me, you need a tooth brush and towels." Lynne stated, before walking down the hallway to the linen closet. "Be right back."

Jelly peered around the doorway and noticed that Ben had come upstairs and for a split second he thought about keeping his deepest secret. He stopped and kissed Lynne on her cheek before looking down the hallway, and that's when he noticed that Jelly was trying to get his attention. The young inner city teen looked cute wearing Joshua's hand-me-down sweets and a Sportster t-shirt while Hexe stood by his side. He motioned to Ben with a beckoning wave as if pleading in silence and Ben acknowledged back by holding up a 'wait-a-second' index finger.

"I think Jelly wants to tell me goodnight." He whispered to Lynne.

"Here, you might as well give him these, then." She stated, handing him the towels and toiletries.

"Hey Jelly, we're very happy that you're here with us." He mentioned, placing the items next to the sink in the bathroom.

"Thank you Ben, I'm happy too and I'm sorry that you guys got put in the middle of…"

"We were put into this, the day Joshua was killed." He said with raised eyebrows. Ben's appearance had changed from earlier in the day, and the once cool and energetic looking older biker gave way to dark rimmed eyeglasses, barefeet and a tired look upon his face. Ben Ladd looked his age.

"Remember when you mentioned some of the reasons for Blaze wanting me killed?" Jelly asked, looking into his eyes.

"Yes, I remember." Ben replied, sitting down next to him on the bed.

Jelly's head dropped and he began to weep.

"I was physically and mentally abused as a kid and most of my life I was an outlaw biker. At times, I did things to others that I will regret until the day I die. I was convicted of attempted murder and spent many years in a federal prison. To be completely honest with you Jelly, in a lot of ways we were no different than those punks up in Philly. However, we had class. A one percent club does not target or harm innocent people and they sure hell don't go after kids. It's about being a stand up man, looking out for your brothers and living by the ultimate code of loyalty."

Jelly looked at him with awe, like a child who was hearing his grandfather talk about the war.

"Jelly, I never had a damned thing in my life. I didn't have a home, a wife or family and I knew that the lifestyle that I was living didn't jive with settling down. Hell, I didn't even have a credit card!" Ben teased, poking the boy in the ribs. "All of that changed the day I met that woman down the hall, because the second I laid eyes on her, I knew that I had met the most beautiful woman in the world. She invited me to join her and her friends from Lighthouse church, and instantly something inside me changed. We ended up getting married and I adopted Joshua, he was the son I never had…"

"I have the gun." Jelly suddenly admitted, as tears began to fill his eyes.

Chapter Twenty Seven

"How come you never remarried, George?" Alicia asked, wiping away the tears from her cheeks and blowing her nose.

"Oh I don't know, maybe it's because I got hurt so bad after Francine left me that I didn't want to set myself up like that again." He replied softly, with a sympathetic smile.

"Was it another man?" She inquired, looking out into the rain drizzled night through the passenger window.

Richards had been around people who had experienced high levels of stress and been subject to psychological trauma most of his adult life. Therefore, he realized that the questions that Chris's wife was asking him (that seemed aloof) was her mind's way of protecting itself from the shock of the current circumstance.

"No, I was drinking pretty heavily back then and blacking out. I'd wake up in the morning and not remember most of what I had said or done the night before." George admitted. "Then it got so bad that I'd sneak out of the house after she fell asleep or I wouldn't come home from work at all."

"She couldn't put up with it anymore." Alicia whispered, more to herself than to him.

"That's correct, she was a good woman. She waited for me to get home from the Army, and kept a good home." He said with a nod. "It was all me, and I knew it."

"When did you get sober?"

"The night that three of my fellow off duty officers and I had a little disagreement in a bar." He chuckled to himself and shook his head. "Twenty five years ago, I woke up in a locked room at the precinct with a black eye and the assholes put lipstick on me and painted my fingernails!"

Alicia squealed a high pitched girl laugh before losing it all altogether. "They did not?!" She could barely ask, while gasping for air.

"The hell they didn't!" He exclaimed, as he began to laugh. "And girl, let me tell ya, it was all in hot pink too!"

"Oh, my God!" She cried out.

"He's going to be fine." George said gently, taking her hand in his.

"I told him… I just knew this was going to happen!" She exclaimed, bursting into tears.

"Now, now, Alicia, c'mon girl he's almost out of surgery."

"I was so worried about you Chris!" Alicia exclaimed, rushing over to his bedside in post-op. "I don't know what I'd do if…" She could barely speak before losing it altogether.

"Alicia." Clayton whispered, reaching for her hand and forcing his best smile.

"Hey Chris, everything is going to be just fine." George said, trying to alleviate her stress and also guarantee his friend that all was under control.

Clayton was groggy and fighting the remaining effects of the anesthesia; his head felt heavy and a dull buzzing sound accompanied with an echo came from somewhere deep inside his brain. He could see their mouths moving but it took a couple of seconds for their voices to catch up with their lips. For a moment he had to stop and think about what he was doing laying in a hospital bed looking up at his wife and boss. Richards let out a slight chuckle before tapping Alicia on the shoulder.

"He has no idea what the hell is going on here." He whispered into her ear. "Do you remember the shootout earlier today on Fitzwater, Chris?"

"Yeah, I do but everything is a little foggy." Clayton replied, rubbing his forehead. "Like a radio station with a lot of static."

"I just knew this was going to be bad, Chris." Alicia added.

"Don't worry dear, it won't be long until you get your end of the bargain." Clayton stated, giving her a wink.

"You stop!" She squealed. "Goerge is standing right here!"

"Well he knows about making babies!" He joked, looking over at his boss.

"Oh Lord, do I need to give you two some room in here?" Richards asked, using his famous grumbly old man's voice.

After the tears had been turned to laughter; which is the best known cure for stress and heartache, Alicia excused herself in order to use the ladies room. Richards asked for a soda if she happened to come across a vending machine in the hopes that this would give him a little more time alone with Clayton.

In the short fifteen minutes that she was gone, Clayton answered his boss's question as to how he ended up playing the role of the contact on such short notice. Jocko's neighbor, Darius Moore is a delivery route driver for FedEx and also a DEA informant. Two years ago he was delivering a package that was being tracked by the agency, it contained 5 kilos of Fentynal and was dropped off at a wrong address intentionally. Those waiting for the drop had managed to evade capture by simply waiting in an alleyway until receiving a text to grab it. Afterwards, DEA kept a close eye on Darius and their conclusion was that he was a hard working and honest man and also a pretty good guy. He accepted the agency's offer to become a paid informant. His reasoning being at the time was, who would ever suspect a FedEx driver, who had the same route for as long as he, could possibly be a narc? One evening, Darius and Jocko were drinking beer by a pit fire and he asked Jocko (knowing of course that he was an old Sworn member) if he happened to know Joshua Ladd's dad.

"Yeah man, are you kidding me? He's a past national president, I've known Towers for years!" Jocko explained, his happy beer face turning into a frown.

"I know a guy on my route, who says he knows who shot his son." Darius said in a low voice.

Unbeknownst to DEA, Darius and Jocko, FBI field operatives had previously gained surveillance of Darius communicating with an unknown source. Timmons pulled a string and had Darius's phone tapped, before scrambling to instill Clayton (undercover) as the man who claimed to know the shooter.

"We need to talk." Richards said softly into his phone.

"Okay, name the spot." Timmons replied, while sitting up in bed.

"How about the Morning Glory Diner on South 10th and Fitzwater?" He suggested in a satirical tone.

"The irony!" Timmons replied. "Shame on you George, returning to the scene of the crime so soon."

"The best breakfast in town!" Richards added, as if he were in a television ad.

"Seven-thirtish?" She asked, turning away from her phone to yawn.

"Sounds good, and I'll see you then. I'm staying here at Penn as long as Chris's wife wants, then taking her home." He added, the fatigue in his voice could not be mistaken.

"I've been getting updates all night and I'll visit him tomorrow after you and I meet." Timmons also sounded concerned.

"He'll be fine." Richards stated flatly. "Clayton is that kind of guy."

"Yes, he is George, yes he is." She agreed.

The sidewalk under their feet pulsed and vibrated momentarily as a Philadelphia Fire Department pumper screamed past in a flurry of red and white emergency strobe lights, its deep raspy air horn blast and high pitched siren was deafening. They turned their heads away from the controlled confusion and in a frozen moment of surprise caught one another's gaze.

"Do you want to know what I always wondered?" Timmons asked, in an attempt to deflect the uncomfortable situation.

"What's that?" Richards asked, exhaling smoke from his nostrils.

"How come fire trucks never look old?"

"Probably because they're always clean and well maintained." He responded, looking away towards the direction of the pumper.

"Unlike us?" Timmons added under her breath.

"Yup, something like that." Richards agreed, straight faced and hard nosed.

They sat at the end of the counter on stools that were fondly referred to as the 'U-Turn' seats, (those that were placed on the curve) and were lucky enough to arrive in the middle of a lull. After the waitress brought water and took their order Richards decided to go for the gusto, just as Timmons knew he would.

"Dryer?" He asked, stirring his coffee.

"Yes, most definitely." Timmons replied, fishing around for a tissue in her purse. "Problem is, I can't be one hundred percent sure that he's the leak."

"Oh please, give me a fucking break!" Richards barked, his head cocked over to one side. "Are you kidding me? You were right there the night he gave us his suggestion for dealing with Blaze."

"He lost a good friend and a good agent…" She began to reason.

"And you lost Moss, and now my boy is recovering from a gunshot wound to his gut." Richards cut in greedily. "Which, if I'm not mistaken is the reason we all got involved with this shit in the first place."

"Hold on, please let me finish?" Timmons asked, holding up her palm indicating that she didn't want to argue. "I could have sworn I had fucking tissues in here someplace!"

"A lot of fumbled balls and feet dragging…" He exclaimed, before Timmons suddenly burst out.

"No one involved with this operation wants this punk more than I do, I can assure you." Timmons interjected. She had a stern look upon her face, and her eyes began to dance with agitation. "I have been putting up with the roadblocks, legalities and all the other bullshit surrounding Blaze and GSM for almost four years now. I didn't think this case was going to be my home!"

"Clayton told me about your fast maneuver getting him to ride as the contact. That was brilliant Deb, seriously." He mentioned softy, in an attempt to bury the hatchet.

"Thank you, I appreciate your compliment, and I didn't mean to snap at you."

"Actually, it was I who popped off first." He offered, with a genuine smile.

"I promise you, as sure as I'm sitting here, that I will find out if Dryer is the leak." She said holding up her right hand as if she were about to testify in court.

"Does it really matter? I mean, what's done is done as far as that's concerned." Richards reasoned.

"Well, he got Clayton exposed." Timmons reckoned, taking a sip of her orange juice.

"Correct me if I'm wrong, but the only civilian who could possibly know that is Darius Moore the FedEx driver, right?" He asked, raising an eyebrow.

"Well, don't forget about Ben Ladd, Micheal Cook and Jocko. Because sure as hell, they all know by now. There's one way to find out for sure while we also keep an eye on Dreyer." Timmons reasoned, as she looked over at a group of elderly folks who had ambled over to their favorite table.

"Outlaw bikers were never my specialty and I never really had any on the job run-ins with them. Everyone in the region knows who they are of course, and I've read some pretty nasty reports; I presume that they'll retaliate." He reasoned, more to himself than to her.

"George, the Sworn is known to be the second largest and most volatile motorcycle club in the country. They've been on and off our radar since the early '70s and I really wouldn't know where to begin the list of criminal activity they're known to engage in. Murder, (and not just rivals) the manufacturing of Methamphetamine, narcotics trafficking and distribution, gun running and weapons sales, not excluding C-4, and hand grenades. We even suspect that they're starting to engage in international smuggling…" Timmons explained, still holding on to the last finger she had counted on.

"They're going to hit Blaze." Richards muttered softly, folding his hands around a crumpled up napkin.

"George, the Sworn has blown up rival gang member's houses and hung people in trees for far less than shooting at one of their ex- national presidents." Timmons declared with a raised eyebrow.

"Of course, that's what they think happened." He nodded.

"Well, what would you think?" Timmons asked.

"Not to change the subject, but the doctors say that Cruz will be ready for questioning sometime next year!" Richards exclaimed sarcastically with a smile.

"Yeah, I heard old Mickey put a hurting on him." She said with a chuckle.

"He's a little more than fucked up, that's for sure." Richards agreed.

"Just say when George." Timmons winked. "Until then, we're still cleaning up surveillance from your shitty street cams and looking at drone footage."

"Deb, do me a favor would ya?" He asked, looking down at his scrambled eggs.

"What's that George?" She replied playfully.

"Pass the Tabasco, please?"

Chapter Twenty Eight

The early spring night air was cold, crisp and damp. Hoodies worn underneath their leather jackets made them appear sinister and daunting as they stood in large clusters within the glow of street lights that cast a large shadow from the ancient brick warehouse off Richmond street. Every so often the low rumble of large V-Twins could be heard approaching by those who waited patiently for their club brothers, and ultimately for KSU (kickstands up). The Sworn, Philadelphia chapter president had received the "go ahead" from the national president (due to inter-State chapters being involved) to rally and represent en masse on this night. Their target run was North East Philly with the primary destination being Blaze's residence on the 900 block of Anchor street; word had been put out that if any resistance was met then violence was guaranteed. Behind the closed and guarded door (by the Sergeant at Arms) of a private room in the Philadelphia club house, high ranking officers were discussing the means by which Blaze would be killed.

A clear and concise message had been passed along from a 'Friend' (a trusted citizen) who had connections with DEA containing information which implicated Andre' Pelts (Blaze) Darius Jones (Cruz) and Preston King (Pearl) as the principal GSM members responsible for the attempted hit on Towers. Word had also bled out from a friend at PPD, that they had Cruz under close supervision in the hospital. This source, (who's cousin had been jumped by Cruz a few years earlier) also assured the club that any information would be provided as soon as it became available. There was even a rumor going around that GSM's president, Breach had attempted to make contact with the Sworn and he himself was invited to come up to Philadelphia and stand alone in the place of his choosing with any single club member. One thing seemed certain in the minds of all who were involved, Blaze was a goner. With an estimated number of three hundred that rode in packs from New York and the Tri-state area, the message was pure and simple; no one, especially a gangbanger punk was going to get away with shooting at an ex national president and wounding a senior club member, absolutely no one.

"Brother, if The General were here, that nigger would be dangling from a rope." Stretch said, narrowing his eyes and flashing an ornery grin.

He had been the Sworn's Philadelphia chapter president for the last ten years and was the veteran of many skirmishes. At one time he and Towers had a love/hate relationship. One drunken night (while Stretch was still a soldier and attending a national rally) he learned a lesson in respect the hard way after grabbing a hold of Ben and challenging him to a one-on-one. Towers laid him out with one solid pop to his chin button and then proceeded to kick the shit out of him, breaking four of his ribs.

"I'm more than aware of how he presided, I sat many a long night with him in war room meetings, Stretch." Ben replied, as the two exchanged a secret handshake.

Even though Towers was considered retired and in good standing, any past national executive ranking officer(s) (of which there are five seats) still received the finger tap on his open palm first, before reciprocating. The five foot, ten inch tall Philadelphia president weighed approximately two hundred twenty pounds, had broad shoulders and walked like a pitbull. His shaved head and blonde, going gray goatee along with squinty light blue cowboy eyes gave him the look of a cage fighter. He bore a one percent diamond tattoo on his Adam's apple and had no neck; overall he was a human D9 bulldozer.

"And I respect that history, my brother." Stretch assured, with a sharp nod and a final firm grip. "And as you know, there ain't know way in hell that anyone takes a shot at Sworn without paying the price."

"I was put in the position of having to get payback on a few occasions." Ben reminisced.

He exhaled slowly and looked up into the darkness that was just beyond the large pine beams, suddenly the image of a cross appeared as a bike's headlight burst through a high window, casting light upon it.

"Then you know, this has to be." Stretch said softly.

Every so often a blast of throttle echoed from the street and resonated into the confines of the vast warehouse. This generation of outlaw bikers had good jobs, mortgages, credit cards and preferred to ride blacked out Road or Street Glides.

"What's up fellas?" Stretch asked after seeing Mickey and Lucy standing inside one of the large open bay doors engaged in a quiet conversation.

Ben and Mickey hadn't been waiting in the parking lot of the Advanced Auto Parts store in Kennett for more than ten minutes when they noticed Lucy's old Lincoln Town Car pull in. The pristine silver 2007 sedan slowly floated like a graceful land yacht until coming to rest in the spot next to Ben's black Sierra.

"More room in here!" Lucy suggested, inviting them to come to his car.

"Alright." Ben replied with a nod.

"I'm getting too old for this shit, Towers." He said, looking back at Ben who had chosen to sit in the rear.

"Hey Lucy, thanks for the meeting and nice hat man." Mickey mentioned, pointing at his black Philadelphia Flyers cap.

Lucius "Lucy" Mcabe, age 55 was a lifetime member and the Sworn president of New Jersey. When he was twenty two years old, The General asked him to steal a car in order for him to become a full patch member, and just minutes before his final test as a prospect was to expire Lucy showed up behind the wheel of a tractor trailer car carrier; its cargo was nine brand spanking new Mercury Marquis that had been relieved from a railhead in Delaware. Shouting, 'General' like a mad man while blasting the truck's air horn not only made him an instant member, but also a living legend. His thick, fire red hair (now turning gray) and beard almost matched the color of his Irish whiskey face, and his large happy blue eyes revealed the affection he had for his old club brothers.

"I called you as soon as I got the news that the Nation gave the green light." Lucy said softly, the smile leaving his face as he gazed into the rearview mirror at Ben.

"Thank you Lucy, I appreciate that." He replied.

"I don't have to tell you…" Lucy began to say.

"Sorry to cut you off, but they weren't gunning for me and my wife." Ben mentioned. "They might as well have been, seeing as how close we were to their target though."

"Who's the kid?" Lucy asked directly with a concerned look on his face. "Jocko thinks that maybe he knows who killed your boy."

"He's an innocent thirteen year old who got tangled up with some streetgang bullshit, because he was buddies with a gangbanger's little brother." He answered in a firm tone.

"Blaze's old lady's kid brother?" Lucy inquired, slowly turning his head towards Mickey. "Word has it, they hacked her up."

"Yeah, that's right, and he's seen more tragedy and death in his life than all of us put together." Ben assured, with a sharp nod. "Look, you know my history brother and you know the places I've been and the shit I did. Now, I'm not going to pretend that I'm some new found saint who wears a white robe and a golden halo, but I am born again. That kid is classified as 'Hands Off' understand? Between the three of us, he doesn't know anything that the law or we don't already know."

"Amen." Mickey whispered.

"Honestly brother, I give you nothing but respect for protecting him, and my love goes out to you and Lynne always. Even more so after what you two have been through." Lucy said with an agreeable tone, reaching back and offering Ben his hand.

"I'm glad to hear that brother, and I feel the same way about you." Ben stated, accepting his grip.

"Philadelphia wants Blaze dead." Mickey added, cutting right to the conversation's finale.

"You better believe it." Lucy uttered under his breath.

"We'll be there." Ben assured him, looking over at Mickey who in turn gave Lucy a broad smile.

"We are what we are." Lucy announced, patting Mickey's shoulder.

"Loyalty."

"Tell them to fire 'em up fellas, let's roll!" Stretch ordered from the open bay door.

Within seconds, shouts of 'KSU' could be heard throughout the masses of bikers who had been busy reconnecting with old friends and partying in small clusters. As if the second hand on a magical stopwatch had frozen, three hundred Harley Davidsons simultaneously blasted to life, and in an instant the world around them detonated with the sound of atomic V-Twin thunder. Ben and Mickey were invited to ride up front behind Stretch and his VP. The formation was standard for most one percent clubs worldwide and had been established after World War II. There was a small gap between each of the nine chapters that were representing this night; their highest ranking members rode up front as road captains managed the formation, and the Sergeant at Arms (the appointed enforcer who also sported a U.S. Army tomahawk) protected the rear. They rode in a double staggered formation and a few members were assigned as 'Signalmen' who rode independently, occasionally breaking away from the pack in order to stop cross traffic at busy intersections, thus allowing the club to roll through unimpeded. The Sworn stopped for no one.

"You're not going to have a lot of time brother." Mickey said, loud enough for Ben to hear.

"I know, but we have to go for it." He replied with a wink.

The massive pack did not go unnoticed as it slowly made its way north up Richmond street. Within seconds PPD dispatch was inundated with calls from units that had witnessed the Sworn cruising slowly, and the number of bikes was enough to span three city blocks. Reports also came in that all the riders were wearing black Balaclava masks and running redlights at intersections that were being blocked off; occasionally those at the front would downshift before throttling hard, launching their large V-Twins into a thunderous blur. The display of raw torque and thrust was glorified when the rest of the huge band followed suit, and after they vanished from a dark city street only their red tail lights could be seen fading off into a ghostly mirage.

They made the four mile run in just under ten minutes and immediately signalmen tore up Anchor street to the next intersection halting traffic flow. Seconds later half of the pack filled the center of Anchor street, while others slowly cruised down to the next left and entered into the back alleyway that sat behind Blaze's address. The young prospects who rode towards the rear of their chapters quickly sealed off any possible routes that could be used to enter or escape the area. Anchor street came alive with frenetic energy and the glowing lights from the big machines added a surreal ingredient to the dream-like and sublime atmosphere. A constant, ever-present muted beam from the street lights blended with those of row homes, creating an eerie strobe-like effect. Occasionally, a flash captured the glimpse of great mischief in a rider's eye.

"Woo-wee! We got a shit pile of Sworn down there on Achor!" Barron shouted, looking at the live feed coming from the surveillance camera at Clayton's cover residence.

"I was expecting that." Timmons replied, holding her phone away from the other customers who were standing in the WaWa checkout line. "Do you know if Blaze is in the house?"

"Not sure, but I'll go back and check it out now." He replied, sounding a little distracted.

"Alright, listen up, keep me posted and give me a yes or no, as to whether he's there." Timmons ordered, as she pulled the cellophane wrapper from around a pack of Newport 100's.

"You got it, boss lady."

"God dammit!" She exclaimed angrily.

"What's wrong?" Barron asked, staring into his monitor and simultaneously checking on the playback time.

"I can't find my fucking lighter again!"

Timmons took a deep breath, looked down at her contact list and pressed Richards' number. "What do you want to do?" She asked, knowing that he had already answered.

"Go fishing in the Gulf of Mexico, how about you Deb?" He replied, his little chuckle brought a smile to her face.

"Cute, but I'll take a trip to Cabo!" She joked back. "Well, I guess you know by now that the boys are back in town?"

"Yeah, I heard dispatch has gotten about a million requests for suggestions on what to do." Richards claimed, while backing his car out of a parking spot at Burger King.

"And?" Timmons asked, pulling out onto East Thompson street.

"I say we observe from the peripheral; side streets and intersections, that way we'll be close enough to respond if need be." He suggested. "Where are you now, Deb?"

"Launching a drone and heading North on Aramingo."

"You're already on the Eastside and enroute? Shame on you!" He teased in a scolding tone.

"C'mon George, you knew what was going on!" Timmons exclaimed with a hint of sarcasm. "Where are you?"

"Just leaving the Burger King off Roosevelt, about three minutes from the biker bash." Richards stated victoriously.

"Okay, I'll wait for you around the corner from the action on Cheltenham." She teased, knowing damned right well that he was way closer.

"I'll already have my people set-up, and see you there!" Richards assured her, as he sat his phone on the passenger seat, hit the strobes and put the boots to his Charger.

Ben was the first to stand on the sidewalk directly in front of Blaze's house and immediately afterwards the bikes that lined the middle of the street shut down. The ruckus trailed off to muted conversations before it became so silent that one could hear a man coughing from a half a block away. Stretch was just about to walk away from his bike and join him when a drone flew slowly up Anchor, pausing to hover over the main action. Not a single man looked up into the night sky.

"Let him be." Mickey said softly, while sitting on his Road Glide parked next to the pack leaders. "He's going to make this personal."

"I'm right here, Towers." Stretch assured him, giving Mickey a wink.

"Good Job!" Ben shouted up to the seemingly empty brick duplex. "My name is Ben Ladd, or Towers if you prefer, and I was once the president of the Sworn motorcycle club. I'm also the guy you took a shot at, as I walked with my wife down the sidewalk!"

Ben turned, faced the Sworn and briefly raised his arms in the air while nodding his head. He could always conjure up emotion through his past experiences and in doing so was able to evoke the passions of those around him. The General himself once told Ben in private that he had never seen anyone who possessed such a natural flair or had this kind of talent. The reaction from the men was just what Ben was hoping for, both approval and unity.

"Preach it brother!" Mickey called out with a sharp clap.

"I'd like to be the first one to congratulate you on being the absolute worst gang leader that I've ever seen in my life. I mean honestly man, you suck!" He yelled. His sarcasm could not be mistaken, and those standing close by roared laughter.

"And to think that all of this started the morning you murdered my son, Joshua Ladd!" Ben vehemently shouted aloud. "That's right! You get a friend of yours killed and then your punk ass runs up on my kid, who's on his way to work by the way, and you shoot him because you want to get away?! An innocent nineteen year old lost his life because you can't handle your business!?"

Just then the neighbor's door cracked ajar and immediately Stretch had his model 640 Smith & Wesson pulled from his concealed holster.

"It's an old woman." The Philadelphia VP said out of the corner of his mouth.

"Please, don't shoot." Ms. Styles pleaded. She was holding up a shaking hand which brought pain to Ben's heart.

"Put that away." He grumbled over to Stretch.

"You're not goin' in there to get him are ya?" The old woman asked with a frail voice and pleading eyes.

"If it comes to that…" Stretch replied, walking closer to her side of the duplex.

"Now hold on a second." Ben cut in, trying as much as possible under the circumstances to be the voice of reason. "No, we're not going to kick his door in and drag him out into the street."

"Well, what are you going to do then?" Ms. Styles asked, nodding in the direction of the cluster of police units that blocked off the nearest intersection. "Because by now son, the whole town knows what's goin' on, up in here."

Ben and those standing closest to the row home stepped out onto Anchor street and momentarily glanced at the cruisers.

"Up there too, Towers." Mickey stated, pointing towards the opposite end of the block.

Ben followed his que, narrowed his eyes and made out about a half dozen cruisers and motor units sitting at the furthest intersection.

"A drone is over the house too!" A Sworn member called out while pointing into the darkness above.

"Shit!" Stretch shouted with frustration.

"What did you think was going to happen? I mean, we got like what, a thousand bikes out here?" Mickey asked.

Stretch's eye's narrowed on him, and Ben, who was saving the best for last, seized the moment to not only defuse Stretch's anger, but also to begin the closing scene of the rally. He slowly walked up Blaze's steps and approached the front door.

"Tower's, he could shoot you through the door, brother!" Stretch warned, reaching for thin air, beckoning him to be careful..

"He doesn't have the balls!" Ben exclaimed, turning around to see the awe and respect on the men's faces. "Blaze, I got more dirt on you than a five dollar whore's got customers. You killed my kid and then you took a shot at me?!"

Ben was giving the performance of a lifetime, and in a bizarre way it also felt therapeutic. He knew to watch out for his ego rearing its ugly head and vainglory justifying the means to an end. Under his breath he prayed for the Lord's strength and forgiveness for what he was about to say.

"Who's the ranking officer here, corporal?" Richards asked the young cop who was slouched by his unit.

"Sergeant Rhoades, sir." He replied, standing up sharply.

"Call him in for me, please."

"Yes, sir." The officer responded, reaching for his hand unit that was clipped to his vest.

"Good evening, George!" Timmons exclaimed, opening her driver's side window.

"Deb, over there!" Richards cried out, pointing to a narrow spot across the street from where he was standing on East Cheltenham.

She gave him a thumbs up and nosed her nondescript white Ford Explorer into the suggested space. It wasn't until after she had shut the door and walked towards Richards that she noticed most of the rear of her car was out in the street.

"Fuck it!" He shouted over to her with a wave off.

"By the looks of things, no one's going through here for a while anyway!" She responded, pointing over to a senior officer.

"Good job sergeant." Richards said, giving his approval and offering him a handshake. "I'm Detective Richards with Division, and this is Agent Timmons, FBI."

"Sir, Ma'am. This is the best I could do under such a short notice." Rhoades replied, turning away from the conversation momentarily and looking in the direction of the situation.

"It's a cluster fuck." Timmons said under her breath.

"Yes, it is ma'am." The sergeant agreed.

"Hang on just a moment please." She excused herself, and walked out of earshot.

"Yes, Barron?" Timmons asked.

"Drone sees guns and Magpie confirms, the action is getting closer to the front row." The young tech reported.

"Okay, thank you and running a route now." She responded, hanging up before anything else could be said. Baron was a good kid but a tad too dramatic at times.

"Bird saw a gun and the party's getting a little rowdier." Timmons said to Richards while looking at the senior officer. This was an old technique that one learned at Quantico; it made all present feel valued and included. The FBI stressed manners and professionalism on every level of protocol.

"What in the hell are you doing, George?" She asked, in disbelief.

He had surprisingly walked away from their little huddle, popped his trunk and grabbed a bullhorn. "I'm taking a little stroll down Anchor street Deb, this here is my turf." He answered, taking off his body armor and necktie.

"Sir, I've worked a few Sworn calls. They are known to be the most violent and unpredictable motorcycle club in the country." The sergeant warned, straight faced. "And they really dig this shit."

"Understood sergeant, but I have a very straightforward solution that will make everyone involved very happy." Richards replied, walking toward Anchor street.

"Hold on cowboy!" Timmons called out excitedly. "You can't just leave a girl stranded on her first date!"

"Blaze!" Ben shouted loudly, his powerful and commanding voice echoed off down the block, as neighbors came out from their homes to listen.

"A leader, leads from the front by example. A leader earns respect from his men and surrounds himself with honorable and trustworthy people. A leader demands the best from his soldiers and doesn't prey upon them. A leader delights in the sacred bond of loyalty and brotherhood. A leader embodies all the things that his club stands for, and would rather die than break the oath that he has sworn to uphold and live by!"

Ben then turned around to face the club again and was surprised to see that many were standing with awestruck expressions and watery eyes.

"I love you, my brothers!" He cried out, looking up into the dark sky.

"Love you, Towers!" The crowd answered in unison.

"Preach it, brother!" Mickey added, coaxing him on once more.

"A loser hides while getting others to do his bidding. A loser tries to lead through lies and deceit. A loser manipulates his people and kills them. A narcissistic, sociopath such as yourself, makes up rules to satisfy their needs and changes the rules as they go along, because they can't live by the code; a coward sheds blood for sport!" Ben took a deep breath and knocked loudly on Blaze's front door.

"I can assure you that there is a hell you piece of shit, and as God is my witness I'm going to make sure you get there!" Ben finished his reprimand with an explosive punch that split Blaze's front door, from top to bottom.

The Sworn cheered and those standing in front of their houses called out for more. The fervor and excitement was elevated to a level that one would experience at a huge rock concert or a mega church revival. All eyes were on Ben Ladd, and many clapped and waved their flashlights.

"Andre' Pelts, this is Detective Richards, Philadelphia Police Department and with me is Special Agent Timmons, FBI. Come out of the house with your hands in the air now!" Richards barked into the bullhorn from across the street.

The two had managed to walk up Anchor street cloaked by Ben's legendary respected stature and captivating address. Everyone present was abruptly awakened from their hypnotic trance upon hearing Richard's orders and turned around.

"If you refuse to exit the premises, Timmons and I will leave! Those cop cars out there will do the same, and then you will be fucked!" He warned, waiving his open hand out to the bikers as if introducing the worst option.

"Oh, he's dead serious." Timmons said, just loud enough for her claim to resonate through the horn.

"Blaze, straight up! I ain't shittin you, this is the best community relations deal you're ever going to get in your life boy! Come with us now or they'll take you apart!" He guaranteed, pointing his finger at the club, who responded with a roar of approval.

"I want him first!" A young biker exclaimed.

Chapter Twenty Nine

After Blaze was cuffed and led away, Ben unexpectedly walked to his bike, threw one leg over the seat and fired it up. "Let me out!" He shouted over the booming exhaust note of his straight shot pipes.

The long line of machines that blocked him in slowly rolled back and parted away from the others that were backed against the curb. A clear passage was made down the entire length of Anchor, and after Ben turned left onto Horrocks street he noticed Timmons, Richards and Blaze walking towards the police barrier that had been set up on East Cheltenham avenue. For a split second he thought about hooking a right and riding off in the other direction but Ben Ladd wasn't through with Blaze yet. He dumped the Road King down into first, popped the clutch and gunned the bike directly at a small opening between the barriers. Making it through with just inches to spare he pulled in the clutch lever, leaned hard and stomped on the rear brake. The nine hundred pound machine immediately quivered as the rear tire shuddered and squealed across the black top in an attempt to find grip. Ben managed to land it exactly where he was aiming, which was directly in front of the target of his anger.

"Ben!" Timmons called out.

"Ben Ladd!" Richards also shouted, holding up an index finger of warning.

Richards yoked Blaze's cuffs and shoved him behind Timmons and against his unmarked Charger. The young gangbanger cowered behind the two as they stood in front of him, and all three had the look of fear and disbelief upon their wide eyed faces. Three or four uniformed officers tore into a run from across the street but after seeing Ben's intentions, Richards held them back.

"You're a better man these days Ben!" Timmons exclaimed.

"Let me see him!" He demanded, shutting off his bike.

Richards grabbed ahold of Blaze's hoodie and yoked him around to face the angry man..

"Look at me, boy!" Ben commanded, with a bellowing roar. "I want you to see the pain and the desire for vengeance in my eyes!"

Timmons gripped Blaze's shoulder and pulled hard on his handcuffs causing him to let out a high pitched shriek. "The man asked you to look at him!" She exclaimed.

"I know you killed my son, and I want you to know that if I had my way, I'd be introducing you to Jesus right now!" Ben shouted, his eyes beginning to fill with tears. "When your end comes, and you walk through that door, you'll have to answer for what you did!"

"Amen." Richards whispered.

Ben headed East until coming to Frankford avenue, where he hooked a right and blasted South towards Kennsington. He occasionally saw a cop car out of his peripheral vision but didn't pay much mind as to whether they were tracking him or if they just happened to be cruising. Looking down at his Iphone which was mounted to the handlebars, he could see the red dot in the center of the GPS app, which had Jelly's address as its destination. Time was of the essence as traffic and pedestrian activity was sure to play a factor in determining the success of his mission.

One of the first lessons learned while engaging in a raid is to get in and get out as quickly as possible, the second is don't get caught, and most importantly, if at all possible, have the front door key. He bumped the shifter into neutral and hit the kill switch to the ignition, allowing him to glide silently against the curb in front of Jelly's. After getting off his bike and grabbing ahold of the rabbit's foot keychain, Ben stepped into the shadow of the front porch. Keeping his head low and eyes forward he then slid the key into the old lock, and with one swift motion opened the door and disappeared into the small row home.

"Are you in here?" He whispered, just loud enough for a potential squatter without any sense to answer back.

Ben was sure that the place was empty and as his eyes adjusted to the darkness he made his way to the couch. While narrowing his gaze he quickly shifted the piece of furniture away from the wall and reached down to wipe his hand gently over the aged and peeled baseboard. Ben discovered the section that could be removed and was thoroughly impressed by the thirteen year old's craftwork and after pulling the board away noticed that a part of the plaster and lath had also been carved out as well. There it sat, as plain as the nose on one's face, the folded Ziploc freezer bag which contained the gun that killed his son.

"We're bringing you a special news report live from our NBC SkyForce10 which is currently over the scene of a police standoff taking place within the 600 block of Anchor street, in the city's North section." The reporter's voice announced into the radio headset.

He sounded synthesized and a slight high pitched buzzing noise bled through the radio transmission which was synchronized with the chopper's twin jet turbines. "We don't really have too many details for you at this time. Eyewitness accounts from neighbors that live in the area said that at approximately 10:00 p.m., calls came into Philadelphia police dispatch reporting that a large number of motorcycles had converged on and around Anchor street. It was soon discovered that they were members of the notorious Sworn motorcycle club, and that they had closed off the area. As you can see below us, police have set up barriers at the intersection of East Cheltenham avenue, and just moments ago two plain clothes officers led a handcuffed black male away from the scene. There's still about two hundred motorcycles parked on Anchor, and the alley that runs behind it."

"Does the area appear to be secure and under control?" Rosemary Connors, the attractive Emmy award winning weekend news anchor, asked from the studio.

"It does Rosemary. Oh wait, hold on a second…" The young reporter sitting in the left seat announced. "A biker just hooked a left onto Horrocks street and barely made it through the police barriers at the intersection of Cheltenham. There seems to be some words being exchanged but what's going on down there is anyone's guess."

Breach was holding a good hand, he took a slow sip of Maker's Mark and looked down at the ten of diamonds and the deuce of hearts that was showing. Just after he pushed another fifty dollar chip forward and tapped the felt at Bally's, Buttons tapped him on the shoulder. He turned his head slightly and noticed that a very large plain-clothed casino security officer was giving the dealer a gesture, indicating that the interruption was permitted.

"Your cuz, up in Philly." Buttons whispered, keeping his eye on the Blackjack dealer.

"Bad?" Breach asked out of the side of his mouth.

"Cops hauled his ass off about half an hour ago and the FBI was there too." Button's tone reached a higher pitch which guaranteed the severity of the situation.

"Damned." Breach growled under his breath. "Alright, go get the fucking car. I gotta cash out and call my nigga Booker the lawyer man."

"I'll be out front, boss." Buttons promised.

"Two babies." Tmmons said sarcastically.

They were standing in a dark observation room and looking up at the monitors, each of which featured a young individual who had unknowingly but voluntarily thrown his life away. Blaze and Pearl sat alone expressionless and intentionally looked away from the impassive lens of the camera's that were mounted high in the corner of both interrogation rooms.

"Do you have anyone onboard tonight who specializes in hardball?" She asked, keeping her attention on Blaze.

"Deb?" Richards replied, not understanding her question.

"C'mon George, look at these fucking kids. Do you really think that they're just going to roll out the information wagon?" Timmons tapped on the monitor that featured Blaze. "That punk right there is a psycho killer with a smile."

"Yeah, I've come across a few bad boys in my day but…"

"Murdering an innocent kid, hacking up a teenage girl and killing two federal agents takes the cake, huh?" She quipped, giving him a nod.

"Yes, it does." His tired and exasperated voice could not be mistaken for anything less than weariness.

"What the hell happened to this country, George?" Timmons asked, narrowing her gaze on the monitor that showed a relaxed looking Pearl.

"Babies having babies, and the music went to hell." He replied, taking off his brown and copper pinstripe Evan Picone suit jacket. "Oh and style, these kids have no fashion sense at all."

"Sir?" A young and very large black sergeant asked after knocking on the observation room door.

"Yeah, Darren?" Richards answered over his shoulder.

"There's a Booker J. Cleveland out here, says he's here to represent the 'hood rats." Darren explained, thumbing over his shoulder.

"We expected that, go ahead and let him in to see Pearl." Richards said, giving Timmons a wink before opening the door for her.

"Picking the low hanging fruit first, George?" She asked, stopping in front of him before exiting the room.

He could smell her natural essence that was blended with the Portofino '97 that she had misted on her neck and wrists earlier in the evening, and immediately became aroused. Debra was a tad taller, had dark eyes and her natural olive complexion gave her the appearance of a woman who could be both sensuous and dangerous.

"Let's just pick em off easy, Deb." Richards said under his breath, and just for an instant he noticed her pupils dilate before she broke off her gaze.

"Easy sounds good, George." She agreed, walking out into the brightly lit hallway.

"Darren, can you please go and remind Andre' Pelts that he is not at his mama's?" Richards asked with a wink.

"Sure thing." He replied, heading directly to the interrogation room.

"Put your Goddamned feet down boy, this ain't your mama's living room!" Darren's voice boomed from down the hallway.

Booker looked up from the table that he was seated at with Pearl, and for a moment thought about interjecting but after seeing the incredible size of the sergeant and the severe expressions upon all of the personnel that were present, he changed his mind.

"He'll be fine, Booker." Richards assured, while holding the door open for Timmons and extending his right hand. "My Name is Detective George Richards, and this lady here with me is Agent Timmons, FBI."

Booker Julius Cleavland, aka 'Bubba the defender man' was a portly jovial fellow who sported a haircut similar to that of his proverbial study mentor Don King, unfortunately he also had the behind the scenes reputation to match. Booker was a slick customer, fast with a pat on the back, a broad grin and a loose wallet. There was a time when dreams of politics knocked on his door but with the seasons of change from the slight of hand maneuvering (and strong arm robbery) that once won (and where a prerequisite) Philadelphia's elected positions, to the popularity game show contest of today, he changed his mind and embraced the decision of holding a license to steal. One didn't stand a chance in the city's political arena (in this era) if they followed the playbook of former mayor, John F. Street and his friend and fundraiser Ron White. However, if you handed out jobs to your constituents and paid them with funneled money from proposed social reform programs, well heck, you were a-okay.

Booker's choice of fashion was that of an old school New Orleans funeral director and he favored shiny silver or gray metallic double breasted suits with bright violet or purple button down dress shirts (that he had custom made and fitted) and thick knotted colorful neckties. He always had a monogrammed handkerchief that was strategically on display in his jacket breast pocket and in the lapel's button slit he wore a small white plastic orchid.

"I'm Booker J. Cleavland, but you can call me Bubba!" He introduced himself with a wide smile and a quick wink.

"How are you tonight, Pearl?" Timmons asked, as if she were speaking to a child. "Oh, I'm so sorry Booker, I didn't mean to be rude. My name's Deb, and it's a pleasure to meet you."

"I can tell by the look on your face that you remember me from the morning we had you hemmed up down on Fitzwater." Richards suggested, using his best street slang. He was giving Pearl an obvious social que to be civil. "Preston King, do you know why you're here this evening?" He asked in a low tone, this time addressing him by his real name.

"Nope." Pearl answered flatly.

"Oh really?" Richards replied with sarcasm. "Then I suppose you also don't remember what happened right after we let you go?"

"Naw, all I know is that you had me out of my girl's whip and then you went through my shit…" The gangbanger answered with a grin. "…and took some pictures." He added, looking at Booker.

"I'm a little confused here Richards, what's the relevance of a stop and go (pulling someone over and allowing them to leave) and something that occurred after the fact, a few blocks away to boot? And, what's that piece about taking photographs?" Booker wanted to know, unfolding his hands that were resting in front of him.

"Relevance, Booker? Timmons asked, with a 'are you serious?' expression.

"Deb." Richards said under his breath. This was his first gesture to the opening act of 'Good cop, Bad cop' and it was intended to give fair warning that the woman from FBI was about to get down to brass tacks.

"No George, let me explain something to this little brat here." She exclaimed, pointing across the table at Pearl. "I'm not going to sit here and listen to your nope's, maybe's and I don't know's and I'm sure as hell not going to put up with any of your junior varsity gangster bullshit. Do you understand me?"

"Now Ms. Timmons!" Booker warned, looking over his glasses.

"I'm going to be very clear about this Pearl." Timmons said, with a stern voice. "It's really simple, so pay attention. There are two federal agents, a teenage girl and another nineteen year old male dead because of that piece of shit sitting down the hallway." She reached down and opened up her briefcase and placed the post-mortem photos of Moss and Trainer (Cleats) on the table in front of him.

"This is Blaze's girlfriend Trina Brooks, and this is the young man, Joshua Ladd who was murdered while on his way to work. Remember the attempted carjacking on Kensington right after Agent Trainer was shot?" Richards asked, looking up at Pearl and placing the photos of Trina and Joshua next to the other two. He was hoping that they would get to this part of the questioning by using a more standard methodical approach, but the preverbal jack in the box had sprung. Pearl's mouth dropped and his eyes fixated on the photo of a dead GSM gang member known as Cleats.

"Cleats?" He whispered.

"That's right son, his real name was Dwayne Trainer and he was an undercover agent with the DEA, and he also had two small boys at home." Timmons stated, tapping her blood red nail polished index finger on the glossy black and white.

"I'm still disillusioned, folks." Booker said, removing his glasses and leaning back in his chair to stretch his legs. "Weren't we just talking about my client being pulled over on Fitzwater?"

"An undercover Philly cop took one in the gut and an old Sworn member got his shoulder blown off because Cruz and Junior opened up on them, down the street from where you were." Richards said, studying Pearl's eyes and looking for the slightest hint that he may be concealing something.

"What?!" Pearl scoffed. "I wasn't with them when that shit went down!"

"They're GSM Pearl, they're your boys, well one of them was but he's dead, as I'm sure your aware." Timmons claimed, posing the obvious correlation of their relationship.

"Circumstantial." Booker mentioned, looking up at the old paint that was peeling from where the wall met the ceiling.

"No it's not, you know how I know it's not?" Richards asked, leaning in closer with a narrowed stare. "Because the target that day wasn't the cop or the old biker, it was a thirteen year old kid that was meeting up with Joshua Ladd's parents."

"That's correct, they actually met at a prayer vigil that was being held for Joshua and the three of them decided to meet up for pizza at Angie's." Timmons added. She uncrossed her long legs and gave him a sideways glance. "Do you know who Joshua's dad is, Pearl?"

"No, I never heard of him." He replied, looking up from the photo of Cleats.

"Benjamin Ladd, aka Towers, is an ex national president of the Sworn motorcycle club. So maybe now you can understand why there's a thousand of them over at Blaze's house right now. They actually think that you guys tried to kill him that day on Fitzwater, if you can imagine that! As it turns out, they also know that you were there too!" Timmons cocked her head to one side and waited to see if Pearl would bite.

"Whoa, wait a second, I don't know nothin' about a Ben or whatever his name is, and I sure as hell don't know nothin' about the damned Sworn motorcycle club!" He exclaimed, pushing the photos away from him.

"Well, they're not considered a one percent club because they sing in a church choir!" She assured, mocking him with a smartass smirk.

"And just as important, do you know who the thirteen year old is?" Richards inquired, raising his eyebrows.

Pearl shook his head as if he were trying to process everything that he had just heard and looked down at the floor.

"I give up, who?" Booker asked for his client, lifting up his hands in mock disbelief.

"He's best friends with Trina's baby brother." Timmons stated flatly. "And he was around Blaze and GSM all the time, Pearl."

"Yo, wait a damned minute! I don't know nothin' about these motherfuckers gettin' killed, ya feel me?!" Pearl's voice cracked with fear and excitement.

"Oh I feel ya, I just don't feel ya, feel ya!" Richards shouted back.

"Kinda makes it look like you're in the know so to speak, do you realize that makes you an accessory?" Timmons explained with a wink.

"Is there anything you want to tell us about your superhero boss now, Blaze?" Richards asked as he reached across the table and picked up the photo of Trina. "She could've been anyone's sister or daughter."

"I call bullshit." Booker hissed, putting his arm around Pearl's shoulder.

"Who told you to sit on Fitzwater that morning Pearl?!" Richard's finger jabbed hard on the metal table.

"I was talking to my girl!" He howled. "I was just on the damned phone!"

"You know what I think, Blaze? I think that thirteen year old kid has some serious dirt on you homie!" Richards announced, following Booker and Timmons into the interrogation room.

"What the fuck you talking old man?" He shot back with a snort. "Nigga, please!"

"Watch your tongue." Booker said out of the side of his mouth. "No need to be ignorant."

"How long have you been living here in Philly, Andre'?" Timmons asked, sliding her chair closer to the table and resting her chin in the palm of her hand.

"Long enough." Blaze curtly replied.

"Andre' Pelts, born in the District of Columbia, April 10th. 2003. Father is the owner of 'Office Brite' a small janitorial service company, he's also a small time numbers and bookie man and was once a member of the now defunct gang, YBM. (Young Black Mafia). Mom is the secretary at the Nineteenth Street Baptist Church, and is an active member of

Prison Fellowship. She got the calling shortly after her oldest son Lemont was murdered at FCI Beckley during a prison riot. He was serving a six year sentence for armed robbery which was pled down from ten, because he was a fucking rat." Richards announced with a hint of sarcasm.

"Fuck you, Richards!" Blaze shouted, barely managing his emotions.

"Your point?" Booker asked, shrugging his shoulders.

"I'll get to my point in just a minute, counselor but right now what I'd really like to know is how a good christian woman, such as your mama, ended up with two losers for sons."

"Do you know any of these people, Blaze?" Timmins inquired, sliding the postmortem photos gently across the table. "Well go on, look at them!" She exclaimed.

"I see em." He grumbled, slowly looking down at them.

"And?" Richards asked, unfolding his hands and raising them up into the air. "What the fuck, we aint asking you to pick out a date, Blaze!"

"I know them, you know that Richards." He replied directly. "What do you want me to say next, that I killed them?"

No one noticed that Agent Timmons had a micro earpiece inserted into her left ear canal and what she was hearing from Barron was unbelievable.

"He's either really, really good or he's a sociopath with a split personality." He whispered into his mic. "I mean his pulse hasn't gone up above seventy per minute, he's not venting off any body heat, and more importantly he's making direct eye contact."

Just prior to the interview Timmons asked Barron what the possibility was of him tapping into the Division's digital surveillance and interrogation camera systems, to which he replied, "I'll do better than that, step out to your car in ten minutes for a cigarette."

"Whatcha got kiddo?" She asked him, while fumbling for her lighter.

Barron opened up his hand to reveal a small pinrose brooch. "This oughta do the job." He said softly, gazing down at it with a smile.

"Honey, you're cute but I'm married." She replied, razzing him with a tug of his elbow.

"Very funny, boss!" Barron exclaimed with a blush. "No, it's a micro digital thermo seeking remote camera. It has similar optics as a military grade TIC (Thermal Imaging Camera) but it's way more sensitive and can detect minute differences in body temperature."

"Operational range?" Timmons asked, removing the brooch gently from his palm.

"The moon if you got WiFi there." Barron answered, letting out a chuckle.

"Seriously?" She wanted to know, spinning the pinrose in her fingers. "How the hell did you..?"

"Look, it's no secret that I'm no social butterfly, this is what I do." He explained, nodding at the brooch. "And an old frat buddy of mine works at Langley."

"Tradecraft." She stated, giving him a wink.

"Yeah, and a lot of Star Trek conventions and expos." Barron admitted, pinning the brooch to her left lapel. "Stick this in your ear canal as far as you can."

Timmons took the tiny cone shaped earpiece and using her index finger pushed it into her left ear. "Got it, now talk to me when I get to the door. If I hear you clearly, I'll wave back to you."

"Run your fingers through your hair if his pupils are dilated." Barron instructed, his voice came through Timmon's earpiece crystal clear. "I can't get in that tight."

"No dilation?" He whispered. "Yeah we got one, he's definitely a savvy sociopath."

Richards decided to cut to the chase and decided to roll the dice; he wanted to see if he could catch him out. His metal chair screeched against the tile floor as he suddenly slid it back and stood up, before placing his open fingers on the two photos of Shey and Cleats.

"When did you find out that Cleats was an undercover agent?" Richards asked, narrowing his gaze.

"I didn't." Blaze replied, the corners of his lips curling up as if he were taunting him.

"I see, and I suppose you want me to believe that he got shot up in your car because of a bad drug deal?" Richards questioned, with a look of disbelief.

"First of all, it wasn't my car and secondly, word has it that Marcus was the one who shot Cleats. Of course, you can't bring him in for questioning because ya'll killed him, ain't that right Richards?" Blaze's dialogue was pointed and curt.

"Word has it?" Timmons asked. A look of disgust came over her and her eyes narrowed like that of a killer.

"It's a black thing, obviously you wouldn't get it." He answered, raising his chin to show his bravado.

"Your a fucking idiot." She hissed, raising her right hand to ward off any further repugnancy.

"Whoa, hang on a second!" Booker shouted, sliding his chair back as if he were getting ready to rumble.

"You killed two federal agents and two innocent teenagers, and you're going to just sit there and pretend in your psycho mind that all this is going to just vanish?" Timmons shouted, her voice had the shrill and passion of a woman scorned.

"Yeah, I heard they was undercover, it must be a dangerous job, huh?" Blaze shot back, folding his arms and nodding his head.

"Can I see you two outside please?" Booker asked, looking across the table at both Richards and Timmons. "Please?" He asked again softly.

"Look, with all due respect, all I've been hearing is accusatory baiting coming from both of you. Please believe me when I say this, if there was a shred of evidence that led to his involvement in these killings, I'd sign on the line and wear a wire myself, that's the God's honest truth." Booker declared straight faced and unblinking. "You don't have anything Richards, you have nothing."

Richards looked at Deb as if seeking moral support and allegiance. He knew of course that Booker was right and he could tell by the look on Timmon's face that she also was disillusioned and exasperated.

"His blood wasn't found in Cleat's car the morning of the alleged shootings that killed Cleats and Ladd." Brooks adjusted his glasses and continued. "No one gets shot in a car and doesn't leave any blood Richards, you know that!"

"That's not entirely true, if Blaze was in the process of exiting the vehicle…" Deb suggested before Booker cut her off at the knees.

"Yeeeeeeah, okay!" Booker exclaimed with mock excitement. "Good luck with that, add one more raindrop of speculation to the lake of mistrial."

"And by the way, another huge hurdle that comes to mind is, if Agent Trainer, aka Cleats was undercover, in an assigned DEA vehicle why wouldn't the tape have been rolling recording all this shit?" Brooks inquired, raising an eyebrow.

"We're still waiting on that." Timmons answered, looking down at the floor.

"And still waiting on a positive ID match of Blaze, from Joshua Ladd's coworker?" Brooks asked with a solemn look. "C'mon man. The only place this would go if it hit the DA's desk is in the trash and we all know it."

The black 2024 Mercedes-Benz S-Class Maybach slowly cruised up Whitaker avenue. Its long seductive and sinister body reflected the overhead street lights that gradually floated over and its sexy skin. The dark tinted windows and blacked out AMG wheels added a menacing touch to its wickedness.

"Yo, over there." Breach instructed Buttons.

"I see him B." His lieutenant replied, looking back at his boss through the rearview mirror.

"Let's him get up to the corner." Breach ordered. He was telling his man, of course, that they had to wait until Pearl had walked far enough away from the division in order to make contact.

Breach reached into the small cooler bag and pulled out two, 22 ounce Heineken bottles. "You want one my brother?" He asked, flashing a sly grin.

"Fuck no! You ain't giving me my last ripple!" Buttons protested, with a chuckle. "Besides, I'm a Stella man. You know that."

"Okay, let's roll up on him." Breach said, clinking the two green bottles together.

"Thirsty?" Breach asked, holding the beers out of the rear window.

"Breach, what the hell?" Pearl asked nervously, squinting to get a better look inside the Maybach.

"Yeah boy, we gonna celebrate! Booker called me and said they aint got nothin' on you and Blaze. Absolutely, nothin'!" He explained, the excitement in his voice could not be mistaken for anything less than jubilation.

"What? For real? Booker?" The young gangbanger asked innocently.

"Now who the fuck do you think called the lawyer man?" Breach assured him with a wink. "C'mon man! I've known that nigga since I was in gradeschool, he's an old friend of my dad's."

"Oh, snap!" Pearl replied, using the classic street slang word which means, 'Wow.'

"Pearl, nobody says snap no more!" Buttons shouted, stirring up a round of laughter.

"Well c'mon, get your ass in here, we wide open!" Breach strongly suggested, thumbing back at division headquarters. "We gonna initiate you into management, I'm making you a lieutenant son!"

"I'm down." Was the last thing Pearl said before getting into the back of the Maybach.

Ascension of Our Lord Church sat on Hunting Park avenue in the heart of Kensington, its once glorious high arched cut granite Romanesque Revival structure now sat abandoned and desolate. The church was once a beacon of hope and a sanctuary for the faithful. It was a place of love and family unity, a place of peace and contentment for the working class who battled life's daily struggles. A half hour before their arrival, Breach ordered a few of his personal crew from DC to clear out the homeless junkies that squatted and sought shelter from the dangerous Kensington nights; those that now came to the temple of the vampire, to draw their own blood and feed off of heroin.

"Place is creepy." Pearl whispered, as the three entered into the main vestibule.

"Yeah, it's a creep show but this is gonna be your new home, Mr. Lieutenant." Breach replied, giving him an assuring nod.

"This is a good spot, what do you think, Buttons?" He asked.

"I like it, boss." Buttons agreed, pointing to the broken water soaked Bishop's pew.

"Okay Pearl, I need you to look into my eyes and repeat after me." Breach instructed.

"Bet, that." He replied, with a smile.

"Rule number one, don't ever talk to the Popo." His president dictated with a stern look. "Go ahead, B." Breach ordered, while keeping his eyes on Pearl.

"Now wait!" Pearl pleaded, seeing Buttons raise his Colt MK IV.

"No one tells you when you get involved with shit, that death is just a heartbeat away." Was the last thing Pearl heard, before seeing the flash of light.

Chapter Thirty

"You're up early honey, you're feeling better huh?" Alicia asked, touching his shoulder.

He was sitting at the kitchen table drinking coffee and reading the Philadelphia Inquirer online.

"I feel great, and I can't believe how well this thing has healed up." He replied, lifting up his t-shirt so his wife could get a better look.

"Chris, I've been cleaning and putting Betadine on it for two and a half months." She remarked smartly, slapping his tummy. "Been seeing that belly getting fatter by the day too!"

"Girl!" Chris played. "I'm still fast enough to catch that ass!" He exclaimed, reaching out for her.

"I let you catch me, Chris!" She teased with a girlish smile.

Clayton's alert for his text message sounded, and after looking down at the phone's screen he immediately picked it up and replied.

'Hey Jelly, how have you been man? I've been thinking about you too!' He texted.

'I'm still at Ben and Lynne's, it's all good but I can't stop thinking about what happened to you. It's all my fault Clay!'

'No it's not, you know the score, and you also know how hard everyone's been working to get that asshole! Now stop with the self guilt trip young man!' Clayton ordered, keying with a frown.

Alicia walked over and sat down next to her husband, he had just read Jelly's last entry and had to put his fist up to his mouth in order to keep himself from choking up.

'I love you, Clay.'

Chris looked up and wiped his wet eyes before turning the phone towards Alicia, so she could read what the boy wrote.

"Bless his little heart." She said, rubbing Chris's forearm. "That boy loves you honey."

"I know he does, and I love him too." He replied, nodding his head and forcing a smile through his sadness. "He's really different, Alicia, you know? I mean he's from the same 'hood as me and knows all the tricks, but he's way smarter than I was at that age."

"He's a special kid alright." She agreed.

'I love you too son, and don't you ever forget that we have a pact!' Clayton answered, narrowing his gaze as his mind wandered off in the direction of seeking vengeance. 'I will get down there to see you. I promise!'

'I can't wait to see you Clay, and give Alicia and Corey my best.'

'Okay, now don't forget we're still in blackout mode, so be cool.' Clayton reminded him.

'I get it, just checking in on you, ya grumpy old fart! lol.'

After hearing a loud crash coming from the living room (due to their son Corey pulling on the small tablecloth that sat underneath her Spider plant) Alicia glanced at Chris and smiled.

"Your son's playing one of his favorite daytime games, I call it driving mommy crazy!"

"Why is it, when he's bad, he's my son?" He asked, while rereading Jelly's text.

"Because I said so…" She replied, before the child squealed ear piercing laughter and the cat screeched hell in protest.

"Corey, you're in big trouble little man!" Alicia warned, getting up from the table and grabbing a hand towel.

The last thing Chris heard the toddler yell before getting spanked was, "No!" Then his phone rang.

"We need to see you Chris, can you meet up?" Richards asked, looking over at Timmons who was digging around in her purse for a lighter.

"Yeah, I need to get some clothes on first, and fill Alicia in." He answered, craning his head around in order to get a better look at the action that had been picked up and carried down the hallway.

"Okay, we'll be in my car at the American Airlines curbside drop off, call me when you're leaving your place." Richards directed.

"Out front, down the end?" Chris inquired, his voice sounding a little skeptical.

"Yup, right out front brother." Richards said passively, assuring Chris that the location was a good one.

"I've done this before…" Chris said under his breath while waiting for the redlight to change.

He and his spotter had been dropped into a remote region about a hundred and fifty miles Northeast of Kandahar to monitor and kill (if necessary) Taliban arms smugglers. CIA satellite images along with Army Intel sources on the ground had confirmed that the route was being used to transport weapons into the Southern region of Afghanistan to attack and terrorize the civilian population; It was the Taliban's savage way of saying: "Stay away from the Americans."

The blacked out C-130 came in low hugging the mountain ridge and as the rear deck came down a gush of cold night air blew through the fuselage's interior.

"God damned we're close Chris!" Jonsie, his spotter shouted over the four Allison T56 turboprop engines.

"Skimming!" Chris yelled back, shaking his head in disbelief.

"I can get you guys about two hundred feet off the deck, but that's about it unless you want to hike back up this bitch!" The pilot announced over the intercom.

Chris looked at Jones and they both instinctively gave the Loadmaster a thumbs up.

"Alright it's a go." The Airman barked into his mouth piece.

"About twenty seconds gentlemen and happy hunting!" The pilot called out again.

The two men and their gear bags hit the slope of the hill hard and were immediately thrown to their sides. Chris dug his left boot heel into the loose rock in an attempt to slow his downward slide, it caught momentarily until the deep layer of gravel gave way and his clumsy butt ride continued for another thirty yards. After switching on the SatNav and dedicated radio they called command to get a precise location of where they were.

"Superhero, Superhero, this is Hammerhead looking for the time. Over." Clayton said softly into his mouthpiece.

"Hammerhead this is Superhero, you're coming in hot and you need to shift a half click (1640 feet) West along the ridge. Over." A young officer's voice answered.

"Roger that, half a click West. Will tag when we're in position. Over."

"Okay, time out at 02:10. Over and out." Command responded.

"Over and out." Clayton repeated.

After reaching their assigned spot on the blind side of the ridge (the side hidden from the combatants vantage point) they began setting up. Chris slid the Barrett M82 50-caliber sniper rifle out of the MAWC (Modular Airborne Weapons Case) and slid the twenty nine inch barrel back over the lower receiver assembly. Next, he unzipped the thick fleece lined custom case for the Leupold Mark 4 telescopic sight, popped the retractable bipod legs down from the middle of the gun and then snapped a ten round magazine into the feed. The last thing he did to make this an instrument of death, was pulling back on the bolt carrier and running a round up into the snout. Jonsie sat crossed legged on his can and peered through his M151 Spotting Scope, it was specifically designed to to make the target the exact same size as the shooters, and its lightweight and durable body that can withstand the rigors of combat and inclement weather make it a favorite scope of NATO warriors around the globe.

"Hammerhead, Hammerhead, do you copy? Over."

"This is Hammerhead, copy that Superhero. Go ahead." Chris replied, adjusting the attached mic arm on the side of his helmet.

"Little Bird says we got 8, I repeat 8 movers headed due West toward your turf. Over." Command informed him.

"Roger on the 8, all I need is a go. Over." Chris answered back, indicating that what he really wanted was permission to kill.

"Situation is hot Hammerhead, take em as you see em. Over." The young officer's voice was encouraging.

"Roger, Superhero, I'm clear to go then? Over." Chris wanted absolute confirmation, because in this day and age the Army couldn't afford to make any mistakes, especially in this politically fuelled arena.

"Hammerhead, I say go, you read me son? Over." Command answered softly, yet with resolve in his voice.

"Roger that Superhero, next talkie will be the score. Hammerhead out."

"How far do you reckon, Chris?" Jonsie asked, not taking his eyes away from his scope.

"About four Superdome's away." He replied with a smile, giving his estimated range of the gun runners at around four hundred yards.

"How close do you want em?" Jonsie asked, smiling back at Chris.

"I dont give a shit." Chris answered, biting off another piece of his Snickers bar. "I love these things."

"Yeah, they're alright but I'm a Kit-Kat guy myself." His spotter mentioned nonchalantly, adjusting the height of his tripod.

"And dick, you like dick too don't forget…" Chris couldn't help but to kick something out but was cut off.

"Only your black dick, and that's our secret girlfriend, you know that." Jonsie kicked back with a chuckle.

"Okay game time cowboy, I spy with my little eye, six sand niggers heading right at us. Range is 228 meters, no wind." His spotter informed him in a low serious voice.

"Thought there were eight?" Chris asked, leaning in to get a better look into his scope. "Yup, there are definitely six."

"Two probably peeled off, or the drone was counting shadows." Jonsie suggested, whisking away a pesky fly from his cheek.

"Let's start from the rear and work our way forward, see if we can trick 'em." Chris was referring to taking out the rear man of the party first in an attempt to fool them into thinking that the shots were coming from behind, thus forcing the enemy into running directly at their line of fire.

"Guy with the Nike t-shirt and tight cargo shorts, c'mon down." Jonsie whispered like a game show announcer, holding his empty fist like a microphone.

The super sonic fifty caliber round caused the rifle to recoil against Chris's shoulder a fraction of a second before the bullet left the muzzle, and the discharge of compressed air once released into the atmosphere created a vacuum ring that resembled a distorted halo. In an instant Chris's target vaporized and everything above the man's chest disappeared into the early morning air.

"One going back for a looksie…" Jonsie started to say, before Chris dropped him. "Nice."

"On the left Jonsie, he's running, gotta lead him a little." Chris remarked, more to himself than his partner while gently shifting the rifle.

"Nice shot Chris, world class." His partner congratulated with an impressed tone.

"Yo asshole, what shade of green do you need?!" An angry voice cried out from behind him, followed by two long horn blasts. "C'mon wake up, would ya!?"

Chris shook his head after being brought back into the present and after flipping the guy the bird hooked a right and made his way to the Philadelphia airport.

"Let me kill this motherfucker!" Chris exclaimed, sitting down behind Timmons and shutting the rear passenger side door. "I take his ass out and all his gangbanger bullshit goes away, it all stops immediately!"

"Chris." Richards said, holding up his hand and peering back at him through the rearview mirror. "Slow down, I know you're anxious right now."

"Anxious?!" He answered with murder in his eyes. "Are you fucking kidding me George?!"

"Chris!" Timmons barked, startling both men. "Shut the fuck up and listen!"

She looked over at Richards and waited for his lead but after seeing the tired look on his face decided that it would be better for her to open. "They got Pearl, executed him in the old Ascension church in Kensington."

Richards acknowledged with a nod. "Right after the interview. The last time we saw him, he was walking up Whitaker and got into the back of a large black sedan, lost him in the night."

"Everybody on the planet knows it was Blaze's cousin, and GSM Godfather, Aaron Pelts, aka Breach." Timmons added, pulling down the passenger sun visor and opening the mirror slide in order to make direct eye contact with him.

"Gee, I'm so sorry to hear that." Chris whispered, turning his head to look out his window at the busy rolling suitcase, pedestrian causeway.

Most of them were in their late twenties or early thirties, wore upper casual dark clothes and had blank expressions on their faces. How they managed to walk while in a semi hypnotic trance while gazing down at their phones was anyone's guess. Occasionally one would glance up and look around in order to check the distance to their terminal and make sure they were safe.

"Well here's the thing, if GSM's upper management hits our boy Blaze, then all of our efforts will have been in vain." Timmons said, turning around to face him. "The murders of Agents Moss and Trainer, Trina Brooks and Joshua Ladd, the attempted hit on Jelly, and of course you and the old biker getting shot. Four years of deep cover goes right down the toilet."

"And you know as well as I do that Blaze's cousin Breach is already loaded for him, that's guaranteed." Richards added, lowering his window and lighting a cigarette.

"Which leaves us where?" Chris asked, looking up and rubbing his forehead.

"It leaves us with the last option that we know will work." She replied, under her breath. "And we get to take him alive."

"What the hell are you talking about Timmons? I'm not following you." Chris inquired, squinting his eyes from the glare of a vehicle's high beams blasting back at him through the windshield rearview. "Asshole."

"We have a plan." She said, blowing her nose into a Dunkin' Donuts napkin. "The air is horrible in this town."

"We're going to bait him Chris, we're going to suck the son of a bitch in and nail his ass to the wall." Richards explained, with a smirk.

"Okay, let's hear it." Clayton muttered, lowering his Phillies cap and laying his head back.

"I think you should read this first." Agent Timmons suggested, handing back her phone to Clayton. "It was this guy's idea!"

'It's a great plan Clay and everyone here is on base with it! Sorry to break our blackout again! lol.' Jelly introduced himself into the plot via text message.

"You have got to be fucking kidding me! I should have known!" Chris shouted through his laughter. "We've created a monster!"

"No, but he's a genius, I'm convinced of that." Richards said, smiling.

'Oh, I bet it's doozie young blood! lol!' He texted the boy.

"Okay, so here's how it's going to fly." Timmons said, nodding her head with approval. "This kid is brilliant."

"Honey, the baby just kicked again!" Lynne, who was now six months pregnant, shouted for joy.

"Let me feel?" Jelly asked with a giggle. "She's going to be a soccer player!"

"Come here Lynne, let me see you!" Ben exclaimed with open arms. "Look at you, all lit up like a girl on Christmas morning!"

"You're burning that pancake Ben, you know I hate them over cooked!" Jelly teased.

"Oh, I'm so sorry your highness, I mean your hiney!" Ben joked back, causing the teen to squeal out loud.

"I feel really good about this, you two." Lynne added, putting her arm around her husband. "Everything is going to work out just fine."

"Amen!" Ben cheerfully shouted.

"Me too. Amen!" Jelly added, hugging Lynne from behind.

"The plan in theory is very simple." Timmons began to explain. "Even Mark Hess, the Kennett police chief, agrees."

"It's a flanking maneuver Chris, just forcing him into what he thinks is his only option." Richards highlighted, in military terminology.

"First step is, Jelly video calls Blaze and suggests a trade. He tells him that he'll return whatever item Blaze thinks he has in exchange for an end to any connection with him." Timmons explained, pinching the cherry off of her cigarette and placing the butt in a plastic bag. "Even Jelly doesn't know exactly what Blaze thinks he has on him but…"

"Blaze is convinced Jelly's got some dirt, and that's all that matters." Richards speculated with a frown.

"Well, Blaze did try to kill him for some reason." Clayton agreed. "Even though Jocko and I got the short end of the stick."

"Step two is, Blaze drives to the Ladd's and a team is outside at the ready." Timmons said, counting down the stages of the plan on her fingers. "You're going to be in the back field with eyes and ears on everything, and that means BDU's and warpaint. (She was referring to him suiting up in his Battle Duty Uniform and wearing camouflage face paint).

"Please refrain from shooting him on sight, Chris." Richards cracked.

"Step three is, that werewolf dog of theirs is let out and chases him right through the cracked open barn door." Timmons added with a chuckle. "And believe me man, Blaze will run for that door!"

Chapter Thirty One

The mid August night was thick with moisture and dense black storm clouds loomed on the Western horizon. Intermittent white flashes of lightning flickered throughout the blanketed sky, followed closely by the deep rumble of thunder. Pesky mosquitoes buzzed and taunted all those who lay in wait before landing on their sticky, sweat soaked skin. Occasionally, cicadas chirped from the trees and moths flew towards exterior lights, some were picked off by the small brown bats that flew amongst them erratically, and with deadly sonar precision. As the barometric pressure dropped the alkaline static charged air got cooler and a light wind began to sweep through the corn fields, rustling the stocks of the rich crop. Behind him, Chris could hear the sound of deer feeding and could sense their restlessness of the impending tempest.

"Dragon Lady, this is Doorman, we have a visitor." The team leader's voice came through softly.

"Roger, Doorman, step one." Timmons replied.

"Roger that, Dragon Lady."

"Don't cheer, but good news, it's game time." She said to those sitting quietly in the dark kitchen.

"Yay." Jelly whispered.

Within seconds of Blaze's arrival and before he could exit the stolen Lexus, the ominous sky opened up and a deluge ensued. He grabbed the Ruger LC-9 from underneath his seat and while looking out of the opened driver's door, slid it down into the back of his pants.

"I got you now, ya little bitch." He hissed to himself, slamming the car door shut.

"Well, I'm at your party, Jelly!" Blaze cried out through the buckets of water coming down. "You got somethin' for me?!"

As if on cue, Clayton cupped his hand over his small Maglite and clicked the button three times, signaling for Jelly to call out from the rear deck.

"Hang on, it's pouring out there!" The teen shouted.

"No shit!" Blaze exclaimed sarcastically. "How do I know you're not setting me up?"

"Setting you up?!" Jelly responded, with a high pitch tone of surprise. "Nigga, are you fucking kidding me?!"

"Nope, straight up!" He wanted to know.

"This shit here makes me an accessory, you idiot!" Jelly had never pulled off such a convincing performance like this, including his days back in the old 'hood.

"Accessory?" Blaze inquired, walking slowly alongside the house.

Jelly suddenly materialized thirty feet in front of him and held up what appeared to be a large Ziploc freezer bag.

"Didn't this go missing from your gym bag?" The teen asked, shaking the bag to entice him.

"What's that there, boy?" Blaze growled, his voice became grizzly and severe.

"You know what it is, and you aint gettin' it until you promise me that we're through, and that means forever!" Jelly's only condition to the proposal rang out clear and concise. "If you can't do that, then you die right here and now."

"Fuck you talking about punk, your telling me what the deal is?" Blaze fired back. "What if I just..."

Both Jelly and Clayton saw Blaze's right hand reach around and lift up his soaked, oversized black hoodie.

"Hexe!" Jelly screamed in fear, just as Blaze had walked directly parallel to the opened barn door. "Get him!"

A clap of thunder and a thick bolt of screaming lightning punched through the balling rain and exploded through a large oak tree, shearing off a large upper section of the hardwood.

"Fuck me!!!" Blaze screamed at the top of his lungs before breaking into a full sprint and heading for the obvious protection of the barn.

The dog shot out from the sliding glass door like a top fuel drag bike launching off the line, and in a split second was on his heels. Blaze's attempt at gripping his pistol failed as Hexe's jaw clamped shut over his wrist, causing him to drop the weapon. The last thought Blaze had before he managed to slide the heavy wooden door shut was that he narrowly escaped a vicious attack by a land shark.

The interior of the barn was dark and the air was still and musty. Blaze inched his way carefully across the creaky wide planked floor with his arms extended outward. He slid his right foot forward and out into nothingness; unable to regain his balance after his left heel cleared the edge of commitment, he fell downward into the pit.

Ben Ladd stood holding his trusty 1950's era Rayovac, and after flipping on the switch aimed it directly into Blaze's eyes.

"Just the man I want to see." He growled, with hot iron in his voice.

"Wait a second, mister." Blaze whispered nervously, as he trembled in fear on the earthen floor.

The only thing Ben had on was a pair of faded Levi's 501's, and as he angled the flashlight back against his broad naked chest, Blaze pissed himself at what he saw. Towering there before him was a six foot six, solid muscular framed man with a long gray beard. His face was expressionless except for a pair of fixed, narrowed dark eyes that pierced right through his soul. Ben's glistening ivory skin was wet and streaks of sweat ran down the length of his torso soaking the waistband of his jeans. A small scar sat high on his left cheek bone and tattooed horizontally, down the center of his breastplate in bold Old English font was the acronym 'SFFS' (Sworn Forever Forever Sworn). Out of the shadows that surrounded him and in one swift motion, Ben lifted the .44 Magnum and cocked the hammer back. His thick forearm bore another Tattoo, that being the familiar "Sworn MC" that also resembled the rocker on their colors.

"When I was your age, I served under a man who demanded nothing less than loyalty." Ben said with a nod. "You would have never made it past your first week. I guarantee it!"

"What do you want from me?" Blaze pleaded, as tears began to fill his eyes. "I'm gangland just like you."

"No, you're not! You're a scared, manipulative little rat who's never sacrificed or fought for anything in his life!" He replied, glaring down at the frightened gangbanger.

Out of the darkness, Ben lifted his left hand to reveal a Ziploc freezer bag that contained what Blaze had been missing; the item was the only thing that directly linked him to the series of murders.

"This is the gun you used to kill my son." He said, holding the bag closer to Blaze's face. Ben unzipped it and the weapon spilled out and onto his lap. "Take it, and get up that ladder."

"What?" Blaze asked, reaching down and taking ahold of the gun.

"You heard me, and if you ever go near that boy again, I'll kill you with my bare hands." Ben promised him, waiving his pistol toward the small ladder. "That's the trade, a life for one who is living and a prayer for the forgiveness of your soul."

"That dog's gonna eat me." Blaze said, looking up through the rungs that eventually faded off into the darkness.

"No, that's not what's going to eat you son." Ben answered.

Blaze swung his leg over the edge and took his first step up and into the barn.

"Freeze, don't move, let me see your hands!" Clayton shouted from the doorway. "Now get on your knees and put your hands behind your head!"

About ten other agents stormed in, while Timmons, Richards and Mark waited outside with Lynne and Jelly.

"Ben honey, come out now!" Lynne shouted through the downpour as the blue and white strobe lights pulsing from the vehicles floated up the driveway. "We're all out here waiting for you!"

"I'm here Lynne." He whispered into her ear, grabbing ahold of her gently and reaching out for Jelly to come and join them. "I'm right here."

The End

Epilogue

"Let's welcome all of these nice people here today!" Pastor Walt exclaimed, his smile beamed from ear to ear and his words were sincere. "Welcome to Lighthouse church!"

"Welcome!" The congregants announced in unison.

"What I see here before me today is nothing short of love, a love that is pure and kind, a love that is true, a love that is God given and right."

"Amen!" His flock responded with joy.

"From Benjamin and Lynne having their new baby daughter Zelda baptized here today, to a young man, who is also the brightest and bravest teenager I've ever had the privilege of meeting, sitting next to his parents."

Clayton immediately put his arm around his son and squeezed his shoulder, and Jelly responded with a smile as tears filled his eyes.

Mark reached for his wife's hand and they shared a silent moment of affection and Mickey who was sitting next to Amanda suddenly felt her gently touching his leg.

Zelda, who was wearing a white dress and wrapped in a hand knitted baby shawl let out a small cry and Lynne rocked the infant until she settled down.

"Calm yourself girl, it's almost time for you to go on!" Pastor Walt teased with dramatic flair, stirring a round of laughter.

"Joshua is beside himself in our Father's heavenly kingdom, and he is looking down on us, feeling this pure love!"

"Amen!" Could be heard from outside the church, as the word was raised and carried throughout their hearts.

"The trials and tribulations, the struggles for our immortal souls and the quest for His light is a lifelong venture that is, at times, filled with the highs and lows of everyday life, and at others is a fight for the survival of our very souls." Pastor Walt reached out towards Ben and Lynne and they responded by raising their hands.

"Righteousness and justice are the foundation of your throne; steadfast love and faithfulness go before you." Psalm 89:14

"Amen!"

"Yeah?" Agent Dreyer asked, after answering his phone.

"Tom?" Timmons asked, needing confirmation.

"That's right, who's this?"

"It's Deb Timmons over at FBI." She replied softly.

"Oh?"

"Tom, I'm going to give you the opportunity to turn in your badge."

Milton Keynes UK
Ingram Content Group UK Ltd.
UKHW010237111224
452348UK00011B/847